MURDER ABOARD YORKTOWN

07/22/99

by Roy Latall

*To Frank
Best Wishes
Roy Latall*

Also by Roy Latall
Books

The Memoirs of LeRoy & Viola, the Early Years 1992

Short Stories

Walnut Shells, Buttons, Imagination and Reality 1997
Do We, or Don't We, Pledge Allegiance 1997
A Father's Letter to his Son 1996

Copyright © 1998
Roy Latall
All Rights Reserved

Cover: by Roy Latall

ISBN: 1-57502-830-1

Published by: L & L Publishing
2314 Lakeshore Drive
Pier Cove, Michigan 49408
(616)543-4297

Printed in U.S.A. by Morris Publishing
3212 East Hwy. 30, Kearney, NE 68847 (800)650-7888

ACKNOWLEDGMENT

A very special thanks to my wife Viola without whose invaluable information, advice, endless patience, gentle criticism, and editing, this book could not have been written and published. I am always amazed at her ability to turn my ramblings into a readable piece of work.

TO THE MEMORY OF

Robert Charles Latall
(1949-1993)

ABBREVIATIONS

Adm	Admiral
AM1	Aviation Metalsmith 1st Class
AMM3	Aviation Machinist's Mate 3rd Class
BB	Battleship
Betty	Mitsubishi G4M medium bomber
BM1	Boatswain's Mate 1st Class (Bosun Mate)
Bogies	Unidentified aircraft
CA	Heavy cruiser
Capt	Captain
Cdr	Commander
CO	Commanding Officer
Cox	Coxswain
CV	Fleet aircraft carrier
DD	Destroyer
Ens	Ensign
Exec	Executive Officer
F3	Fireman 3rd Class
F4F	Grumman Wildcat fighter
F4U	Voight Chance fighter
F6F	Grumman Hellcat fighter
1stLt	First Lieutenant
Kate	Nakajima B5N torpedo bomber
LCdr	Lieutenant Commander
LSO	Landing Signal Officer
Lt	Lieutenant
Lt(jg)	Lieutenant Junior Grade
MM1	Machinist's Mate 1st Class
PB	Patrol boat
PBY	Consolidated Catalina patrol bomber
Pfc	Private First Class
PhM1	Pharmacist's Mate 1st Class
PT	Patrol torpedo boat
RAdm	Rear Admiral
S1	Seaman 1st Class
SBD	Douglas Dauntless dive-bomber
2ndLt	Second Lieutenant
SB2C	Curtiss dive-bomber
TBD	Douglas Devastator torpedo bomber
TBF	Grumman Avenger torpedo bomber
Val	Aichi D3A dive-bomber
VB	Navy bombing squadron
VF	Navy fighting squadron
VT	Navy torpedo squadron
Y2	Yeoman 2nd Class
Zero	Mitsubishi A6M fighter

§§§

"OK, who's the smartass now! I catch you pulling those childish boot tricks on me an' I'll break your balls," yelled Bosun Mate 1st Class Ed Hill, as he watched the pink then reddish stream flow past under his private parts, this while he sat perched on the substantial Navy hardware known as the latrine.

Ed Hill had signed over for another 6 year hitch back in 1940. The Navy had been good to him, given him a home, good food and rapid rates of promotion, especially fast for a boy off an Oklahoma farm with only two years of high school, promotions mainly since December 7, 1941, when as a seaman 1st he was blown over the side while aboard the Pennsylvania.

Ed's assignment prior to that fateful day had been captain of the head on this proud battleship. His duty had been to supervise the apprentice seamen whose job it was to see that all the heads were kept spotless. This included swabbing the decks, cleaning the washbasins, mirrors, and making sure that the latrines flowed smoothly, that all toilet paper and fecal matter moved along the 30 foot long metal troughs to its designated depository.

Ed over the years had become wise to the many tricks bored sailors would pull on each other in these same heads, such as lighting a roll of toilet paper at one end of the trough and floating it down the ways toward some poor unsuspecting swabby, sitting on his solid plank seat with his pants down to his ankles, reading a letter from home, doing his duty, when "whow, goddam that's hot" could be heard echoing through the compartment as the flaming pyre floated by. Yes, Ed Hill had seen all kinds of tricks of this type, but dye or coloring added to the cascading flow was new to him.

As he looked out past the partition separating his area from one fifteen feet away, he could see a pair of dungaree-covered legs, feet firmly planted on the deck, motionless.

"What the hell is this guy trying to pull," yelled Ed as he sprang from his seat, half pulling up his boxer shorts and pants with one quick swoop, this as he headed toward the assumed culprit. Dam, this guy is sleeping, sitting up, thought the surprised bosun, as he both screamed and grabbed at the sailor's shoulder. Sleeping hell, thought Ed, as the once motionless body tumbled over to the deck exposing the handle of a hunting knife buried deep into his back just behind the heart. That wasn't dye, that was blood!

§§

The Yorktown had put into drydock at Pearl just 76 hours ago for fairly major repairs, this due to damage she received at the Battle of the Coral Sea. Her F4Fs, SBDs and TBD Torpedo planes along with those of the Lexington had sunk one Japanese carrier and badly damaged a second, but only after the Japs had sunk the Lex and damaged the Yorktown, not too bad because she could still make 20 plus knots and limp back to Hawaii where after a super 72 hour effort by the yard workmen, she would be patched up, declared seaworthy, and sent on her way for further action back in the deep blue, scary, unfriendly waters of the South Pacific.

At 0001 the Yorktown was floated out of #2 drydock and with the help of three tugs guided through the mine fields protecting this once palatial paradise. She was soon joined by her screening vessels which included five 400 class destroyers, one light and two heavy cruisers.

Once out to sea, Capt. Bill Fielder, the Yorktown skipper, would open his orders that read proceed to a position 220 miles north-northwest of Midway where you will join up with Vice Admiral Ray Spruance's two carrier task force and prepare to engage the enemy Japanese fleet assumed headed for the invasion of Midway Island.

At 0020 hours Capt. Fielder had ordered the ship's mid watch be set. BM1. Ed Hill had taken the duty and responsibility for seeing that all posts were manned, and it was at 0400 when this watch had been completed that Ed had sought relief in the ship's hangar deck head, aft, just forward or outside of the aviation metalsmith's shop. Upon entering the area, he sat down on the first available toilet, not noticing anyone else around, assuming he was alone, not too many swabbies normally out of the sack at this ungodly hour unless assigned duty of one form or other.

This is why Ed Hill had been so startled, first by the reddish flow and then noticing another person just a short distance away. And now this person, this fellow-shipmate, lay bleeding on the deck with a pig sticker in his back. As Ed knelt down to take the victim's pulse, he couldn't help but notice that this fellow's shirt had stenciled on its left sleeve a rating badge of aviation metalsmith 3rd class. This fellow wasn't far from home in one sense, but in another, he was. He was dead! Now what, who do I report this to, the officer of the deck was most likely up on the bridge. Let him wake Lt. Craiger, the ship's provost marshall, to see what the next step should be, he thought. How many knifings do you find on a ship out to sea? Not many, Ed guessed. This was his first experience with this type of out to sea ghastly deed.

Oh, Ed had taken part in many a knifing altercation while on duty as part of the Honolulu Navy Shore Patrol. That's for sure. He could remember the two months he spent assigned to the Front Street Bistro appropriately called the "Bucket of Blood," a large one-story building having a bar that would open at 1630 in the afternoon to accommodate the factory workers getting off the day shift.

The servicemen would start piling in around 1800 and by 2000 things were really humming, seven nights a week. The MP's and Shore Patrol had a station right in the nightclub, but that didn't stop the fists, chairs, and bottles from flying. All it would take to set off the melee would be for a sailor to walk up to a civilian table, the sailor to ask the lady of the party to dance, and all hell might break loose. The service personnel and civilians would choose up sides. What had been an incident between three people might end up involving hundreds. The "Bucket of Blood" was a good place to avoid.

§§

But this was different. This rowdy lifestyle didn't exist aboard ship, especially during wartime.

"Don't touch anything," bellowed a sleepy-eyed Lt. Craiger. "I want all the evidence preserved and an autopsy performed immediately. Wake up Capt. Fielder and ask him to meet with me, Dr. Chamer, and Bosun Mate Ed Hill in the #2 ready room and let's also have the on-duty yeoman match the victim's dog tag with his records, and get that dope up to us on the double," he added.

Marine Lt. Humphrey Craiger might have been a 90 day wonder, but he sure knew how to take charge of an investigation, marveled Ed Hill. Ed had worked with the Honolulu police during his stint with the Shore Patrol, but he had never seen an investigation start out as smooth as the one he was experiencing on this fateful morning.

"Tag shows he is Fred William Daukins, Serial Number 611-02-24 - USNR-A enlisted 10/39. Records indicate he was promoted to aviation metalsmith 3rd class on 01-42 and assigned to the Yorktown yesterday just prior to its leaving port. Records

3

indicate the victim was transferred from the Ford Island aviation metal shop where he had worked for the last 5 months. Duties were liaison between the shop and office, cutting orders and setting priorities."

"Daukins went through boots at Great Lakes Naval Training Station in '39 and Aviation Metalsmith School at 87th & Anthony in Chicago prior to the Ford Island assignment. Born and raised in Columbus, Ohio; John B. Sawyer High School graduate 6/10/39; no prior work experience."

If Lt. Craiger seemed efficient, Yeoman 2nd Class Herb Andrews echoed the impression. He was on the stick, not hesitating to fill the room with statistics and information about the deceased. Daukins had been up before Captain's mast three times, twice for open gambling, once for being AWOL for two days, found with an underage girl in a Honolulu hotel room, the charges later dropped.

"And what were your findings, Doctor?" asked the hard-pressing, ever-eager Marine.

"The deceased died at approximately 0340, cause of death stab wound through the heart, caused by a 9" long hunting knife blade buried to its hilt, through the back and between the ribs. The blade's handle was wiped clean of prints, but its very tip showed signs of grey paint similar to the color and kind used to paint the bulkheads in the ship's heads," Dr. Chamer reported.

He continued, "I would guess that the victim laid back against the bulkhead after the incident, causing further penetration of the knife blade until the hilt of the knife pressed against the back partially retarding the flow of blood from the wound. The knife is of a very common type, made by the R. J. Miller Company, distributed through many hardware and cutlery outlets."

"Other than a silver chain and dog tags, the deceased wore a Bulova gold watch on his left wrist, no other jewelry, but the right hand ring finger showed signs that a heavy, boldfaced ring had been in place recently. No ring was found."

"No other bruises or cuts on the body. Fred Daukins' wallet was in the rear lefthand pocket of his pants, contents of same listed in a separate manifest. The typical hunting knife holster with its knife encased was found fastened through his belt. Regulation issue skivvies, socks, shoes, dungaree pants and shirt were worn. No hat was found."

§§

At this point, the tall lean Texan paused, picked up a slide and placed it in the waiting projector. Lt. Commander Hilton Chamer was as smooth and methodical with this report of his investigation as Ed Hill remembered him back at the Pearl Harbor Naval Hospital treating patients soon after the December 7th tragedy. Although Chamer had been in charge of the base hospital Pathology lab, on this day all M.D.s no matter what their specialty had been pressed into service, treating wounds, burns, mending broken bodies and bones as well as doing general surgery.

LCdr. Chamer had graduated from Duke University Medical School doing his internship and residency in General Medicine at Evanston Hospital in Illinois. He went into private practice for six months, then decided to accept a two year fellowship in Pathology and Forensic medicine at Northwestern Memorial Hospital. Upon graduation, he found positions in his field few and far between. Hence, the service. The Navy was begging for well-educated doctors.

After being picked up from the burning waters of the harbor at Pearl, Ed had been taken by truck on a makeshift stretcher to the same hospital and burn ward where Dr. Chamer was assisting. The good doctor had cleaned and treated his burns and assigned him to a nurse and eventual bed where he would spend the next three months recovering, this prior to his being assigned to the Honolulu Shore Patrol. BM1. Hill had not been aware that the lieutenant commander had been assigned to the Yorktown medical staff, but when the good doctor entered the ready room with the rest of the team, he felt a sigh of relief. This man knew what he was doing. This case had come a long way.

The slide showed a close-up facial view of the victim, heavy, dark, pompadour style hair, swarthy complexion with Grecian features. It was reported he had dark brown eyes, stood 5 foot 7½" tall, weighed 154 lbs, all in all, a handsome guy.

Dr. Chamer replaced the slide with another showing the back of the naked victim with a 2" long by ½" wide wound, just over the area of the heart.

§§

At this point, the discussion and investigation was interrupted by the familiar call to flight quarters: "Pilots man your planes." Two F4Fs stood ready, one on the port, the other on the starboard flight deck catapult, the pilots scurrying from the #3 ready room, up the ladder, through the hatch onto the flight deck and into their cockpits.

The ship's bow had been turned into the wind and its speed increased to 29 knots. Within 30 seconds the powerful nine cylinder Pratt Whitney engines could be heard revving up, then the starboard pilot giving thumbs up to the catapult officer whose arm came down with the signal to the aviation machinist mate 2nd class stationed in the nearby catwalk to press the button that would alert the crew below to release the powerful thrust that would physically throw this heavy single seater fighter off the carrier deck and into the wild blue yonder, all within a distance of about 90 feet.

Then over to the waiting plane on the port side of the deck; two windblown crewmen had just attached the catapult bridle to the eager aircraft. Within seconds, a second plane had been launched. The morning's CAP had been set giving the Yorktown's task force the much needed air cover against possible enemy air or submarine attack in the unfriendly waters of this treacherous sea.

§§

Back in the #2 ready room, Capt. Fielder sanctioned the resumption of the investigation. "Lieutenant, have you anything to add to the reports given by BM1 Hill, Yeoman Andrews, and/or Dr. Chamer?" he asked.

"No sir, not at this point, other than to say I have assigned three Marines to interrogate Mr. Daukins' fellows in the workplace, finding out if he had friends or enemies aboard, where he bunked, to check the contents of his locker, sea bag and wallet, and why he was found fully dressed at 0400 when he had not been on the duty roster. I would also like to know more about his lifestyle, the three Captain's masts and especially the details of the AWOL charge," the lieutenant replied.

"But as you know, Lieutenant, being out to sea with the possibility of engaging a large enemy task force within a few days stifles the maximum effort this crime should have precipitated. You also know that all communication between fleet and home base has been curtailed, so your information must come from people and evidence aboard. Keep in mind your first duty is to your Marine contingent and their General Quarters gunnery assignments," the captain responded.

Craiger knew this was not going to be easy. Murder cases in general never were, even under the best conditions. He had been involved in several as a civilian federal prosecutor, working out of the courts of Newark, New Jersey.

Humphrey Craiger came from a long line of law enforcement people, dating back to his great-grandfather in the old country.

His grandfather had emigrated from Ireland in 1902, met and married his grandmother while in the bowels of an overcrowded, rusty old passenger ship, both traveling steerage because that's all the passage money they could scrape together, this at a time of famine and depression back home, landing at Ellis Island with just enough money to be allowed to go ashore in this land of milk and honey "where the streets were supposedly paved with gold!"

Grama Craiger's entry had been held up for a day or so because the examining physician thought she might have trachoma, but further testing proved this was not true. They would live in a crowded Bronx apartment with relatives until Grampa would give up his garbage collector's job, this after passing the written and physical exams for the New York City police department. Humphrey's dad followed in Grampa's footsteps, moving up to the rank of sergeant.

Humphrey marveled and respected both his father's and grandfather's honest and dedicated efforts to the duty and service of the New York police department. But when it came time to decide on his education and career, he wanted more. A good student in high school, he would attend junior college and stock grocery shelves in the evening, this while graduating third in his class of 600. Upon graduation from a junior college two-year liberal arts program, Humphrey applied to New York University taking three years to complete the two years of work necessary to receive his B.A. in pre-law. You couldn't carry 18-20 credit hours in school while working a full eight hour shift loading mailbags into boxcars located outside of the main post office.

Law school seemed a long way off, maybe in the future, thought the hard-working Mick. Then along came an unexpected break, a real godsend. Craiger's mother had been working as a part-time cleaning lady for a Long Island family, the husband a professor at Columbia University Law School. Mildred Craiger had often mentioned her son to her employers, praising his hard work and success in the field of pre-law.

From time to time Prof. Kramer would ask Mildred how Humphrey was progressing. When told he would not go on to law school, at least not at the present, the inquisitive professor asked why and was told that although her son had graduated with honors, continued working while attending law school was more than he could handle. He would take the New York City police department's examination, hope to pass and maybe in years to come after saving the necessary finances, go on to law school.

The professor was wise to the many potential students whose thoughts were of a similar vein, knew that maybe one in ten would eventually seek out their dream.

"Have Humphrey visit me in my office next Wednesday, Mrs. Craiger," the kind professor proclaimed, "let's see what we can work out."

And so it happened. Scholarships, grants and loans would provide the necessary vehicles to propel the youngest member of the Craiger clan through school, the bar, and eventually a position of prosecutor.

§§

Again the call to flight quarters broke up the heated discussion surrounding the investigation into Daukins' death. All aircraft on the aft end of the flight deck had been moved forward of the #5 barrier. Four more fighters were readying for catapult launch while the arresting gear crew and landing signal officer prepared to take back aboard the two fuel-starved F4Fs launched earlier.

As the Yorktown headed into the wind, two small objects could be seen side by side heading toward the aft end of the massive giant. Lt. Crantz, paddles in hand, paced the landing signal platform like a ballerina readying for her debut. Crantz, a Navy pilot himself, had just returned from a two week training course provided potential landing signal officers, this before being assigned to the Yorktown to replace the ill-fated Lt. Arrey, killed during the last hours of the Coral Sea action.

Soon the two distant objects became larger and larger until they could be recognized as F4Fs. As they passed by the starboard side of the carrier about 150 feet off the water, Lt. Shingleton waved his two agile green-shirted hook men into position, one on each side of the deck in the area of the #3 wire rope. After surveying the deck to make sure that all five of the barriers were in the up position, all deck pendants straining against the opposing forces provided by their sturdy cylinders mounted just below the flight deck, noting that each critical apparatus was manned by its well-trained and tested crewman, the lieutenant motioned to the landing signal officer's communications assistant that landings could commence.

The two fighters moved to a half mile ahead of the carrier. One broke off, made a sharp 180 degree turn, then the other followed, keeping at a manageable distance behind. The planes were now on the port side of their airfield traveling toward their goal.

Once a safe distance past the island another 180 degree turn brought the first plane in line with the flight deck, and gaining on it fast. Lt. Crantz waved his paddles to indicate to the pilot that he was coming in high and fast. He corrected and as the F4F neared the edge of the flight deck, the lieutenant's right paddle crossed his chest, the pilot cut his engine and seemed to float over the deck and down, his tailhook picking up #2 wire and within a hundred feet or so, the plane came to a screeching halt.

Out of nowhere came the two nimble hookmen while Lt. Shingleton signaled the pilot to release his brakes so that the aircraft would roll back and its arresting gear hook could be disengaged from the deck pendant. All five barriers came down, while #2 wire was being retrieved, and the F4F engines gunned to move it both forward and beyond the devices so necessary for safe aircraft operation, all this occurring in a matter of a few fleeting seconds.

Once past the last barrier, all five were again moved to the up position along with the deck pendants, while the signal officer was given the go-ahead to land the second aircraft.

This was not going to be easy. The second F4F was coming in high and fast, not responding to Crantz's frantic signals to correct for same. Instantly, the lieutenant's paddles went up over his head giving the well-known wave-off signal. In response, pilot Ensign Lopez gunned the multi-cylinder radial engine, set his control to dip the port wing, then raise the plane's nose high over Yorktown's flight deck in a maneuver that would allow him once again to move along the ship's starboard side until at adequate distances perform his two, 180's and eventual heading back to the deck, where a successful landing would be made.

The end to flight quarters had sounded, all non-participants heading back to other duties. Ensign Lopez taxied his fighter into a forward position helped by the yellow-shirted plane handling crew members while his plane captain jumped onto his starboard wing, smiled and helped the weary young man out of his seat belt, shoulder harness and seat pack.

"Great job," shouted AMM2. Pat Riley, "you brought her back in one piece, and you were worried."

"Not half as worried as I am now," volunteered Ensign Lopez as he climbed from the office aboard his wildcat fighter, the fighter that brought him safely home on his maiden combat flight.

He could see Lt. Crantz heading straight for him, face flushed, jaws moving a mile a minute. "What th' hell you think you're doin' up there, Ensign? Did you get those god-dam wings at the dime store? When I give you signals I expect you to respond accordingly. That stupid wave-off could have cost us a plane or maybe a couple of planes and their pilots."

"I hear you, Skipper. It won't happen again," this as the embarrassed youngster, head down, walked toward the island hatch. He knew what the landing signal officer was saying. Planes returning aboard could be low on fuel, maybe only enough for one pass at the deck, and a wave-off being the difference between making it or the deep blue alongside.

§§

"I really never got to know the kid. Assigned him to rack and locker #42 yesterday when he came aboard, saw to it that he got the necessary mattress, sheets, pillow, and so forth to make up the sack, then on my way. Being master at arms for this compartment takes up a lot of time, a whole mess of new guys assigned since the Coral Sea gig."

"Did I notice anything different about him? Hell no, just another swabby, but wait. He did ask if there was any action aboard, and I set him straight in a hurry. I don't stand for any of that crap in my area."

Bosun Mate Harry Canter had been aboard Yorktown for several years and in the Navy for over nine. He had struggled through the peacetime service, just recently promoted to 2nd Class and given the assignment of tending the flock billeted in the below flight deck starboard compartment, housing mainly the catapult and arresting gear crew. A few extra racks were available in the four high stacks of metal frames lining the compartment bulkheads, so Fred Daukins, for whatever reason, had been assigned to #42. It was considered good duty to live anywhere above the hangar deck.

"Well then, how about his locker combination, Bosun?" asked Marine Corporal Gene Spies. "I've been assigned the job of investigating his past, so let's start with an inventory of his sea bag and whatever other possessions he had."

Two pairs of dress blues, one tailormade, three sets of dress whites, two neckerchiefs, three white hats, one dress blue, one pea coat, two pairs of issue black oxfords, six pairs of black socks, six sets of issue skivvies, two sets of dungaree pants and shirts, all neatly folded in a regulation style and stored in the compact 2x2x3 foot locker. In addition, an $8\frac{1}{2}$ x 11 framed picture of what appeared to be a family, mother, father and two boys. At this point, Corp. Spies had to assume one of the boys was Fred, the other a younger brother.

A small leather bag contained the usual toilet articles, safety razor, shaving cream, toothpaste and brush, several combs, a military type hairbrush, a container of shampoo, and, of course, a bar of salt water soap so necessary when washing or showering out to sea.

Several towels were also neatly folded and stacked next to the leather container. There was a 12x14 leather-bound book, which after careful scrutiny yielded the fact that Fred Daukins had attended John B. Sawyer High School and this was his yearbook. This confirmed Y. Herb Andrews' report earlier that the deceased had graduated from high school. There were two fountain pens, a half-filled bottle of blue ink, blotter from a Central National Bank in Columbus, Ohio, and a 4x2 address book. That could be interesting, thought the corporal as he absentmindedly thumbed through the book. Wow, this guy either had a lot of cousins, mostly female, or he sure must have been a Don Juan. Might not help with the investigation, but then again, who knows. We'll let the lieutenant decide that, he thought.

Continued search of the locker yielded a lined writing pad, three #2 pencils, and a neatly rolled bundle of receipts held together by a rubberband, five Hawaiian one dollar bills, three fives and thirty-four cents in change. A further hurried investigation by the corporal showed the receipts had been issued by a Honolulu Western Union office for big bucks and over a period of several months. This could be important, thought the Marine. He better get this information to Lt. Craiger on the double.

§§

"Lt. Shingleton, could you muster your crew and maybe Lt. Meyers' catapult crew outside the arresting gear shack as soon as possible? BM. Canter has given me a list of the men assigned to his compartment and it looks like with few exceptions they work for either you or Lt. Meyers." The short stocky homely Marine sergeant assigned by Lt. Craiger as part of his investigative force had explained the little known details of the aviation metalsmith's murder to the handsome keeper of this important group, the group responsible for safely bringing the Yorktown birds back aboard.

Sgt. Milkusky knew that there was a very narrow window as far as time was concerned. Flight quarters, or worse yet, general quarters, could blow any minute requiring all men to man their stations, taking precidence over his desire to learn if or when any of the men living with Fred Daukins, no matter for how long, could shed light on his background, friends, enemies, or if he got lucky, his assailant.

"I showed him how to secure his rack to the bulkhead when not in use. He had never been aboard a ship before, looked for help, and I gave it. Seemed like a nice enough guy, was surprised that four bunks were chained together and that all four had to be hinged in one operation."

"Joe, the sergeant is looking for information that might help in his investigation into the young man's death. Did he mention anything about family, friends, shipmates, etc?"

"No, Lieutenant, he didn't." Indian Joe Begono had been a member of Yorktown's catapult crew for several years, a funny little guy, always in the company of his buddy Terry Cassesis, another catapult crewman, former professional hockey player. Joe had a dark brownish complexion and a hook nose that presented the typical profile of an American Indian, thus properly nicknamed Indian Joe.

"Anyone else know anything?" asked the impatient sergeant. "OK, then if not, let's take muster."

Milkusky pulled out the list of men assigned, reeled off the names, marking the list when a name was not answered. He would have to find and talk with these six fellas when and if time allowed.

§§

2ndLt. Herb Shacter was the third Marine assigned to Lt. Craiger's team. He had finally cornered the air group engineering officer, Cdr. Billy Blake, down on the hangar deck with a group bent over a faulty release mechanism of a TBD.

"You know, Lieutenant, I'm one hell of a busy guy, and although I'm really concerned that one of my men has been murdered, with this potential skirmish with those Jap bastards coming up, I've got about two minutes to answer any questions you have."

The lieutenant commander was responsible for all maintenance on the aircraft that made up the three squadrons. This was a horrendous job. Billy Blake had been chief engineer for the Grumman Aircraft Company in civilian life, a real rollup your sleeves type of person.

He had more or less been drafted into his Navy position. When the United States began to arm in one sense or another around '40 and '41, finding people, experienced people like the commander, was not easy. You could draft bodies and in a short period of time teach them to march, shoot a gun, drive a Jeep and so forth, but flying an airplane, fixing an airplane, was another story. Those radial engines, hydraulic systems, mechanical devices were complicated. This took experience and the Navy didn't have enough of this experience to go around. They were stretched thin.

No, Billy Blake was not actually drafted. The Navy would proudly proclaim that they didn't draft their men. They were all volunteers. But Billy's bosses at Grumman, along with many other companies supplying arms and machines to the government were being squeezed by Uncle Sam to encourage some of their capable, especially younger, managers to enlist. Blake was a mechanical engineering graduate from M.I.T., came to Grumman as a design engineer, working on the board the first two years of his employment. His talents were soon recognized and within another three years had moved up to assistant chief engineer for aircraft design of the future, and when his boss retired, given the job of chief engineer.

"Well, Commander, tell me about Fred Daukins."

"I never heard of Daukins before this morning," voiced the irritated Blake. "In fact, I didn't or don't know anymore than his name, that he came aboard in Pearl, he was a metalsmith and was assigned to Jeffery Klein as one of the replacements for Chief Carpenter and Seaman Wagnor. Talk to Klein. You should find him in the metalshop. Tell him I expect his full cooperation, but don't hassle him. Getting our planes ready for this coming operation is #1 priority."

§§

"Klein's down having chow. Should be back before too long. How can I help you, Lieutenant?"

"You know Fred Daukins?"

"Yeah, I knew Fred," amswered AM2 Milt Tarry.

"You knew him or know him?" asked Herb Shacter.

"Knew him, Lieutenant. We heard about his problem during muster this morning."

"What can you tell me about Fred?"

"Well, he worked on the base with me for awhile. Only knew him through work. We never socialized. He ran orders between the shop and office, more or less of an administrative job, seldom saw him work with the tools, but he did have a 3rd class rating."

"What kind of a guy was he?"

"OK I guess. Never gave me any trouble but as I said, he pretty much shuffled papers and was sort of a goffer between the shop and office. Hey, here comes our leader, Jeff. Lieutenant, meet AM1. Jeffery Klein. Jeff, this is Marine 2ndLt. Herb Shacter. He's investigating the death of Fred Daukins."

"Did you know Daukins before he came aboard?"

"No, I didn't, Lieutenant," answered the husky blonde-haired Swede. "I was put in charge of Yorktown's metal shop just a few days ago as a replacement for Chief Carpentor who was killed at Coral Sea. He and another fellow were repairing a few bullet holes on the tail of an SBD when a Jap Val came in strafing. Killed both Hal and Jerry. Same plane got our landing signal officer and one of the arresting gear crew. I'd been the #2 man in the metal shop, they didn't have another chief handy, so I'm filling in."

He continued on. "Personnel at Pearl sent Daukins and Milt Tarry as replacements for Hal and Jerry. Claimed they were all that were available. Never got to know Fred. He only came aboard yesterday, sent him up to get settled, you know, bunk, locker, pay office. Claimed he had to get an allotment straightened out. Told him to report to Aviation Stores so that he could be issued special clothing for flight and hangar deck crew and if he was eligible for flight skins, to draw flight gear. Told him to report back to the metal shop for muster this morning, but, of course, he never showed."

"Had you assigned him to a watch last night or early this morning, Klein?"

"No, as I said, Lieutenant, my last words to him were to report for morning muster. Lieutenant, I can't help you any more. We're shorthanded as it is and have two TBDs that need Milt and my attention before they fly again."

§§

Later the same evening after flight quarters had been secured for the day and watches set, a busy Jack Fletcher had excused Humphrey Craiger from the high level, critical strategy meeting occurring aboard CV-5, a meeting that could determine the life or death of TF17, in fact would also affect the success or failure of Fletcher's partner in this massive operation, Admiral Spruance, who was presently speeding toward a rendezvous point aboard Enterprise. Yes, Enterprise, Hornet, along with six cruisers and destroyers making up TF16 would be a major part of the combined fleet's strategies.

Fletcher had been notified of Fred Daukins' death by Captain Fielder. Normally, the death of one person, out to sea, in the middle of a war zone, would not have created the distress that this incident had. Being killed due to injury caused by one doing his duty was one thing. But murder. This just didn't happen aboard ship in this man's navy. So although Craiger was an important part of the total fleet operation, his subordinate would suffice. Let the lieutenant continue the murder investigation.

§§

"OK. Let's pull our information together. Let's see if we make sense out of what we've found. You say Harry Canter could be of little help other than to get you into Daukins' locker, but he did say Daukins was looking for some action, crap game or poker. Well, that could be a factor. Let's keep gambling in mind and that may also tie into the roll of Western Union receipts found. How does a 3d class petty officer send home over $2300 in a period of five months? There's no moonlighting job or jobs that would pay that kind of dough." Craiger frowned after Corp. Spies came forth not only with the receipts but the total amount of money they represented.

Daukins was pulling down $61 a month working for uncle, times five months would be about $300, and then only if all money earned had been sent to the bank. The Navy fed you, gave you a roof over your head, a clothing allowance, really took care of all your basic needs, but this fellow was living on the beach, most likely went to movies off base, smoked, pogey bait, maybe girls.

Sixty-one dollars a month really didn't go that far. Yeah, you could get sea stores for a nickel a pack and other than tailormades, you just didn't have to spend big bucks to be well-dressed, but some guys liked the comforts of home they remembered. There was that sick sucker in the black gang that would wear a silk smoking jacket when lounging around off-duty. Takes all kinds.

And that address book. Over a hundred names, addresses and telephone numbers. That could be a gold mine.

"Spies, I know all communications between the fleet and Pearl are curtailed until after our operation, but let's sort out the categories, the names and addresses from Columbus, from Chicago, Hawaii and see if any of the names tie in with the existing Yorktown roster. Herb, you can help the corporal with that one, and Yeoman, while we got you under the gun, why not give us a report on what you found in Daukins' file regarding the three Captain's masts."

Yeoman Herb Andrews smiled, took three 8½x11 pieces of paper from a folder and startled the group present by informing them that the first two disciplinary actions had been due to Daukins' love of gambling.

The first was while he was a boot at the Great Lakes Naval Training Station in North Chicago, Illinois. He had been assigned to Barracks #10 located at one of the new camps being built at the time, Camp Moffett.

The original training station had stately buildings of brick, mortar and concrete, all centered around a magnificent drill field located in an area on the western shores of Lake Michigan, about 35 miles north of the heart of Chicago, yet only a few miles north of one of the most magnificent suburbs in the country, Lake Forest.

The 2-story wooden barracks being rushed to completion were not only a far cry from the original station facilities, but considered an eyesore by the mega-rich owners of the many stately mansions surrounding the area, people like the meatpacking families Swift, Armour, or the newspaper magnet Col. Robert McCormick, as well as the farm machinery marriage responsible for creating the 35 acre Edith Rockefeller McCormick estate.

Although not a thing of beauty, barracks like Camp Moffett were necessary to house the overflow of patriotic young men anxious to receive the basic training that would allow them to man the ships and fly the airplanes that would bring a sneaky aggressor to its knees.

Apprentice Seaman Fred Daukins had been at Great Lakes for only a week when he was found shooting craps with five other men, all civilian workers from the Camp Moffett project. Poker, pinochle, cribbage, card games in general were not frowned on by the Navy, but when good old American cash was found on the table, or in the case of a crap game, on the floor, this was off-limits. This could get you 5 days in the brig, and in Daukins' case, it did. Not a good start to a career.

"What about the five civilians?" asked Gene Spies.

"Nothing in the record regarding them other than they worked for a large architectural building contractor located on the near west side of Chicago. The company was owned by the Ellis Brothers. They had low-bid the Moffett job, lock stock and barrel. When the company heard that five of their carpenters were about to be taken into custody, bang, a Jim Heller lawyer was knocking on the base commander's door, the 5 guys were back on the job, nothing more said. We don't even have their names in our records."

Though the shells being built to house the recruits were nothing more than 2x4 stud walls, with 1x6 pine bevel siding on the outside, bare inside, no insulation or drywall, rough wood floors, 4/12 pitch roof with roll asphalt roofing, it was shelter and the base commander was not about to create a situation that possibly could halt or slow up work on a project so necessary to our national security. Let the seaman take the fall. Most likely teach him a lesson.

§§

Ed Hill found himself doping off, only half listening to Herb Andrews' report on Great Lakes with one ear, thinking back some years when he had gone through this same training station, this as a young man who had dropped out of high school after just two years, tried to find a job, ended up joining the Navy. No, he didn't know about Camp Moffett. He had gone through that magnificent facility called Camp Dewey. There wasn't any Camp Moffett at that time. Where it stands were farmers' fields, a rifle range and football stadium.

Yeah, Ed could remember being sent to the old post office building in downtown Chicago. Seemed a long way from Oklahoma.

"A through L over here, M through Z form straight lines to the right of those chairs," bellowed the barrel-chested chief bosun mate. "Listen up. I'm going to give you instruction once and only once, so get it right."

The day had come. Ed and Freddie had taken a train, in fact two trains, to get downtown to the Post Office in time for the swearing in. There were 132 fellows grouped together, waiting for this most important event in their lives, but it would be awhile before the actual swearing in. First, another physical! How one's overall condition could change in a matter of a month or so, the guys would never know, but for some reason or other, the Navy was skeptical so, strip down, bend over, pull back the foreskin, cough, read the chart, breathe in, breathe out, all over again. After placing their stamp of approval, the Navy asked the young men to assemble again in neat rows, raise their right hand and take the oath of allegiance.

"Any of you guys have any military training?, the CPO barked.

"I have," answered a tall, broad-shouldered, husky, pug-nosed, deep-voiced gob in the front row.

"OK. It's your job to get these recruits out to Great Lakes. I'm going to give you 132 tickets for the North Shore Electric train. You can pick it up on the elevated platform at Wabash and Randolph. Should take you about an hour and fifteen minutes to get out to the Navy Station. Anybody who misses the train will be considered AWOL, and you know what happens to AWOLs - the brig!"

"Boy, Freddie, this guy sure has guts," Ed smilingly commented to his newly sworn-in friend as he marveled at one of the fellows having the nerve to come out of the group to take on such a monumental responsibility.

"Alright, guys, let's look sharp as we parade through the Loop toward the "L" station. Let's show these civilians what a good Navy bunch looks like," shouted the big Polack named Stosch over the rumbling of 131 other voices.

The train ride was pleasant. It was a warm day so the car windows could be opened which seemed to make the 35 mile trip from the hot, muggy city to the cooler lands of North Chicago more meaningful. What were they getting themselves into most of the guys silently questioned as the green, lush countryside sped by outside. Here were 132 young people, some just 17 years of age, most of them city boys, most of them had never so much as fired a 22, let alone a three or five inch gun. Most of them had never been outside of the midwestern part of the country. Indiana, Wisconsin, Michigan, Oklahoma, Illinois, these were places they knew. What were these lands called Germany and Italy? They knew about Lake Michigan, but not the Atlantic or Pacific Oceans.

§§

"Alright, men. Let's form ranks, four in a row and down the steps to the right," yelled a smart-looking 2nd class petty officer who met the North Shore train carrying the recruits to the Naval Training Station stop.

"Hup, two three four, Hup, two three four, let's not straggle in the rear. Pick up the rear, pick up the cadence, let's look smart. You're in the Navy now," and so it went as the raw, untrained group headed down Buckley Drive toward a large fenced-in area protected by still another high steel reinforced wire mesh gate guarded day and night by a stiff and proper Marine contingent.

"This is Camp Dewey," yelled the 2nd class bosun mate as the civilian-dressed detachment rounded the corner and headed up the one-lane asphalt path past a series of 2-story red brick buildings. "This is Building #2304, your new home for the next six weeks."

"Halt, one two three," commanded the petty officer in charge. "Stand easy, men. We're going to file into the building as a group for basic indoctrination. Then men with last names starting with A through L will sling their hammocks on the lower deck pipe stanchions, names M through Z on the stanchions located on the upper deck."

"Heads are located on the starboard side of each deck. Keep 'em spotless! You're Battalion 'Zebra.' The company commander CPO Larson has his stateroom located forward on the portside of the lower deck. You'll meet your commander after chow at 1400 hours after which you'll draw your clothing allowance, hammock and sea bag, sign your pay chits, string your hammocks, chow down again at 1800 hours, then march over to Camp Dewey's infirmary for the first series of three shots, back to barracks for lights out at 2100 hours."

Wow! Freddie looked at Ed, Ed at Freddie, both with sort of confused expressions. First, this building #2304. It was nothing more than bare wooden floor, drywall ceilings and walls with a series of large diameter pipe railing standing about 4 ft. high dominating the otherwise vacant area.

And this business of sleeping in hammocks. That was something new. And what are these heads boats keep talking about? Where are the bathrooms? Could they be the heads? And why not right and left? Why port and starboard. We're not aboard ship. Chow 1400, 1800, they're going to pay us already? We just got here. This all added up to a confusing morning for the two guys from Oklahoma City and most likely to most of their assembled buddies.

"And three shots before bed? I don't even drink on a social basis," Freddie laughed.

"Alright, sailors, let's line up again but before we fall in, we'll line up according to height, the tallest in front and so on. Remember your spot and from now on, whenever we march, drill, or make ranks for any reason, be in that spot."

"Alright, forward march, hup, two three four, hup, two three four, 'Over the sea let's go men, we're shoving right off, we're shoving right off again, Sally and Sue, don't be blue,' Let's hear it back there!" shouted the recruits' mentor breaking into his burst of song. "Whenever we march, we sing. Whenever we sing, we sing loud and clear. What do we do when we march?" boats yelled.

"We sing," Zebra Company yelled back.

"And how do we sing?" boats asked.

"We sing loud and clear."

"Any of you guys ever work in the restaurant field?" boats asked as the recruits filed into the mess hall, single file, and picked up their trays. There were a few hands of acknowledgement and later that evening, to their sorrow, they would be assigned to a duty known in the service as KP, Kitchen Police.

"You'll all get a shot at it before you leave boot camp, so don't feel bad that you missed out today," Chief Larson explained. "You'll learn to march, swim, handle whale boats, go through gas mask drills, shoot, tie knots, review the Navy manual, trim down on the obstacle course, receive your shots (and not the kind Freddie was thinking of), take a battery of tests so that we have a better idea of how you can best serve the Navy and our country in these times of stress."

"Some of you will go right out into the fleet, some into the armed guard, some of you will go to service schools for further training in gunnery, learn to be motor machinist mates, bosun mates, aviation gunners, metalsmiths, yeomen, and so on. Uncle Sam has a place for each one of you."

This Chief Larson seems like a nice guy, Ed thought, more refined than the rough and ready stereotype portrayed in the movies. Chief Allen Larson was a college professor up until four months ago. He might not have been able to recite the Navy manual from memory like some of the old salts, but he did have vast experience in dealing with students, and these raw recruits were students, eager to learn what was needed to make them capable of doing the job they enlisted to do.

§§

"What size shoe?"

"Nine and a half C," Ed called back.

"There's no C or whatever. Here's two pairs of nine and a halfs, one oxford, one high top. Next," was the answer he got.

And so the recruits passed through the seemingly endless racks and shelves of Navy gear, stopping at each station for the item of issue that would have to last them for many months to come.

"How do you know if these pants are the right length?" one of the gobs asked.

"If they're too short, bring 'em back. If they're too long, roll 'em up. There's no tailor shop here. Take 'em home on leave. Let your mother or sister take care of it."

Later in the barracks, a once-in-a-lifetime fashion show was to take place, shirts, pants, hats, underwear, even shoes were being tried on and exchanged among the fellows. It was not uncommon to see Navy bellbottoms with rolled-up cuffs, rounded instead of squared off hats, ties with knots looking more the fore and hand civilian version of the Windsor than the tried and true tradition of a great service, but these were young men who were making the best of coping with a difficult situation, but of course not without the normal expected amount of good-natured griping so typical of human nature.

§§

"String 'em tight, string 'em high," boats disciplined voice rang out as lessons in hammock-rigging reverberated throughout the building. "If you don't and the officer of the day comes thru during the night, he'll dump you and that's a long fall!" boats warned.

"Gee, Mr. Hill, this hammock doesn't look too comfortable," voiced Ed's new next door neighbor, a young 17 year old boy from Milwaukee, Wisconsin, named Ron Homer.

The company billeted in Barracks #2304 had just been brought up to full strength an hour or so before with the addition of eight recruits from the Wisconsin area and Ron was one of the eight. He had come to boot camp fully prepared. Golf clubs, tennis racket, baseball mitt! Some recuiter really must have sold him a bill of goods.

"What the hell do you think you're going to do with that crap," boats bellowed when Homer appeared on the scene dressed for battle (yeah, maybe battle on the golf course or tennis court).

"Well, sir, I thought there would be time for a little relaxation, and I didn't know if the Navy furnished the things I brought along."

"You get your ass and those items down to the base storage building right now, and I don't want to see hide nor hair of any of 'em until you finish your training here at Great Lakes, or there won't be any leave."

Homer, although not too bright about the ways of the world, was an exceptionally pleasant person to be around, always smiling, always happy, and because each hammock support area provided room for six hammocks and only five had been strung in Ed's area, plus the fact that Homer's last name started with an "H," well, voila, Hill-Homer side by side for the duration, the duration of boot camp, that is.

§§

A group of tired, apprehensive sailors marched to the mess hall that evening, thinking about the yet to come needle session and then the first night in those tricky canvas torture chambers.

"You call this chow?" Freddie cried out, as the spoonful of mixed vegetables was ladled onto his tray. "And, God, those potatoes! They don't look done!"

This was the first opportunity Ed and Fred had to talk over the happenings of the day since the noon meal because of Schumacher falling into the M through Z category and, of course, being assigned to the upper deck of the barracks. Fred sure looked different in his sailor outfit, Ed thought, you know actually sorta funny. Wonder what he thinks of my outfit.

"Ya know, one guy on my floor, oops I mean deck," Fred quickly corrected, "spit on the deck and he's back at the barracks. They have him scrubbing that same deck with a toothbrush. Can you imagine! A toothbrush! Another one of the fellows called the bulkhead a wall and he's been given a week's extra duty in the head. I'm just waiting for someone to slip and call the overhead a ceiling," Fred confided.

To himself he thought, boy, wouldn't it be nice to be laying out on a Lake Michigan beach with the girls, all the time thinking that we'd be going home to some of Ma's great homecooking.

"I wonder if we made a mistake by signing up," Freddie sighed.

§§

"Alright, guys, let's make that trip back, and let's look sharp doing it," Chief Larson boomed as he walked up and down reviewing the newly-formed body of men fresh from their first evening meal in this man's navy.

"You know that upon graduation, the company that has the best overall record for the same period of time here at Great Lakes will receive the coveted 'Red Rooster' award. This award is the top honor that can be given a company and each man in the winning company has this citation permanently engraved in his service record," the chief concluded.

"Let's go for it!" an excited Stosch shouted, arm and hand raised high. "We have the makings of the best bunch. Let's show the judges we should get that award."

The big, enthusiastic Polack had been voted recruit company commander earlier in the day, an honor he surely deserved and was capable of handling, an earlier example of his abilities being the excellent job of shepherding the 132 man contingent from the Chicago Loop to Great Lakes without incident or loss of personnel.

"Take over, company commander," Chief Larson ordered.

"Company, about face, forward march. Let's keep in step. Let's look sharp," as Stosch proudly stepped off and voiced his cadence and song. "Greenberg, you have two left feet! To the left, to the left, left, right, left..."

Back down Buckley Drive, under the viaduct, then right the contingent moved with a precision seldom seen so early in a training program, and on to the infirmary.

§§

"Is this Zebra Company?" the 1st class corpsman asked Stosch.

"Yes, sir, it is," Stosch snapped back as his heels came together and hand went up in a snappy salute.

"Save your salutes for the brass," the corpsman sneered. "Let's get the company in line alphabetically and single file, pass down the aisle between the hospital people, sleeves rolled up to the shoulder. The men will receive a shot in each shoulder as well as one in the right forearm."

"After receiving the shots, pass on down to the doctor, open your fly, break out your penis, roll back the foreskin if you have one, for short arm inspection. Let's get started."

One fellow didn't make it through the line. After the second shot, he passed out cold. Fortunately, the man in line behind him saw his knees buckle, reached out, and broke his fall.

"Greenberg, knock the cheese off your pecker," the doctor disgustingly barked as the little Jewish kid showed up for his turn in the limelight. "If you have a wet dream, clean yourself up!"

In less than one day this fellow was fast becoming the company celebrity, not really a coveted position to be in, especially in the service. "Boy, I can see why they call these corpsmen Pecker Checkers," Greenberg sighed. "They come by the name naturally."

§§

"Lights out in ten minutes," boats warned as, arms swinging, members of Zebra Company tried all known forms of remedy to ease the pain brought on by the medication used to immunize the recruits.

"Have you tried the sack yet?" Homer asked. "Gee, that rough canvas is sorta hard on the sore arms." The tight drawn hammocks left little free space between the occupant and its surfaces, causing two basic problems for the men required to sleep in them.

One, as Ron mentioned, the canvas rubbed salt into the already wounded body parts, and two, as a person swung up into the hammock, if fortunate enough in doing so not to roll over and either hang upside down or fall to the deck, it was OK. But if you once became situated in a lying position, just the slightest amount of motion side to side or fore and aft could cause a spinning or rotating action by the hammock, and boom, out you would go.

"Lights out!" boats ordered as taps could be heard off in the distance.

Now for a well-deserved rest after a very busy day, Hill thought. Wow, boom, damn! were comments that could be heard throughout the night in the barracks as unsuspecting occupants rolled out of their hammocks and down on the deck.

"Did you hear about George Coleman?" Freddie asked the next morning as the two waited in line for morning chow. "He fell out of his hammock and now he's in sick bay with a broken arm." What a beginning, what a first day!

§§

"You have any comments on that report, Bosun?" asked the persistent lieutenant, awakening the wandering thoughts of a man deep in nostalgia.

"No, sir," replied Hill after an embarrassed second. He felt he had to contribute something to this meeting. If we don't have this case solved by the time we get back to Hawaii, he might suggest contacting the Ellis Brothers or their lawyer on the outside chance they might have information to help.

§§

"Go on, Andrews. How about that second captain's mast? There sure wasn't much meat in the first report other than to verify the fact that this kid liked to gamble."

"Well, Lieutenant, I don't know. We might have a little more help, at least a few names. Daukins was caught, along with four other servicemen, playing poker for money this past February. About 0130 there had been lights out in their Ford Island barracks for some time. The master at arms thought he heard noise in the unoccupied rear part of the building, and sure enough, he found five fellows gambling by the light of a couple of flashlights. Picked up the money and put them all on report."

Andrews continued, "Other than Daukins, there was aviation ordinance man 1st Harry Jennings, Seaman 2nd Jim (Rusty) Pattern, Ben Cliner, another seaman 2nd, and a Marine Corporal, Heine Schuster. Daukins was given another five day tour of the brig and told that his 3rd class rating would be lifted if found gambling again."

"How about the other four? Anything on them?" the lieutenant asked.

"No, nothing. I do have their service numbers that might help."

"It sure might, Herb. First chance you get after we secure from this meeting, check our ship's roster, get some help down in your office, see if any of these numbers check with our present crew. Ed, how about you helping on this one? I talked with Capt. Fielder earlier today and he's assigned you to the investigation. Your normal duties will be taken over by others."

"And you say Daukins was exonerated on the third charge just this past month?" the lieutenant continued.

"Yes, and lucky for him he was because this would have been major time if convicted. Could have been life in the brig. He was charged with statutory rape of a 16 year old girl. The two were caught in a $25 a night room in the Royal Hawaiian Hotel, not only naked but in a compromising position."

"It seems the house detective was alerted by a civilian guest who had the room next door. Lots of noise, loud music, drinking and etc. When the detective knocked on the door, he got no answer, so used his pass key. One thing led to another and when it was found that the young lady was underage, the military police and juvenile authorities were brought in. Daukins was charged and brought before the base commander, but then strange things began to happen."

"Daukins claimed he met the girl at the Honolulu Bucket of Blood just that evening. She'd been partying with friends, drinking Bloody Marys, dancing, singing, having one hell of a time. He took a chance, asked her to dance, and the rest was history. She thought he was one good-looking, fun guy. He thought she was 21, IDs were checked at the door, and sure enough. She had an ID showing she was of age, but when it came down to cases, it wasn't hers."

"The real surprise turned up at the hearing later. This girl was married to a young Army Air Force lieutenant, a navigator on a B17 recently assigned to an airbase on Midway Island. All sides looked at the case and agreed that in the eyes of the metalsmith, he was having sex with a consenting adult. He didn't know she was married, and all charges were dropped. There was no further information in Navy records regarding the young lady."

§§

The lieutenant asked Ron if he was able to talk with the six men assigned to Daukins' compartment, the fellows who weren't available during the first muster. He had, but drew a blank. Nobody knew anything about Daukins. They really didn't know who he was talking about.

Further check with the people he worked for, how he happened to come aboard, what his duties were, etc. also drew a blank. While Daukins came under LCdr. Billy Blake's group, the commander had not even met him.

Klein in the sheet metal shop said that both Tarry and Daukins had been sent aboard as replacements, came from the personnel pool on Ford Island. Tarry had worked with Daukins in the base sheet metal shop but only a nodding acquaintance.

Klein had met Daukins when he came aboard, gave him the day to get settled, told him to report for duty next morning. Klein said he had not requested any specific replacements because he didn't know anyone on the base.

Disappointed, Lt. Craiger said they'd just have to keep plugging. Cdr. Chamer, unable to attend the meeting, had asked that the lieutenant give the green light to burying Fred Daukins. Not really having a morgue down in sick bay and with high temperatures, bodies didn't last long.

All necessary photographs, blood and tissue samples, autopsy report, locker and sea bag items of the deceased had been preserved and assembled into a watertight, floatable container. Should anything happen to Yorktown during the coming engagement, Ed Hill and/or Herb Andrews would be responsible for seeing that the items were delivered to the Judge Advocate General's offices in Hawaii.

Shacter was asked to take care of the details. Daukins would be buried at first light that morning.

§§

Meanwhile, Jack Fletcher was concerned, and rightfully so, on this June 3d evening as he gathered his flock for a final briefing regarding the job ahead. He was still stinging from the Coral Sea engagement. His flagship, this same Yorktown, had taken a hit from a bomb dropped by a Japanese Val. Fortunate in being hit only once, the 550 pounder sliced down to below the hangar deck level before exploding. She was lucky, although seriously damaged.

In this same battle, the large Lexington (CV-2) was the object of a coordinated attack by 33 unmolested Japanese Vals and 9 Kates. She took two torpedo hits on the portside plus two bomb hits. Unfortunately, insidious danger lay in the fracturing of aviation fuel mains and tank bulkheads. Being an early conversion, the Lexington had aviation fuel tanks built integrally with the hull, whereas later ships had separate containments supported by, but not part of, the structure.

Fumes began to accumulate resulting in a massive explosion an hour after the attack. The crew was transferred to destroyers alongside and shortly after sunset, deserted, the great ship received several torpedoes from her escort and sank.

§§

The Battle of the Coral Sea had been the first real setback for the Japanese. Their invasion plans had been thwarted. New Guinea held out. The small carrier Shoho had been sunk and the ravaged large carrier Shokaku returned home as evidence of the enemy's resolve. But it was not a clearcut allied victory. Lexington was the greatest material loss and it set in train the requirements leading to the recall of the Wasp from the North Atlantic at a time when her presence could have been decisive on the Atlantic route.

§§

Immediately upon docking the Yorktown in Pearl Harbor, Fletcher had been summoned to Pacific fleet headquarters and the highest level conference with its supreme commander, Admiral Nimitz.

Any feelings of invincibility in the Japanese armada were understandable but misplaced, as the Americans, although materially inferior, had the tremendous advantage of having broken codes to a point where the bulk of their plans had been appreciated a month before. They who would surprise were about to be surprised.

Commander Gerald Cummings, in charge of intelligence for Nimitz, had reported a lot of Japanese traffic regarding a spot in the

Pacific known as Midway Island, a U.S. possession. At least he and his men thought it was Midway. Nimitz wasn't sold on the fact that this might be the next step Yamamoto's fleet would take in their attempt to conquer the Pacific. Cummings facts regarding the attack were thin. Maybe 10% of his supposition was fact, the remaining 90% just good old-fashioned gut feeling.

In order to convince the Admiral that the Japanese were going to attack Midway, Cummings devised a plan. He would write a message stating that Midway's fresh water condenser had broken down. He would ask the Admiral to have the message flown to Midway, they in turn would send the message in code in a way that the Japanese could not help intercept it. The next day the Japanese repeated the message, "Canton" - Japanese code word for Midway - "fresh water condenser had broken down." Nimitz was convinced. Yamamoto's next strike would be the tiny bastion in the Pacific.

§§

Knowledge of the impending raid was one thing. What to do about it was something else entirely. Carriers obviously were the key to success and the Americans at that moment were reduced to only two, Enterprise and Hornet. Yorktown, undergoing repair of her Coral Sea damage, would be ready in another 48 hours.

Another disaster was looming. Bull Halsey, Nimitz's top carrier commander, was in the base hospital suffering from a skin disease. Who would lead this task force so necessary in order to deter our hated enemy? He could send Jack Fletcher back out on the Yorktown heading up the group labeled TF17, consisting of 2 cruisers and 5 destroyers, but with Halsey under the weather, who would lead Enterprise, Hornet, the cruisers and destroyers known as Task Force 16?

Halsey had suggested that Admiral Spruance, a cruiser sailor, take over his responsibility. Nimitz pondered this suggestion for some time before agreeing. What would Washington think? They already were skeptical about subjecting a goodly balance of our carrier fleet to an operation that was so uncertain. Now putting this precious commodity in the hands of a skipper who couldn't fly! Well, Jack Fletcher wasn't a pilot either and he had done one hell of a good job leading his carriers at Coral Sea. Fletcher was senior so he would have the final say regarding the combined fleet. The die was cast.

When Admiral King and his staff reviewed Nimitz's plan in Washington, one prominent factor stood out. It consisted of three carriers, nine cruisers, and fifteen destroyers, but what about the wagons? What task force would do battle without battleships? Nimitz' answer: the lack of battleships would be offset by the possession of Midway itself, whose airfields were reinforced until they fairly bulged with aircraft.

§§

Back in Japan, a tenuous balance of power remained. Yamamoto, the able commander of the Imperial Fleet's main body, had evolved a complex plan to take Midway Island, a territory sensitive to America.

Unaware that Commander Cummings and his able staff back in Hawaii had cracked the Japanese secret code and forewarned Nimitz of impending dangers, Yamamoto's main concern was to get his major strength to a suitable ambush position without arousing American suspicions.

Nimitz had great respect for the abilities of the Japanese admiral. He had been responsible for planning the December 7, 1941 attack on Pearl Harbor. Although many in America considered Yamamoto a fiend, a sly, sneaky preditor out to ravage the American nation, he actually was a very intelligent, well-educated, concerned man who had tried to convince his emperor and diet that making war on the United States was like committing suicide for the Japanese nation.

Yamamoto had spent a number of years in the States. He had been educated at the better eastern universities and spent time as a diplomat in Washington, D.C. His stay in the United States allowed him to travel extensively. He envisioned that not only did the country have an abundance of raw materials necessary to build a mammoth war machine, but that it had the steel mills, assembly lines, skilled workers and capital to back it. A sleeping giant.

When Yamamoto came to grips with the fact that the Japanese nation was not going to back down in its effort to seek war with America, he realized that the only chance for victory was one giant sweep of America's Pacific fleet, hence Pearl Harbor, which turned out to be a tremendous victory for the Japanese. Coral Sea was considered more or less a stand-off, but if the balance of Nimitz's fleet could be lured out into the area of Midway, Admiral Nagumo, the ravager of Pearl Harbor, his carriers, and the greater part of the Japanese fleet would be waiting to crush it once and for all, allowing the aggressor to roam the Pacific unmolested.

To effect this, he would have shore stations exchange W/T traffic with a fictitious fleet while the striking force took up its station under a cloak of total wireless silence. In addition, a feint operation was to be mounted the day before against the Aleutian Islands.

§§

Nagumo's striking force consisted of carriers Akagi, Kaga, Hiryu, and Soryu, 3 cruisers and 12 destroyers. His task would be to reduce Midway Island's defenses to a point where the occupation force of 5,000 men could go in. The force was borne in 16 transports, covered by two specialist seaplane carriers, two battleships, eight cruisers and thirty-three destroyers.

Yamamoto himself, with the venerable Hosho and three battleships, would be placed 300 miles behind Nagumo's forces so as to be a mobile reinforcement either to the Midway or Aleutian operations, should such be necessary.

§§

Nimitz in turn was relying for sighting reports on the Japanese fleet by submarine and long range B17 and PBY Catalina flights from Midway. By 2 June nothing had been reported and the U.S. carrier groups had combined, marking time in a position about 350 miles northeast of the island and well-placed to surprise any assault by the enemy.

On the morning of the 3rd of June, a far-ranging PBY sighted a large group of ships about 700 miles southwest of Midway. Suspected of being the invasion force, it was left unmolested until mid-afternoon, when, its identity confirmed, it was bombed by B17s from Midway without results. This low-key reaction puzzled Yamamoto, but Nimitz was after bigger game in the shape of Nagumo's carrier group, suspected of lurking under the thick overcast of a front coming down from the northwest.

CINCPAC retained overall control of the operation from Pearl Harbor. And this further concerned Admiral Fletcher as he discussed strategy with his staff. Fletcher was left in tactical command, given the general instruction that his operations were to be governed by "the principals of calculated risk!" What in the hell is "calculated risk," pondered the confused admiral. It sounds like one of those deals "damned if you do or damned if you don't." Fletcher knew that his responsibilities were considerable, being fully aware that the loss of his carriers would leave the Pacific wide open and as had been suggested by Washington, leaving the West Coast of the United States unprotected.

As the passing hours of the night of the 3rd of June brought no news of Nagumo's whereabouts, Fletcher ended his staff meeting, suggesting that men not on duty get as much rest as possible. The next day could be both a busy and dangerous one. He left orders that as the night hours passed, the task force close on Midway.

§§

As dawn flushed the eastern sky on the day of June 4, the American force was 200 miles to the northeast of the island. Lt. Shacter, in command of the six-man Marine burial detail, gave orders to proceed with the ceremony. A flag covered Aviation Metalsmith 3rd Class Fred Daukins' body, a five inch shell between its legs, had been sewn into a canvas bag and placed in a wire basket used aboard ship to move wounded to and from sick bay. Lt. Jerry Rice, Catholic chaplain aboard Yorktown, gave a short homily, prayers and a blessing. The Marine honor guard, rifles raised, fired a volley while the bugler blew taps, and the body slipped from beneath its American flag and basket into the deep emerald-blue ocean below.

§§

About this same time Captain Bill Fielder was awakened by his aide, given a quick summary of happenings since turning in a few hours earlier, and laid back for just a few minutes of thought before tackling the duties of the day.

He looked around at the furnishings of his very fine sea cabin and thought back to the days just out of flight school at Pensacola when he went aboard his first carrier as a bushy-tailed lieutenant. He could remember sharing a very small compartment with three other fledgling flyers, sleeping in the top bunk, only a few feet between his outstretched body and the overhead, tight quarters, yes, but the compartment had a lifesaver's porthole some times left open to provide God's homemade air-conditioning, necessary in this sultry, humid climate of the south Atlantic. The 12' diameter opening in the ship's thick bulkhead provided Bill with a never-ending panorama of the some times green, grey, then various shades of blue, waters, or the silver, star-like trailings of its screening vessels' wake as they passed in the night. How beautiful.

But these same waters could be deadly, reminisced the Captain. Arresting gear had come a long way from the original mechanism used aboard Langley (CV-1). Heavy ropes anchored on either end by bags of cement, each held by a half dozen men, this would be the means of retarding the forward progress of the old biplanes as they floated over the deck, tail hook dangling in the air, searching, reaching for that precious deck pendant. Miss a rope or come in fast causing the arresting gear device, its crew as well as the airplane to go over the side. This could be fatal. The Captain could vouch for that. He had that experience many years ago.

Bill and his instructor making practice landings aboard this same USS Langley had picked up a rope but the tail hook parted from the rear of the aircraft it was mounted to, causing the machine and its occupants to go over the side, killing the instructor, breaking both ankles of the student. Yes, Captain

Fielder proudly wore those coveted gold wings of a naval pilot. Yes, after the accident his flying days were over and, yes, each morning as he pulled on his socks and shoes and felt the forever remaining pain in the poorly mended bones of his ankles, he would thank the good Lord for another day, and this 4th of June 1942 was no exception.

§§

"Captain, what can I bring you for breakfast, sir?" asked the aging 52 year old stewards mate, this after knocking on the compartment hatch and entering the ship's sanctioned quarters.

"How about some toast and coffee, Jim? You might just be one hell of a busy guy today and I don't want to add to your burden."

"Sir, you're never a burden. You know I'm honored to serve you," voiced the small, slightly humped, muscular Negro man, clad in a stiffly starched, smartly pressed mess jacket typical of the corps traditionally serving the officers of this man's navy.

Chief Stewards Mate Jim Caffrey had spent the past 32 years of his life in the service, the last eight years with Captain Fielder. He had been asked to muster out of the service at 30 years, but Bill Fielder pulled a few strings, got him a chief's rating, and the two continued to serve together, great friends. The Captain considered Jim a confidant. It was not uncommon to find the two in the privacy of the sea cabin, late in the evening, discussing not only the duties of the day, but their private lives.

It was no surprise that the chief's youngest son, Sam, just out of Howard University with a degree in business, had been accepted for training in an all-colored Army Air Force fighter squadron being put together down in South Carolina. Just mention Sam's name when Jim was in the area and you would have thought that the buttons on his spotless jacket were about to pop. Not only had Sam quarterbacked the Howard football team for the past three years, but he had been a straight "A" student, never in trouble, a joy to be around.

In contrast, Bill Fielder's twin boys, the same age as Sam, had been in and out of the doghouse, both at home and at the Academy. Annapolis had not been Mike nor Bob's choice for further formal education, but over their objections, again strings were pulled. The two brothers became ensigns and were presently in flight school down in Pensacola, Florida.

Many nights as the two men sat discussing their families, the subject of race would rear its ugly head. The Captain had real feelings for the Negro, and in his command, whether it be shore or sea duty, had done everything in his power to see that the colored man served with dignity and equality. As mentioned earlier, the Navy wardroom tradition was that the Negro serve the white officer, more or less a carryover from the earlier days of the deep south. Aboard Yorktown, this tradition continued but in addition to serving duties, the colored stewards would be given gunnery assignments during general quarters.

The ship had one 20 millimeter gun tub on its portside aft manned solely by Negroes. The tub was under the direct command of Chief Caffrey and had distinguished itself at the Battle of Coral Sea, being credited with downing a Zeke and a Betty.

This morning as the steward poured his skipper's coffee, he was asked if there had been any comments in the ranks of the serving corps regarding the death of 3d Class Fred Daukins.

"No, sir. I'm not sure that any of our fellows are aware of the incident. I know that I haven't brought it up."

"Well, that's fine, Jim, but I'm concerned. Hard to believe one man could take another shipmate's life when there is so much necessary killing going on with the enemy."

§§

About 250 miles west of the American Task Force position, the same light was catching the wings of over 100 enemy aircraft formatting above their carriers cruising in the darkness below. Nagumo, the task force commander, was moving on his softening-up mission of Midway. He figured that the island might be well-fortified with protective aircraft, so roughly one-third of the incoming armada was made up of Zero fighters.

§§

"Holy cow, Lieutenent, look at those ships below us at about 10 o'clock. Must be the entire Japanese navy. Sparks, send the message, 'Jap fleet located."

The PBY searching the likely sector had spotted Nagumo's ships at 0530, one hour after the carrier aircraft had departed. Nimitz's plan to launch a number of patrol planes from Midway, each searching a given sector, had paid off, but although the message of sighting had been received both by Midway and Fletcher, it did not indicate how many ships, what type, or at what latitude and longitude. About the same time Midway received a ground radar report of the approaching strike still 100 miles out.

§§

Soon after Fred Daukins' burial at sea, Yorktown had launched ten SBDs, scouts, each given a sector to search and forewarned not to exceed a 100 mile range, so that if the Japanese fleet was sighted, they could easily be recovered, rearmed with bombs, and become part of the force necessary to annihilate the enemy. Spruance's Task Force 16 would stand ready with planes from Enterprise (CV-6) and Hornet (CV-8).

"Major Donaldson, how many planes can you put up in defense of the island?"

"Colonel, about 15 Buffaloes and 5 Wildcats are on the runway ready to roll."

"Gosh, Major, those are relics. Radar shows the enemy coming in with over a hundred aircraft. Pearl Harbor and Coral Sea engagements showed Yamamoto using only the latest Zeroes, Vals and Kates. They'll blow you out of the sky!"

"We'll give 'em a fight for their money, Colonel," commented Marine Major Donaldson, as he and his brave band of pilots climbed into the cockpits of their aging weapons. "Don't count us out yet."

At 15,000 ft. the little armada from Midway spotted three levels of aircraft below and to the east, each traveling in tight, precision-like formations.

"Let's go get 'em, Marines," shouted the Marine Major over the intercom, as he dipped the left wing of his F4F and pointed her nose down. "Let's make 'em pay!"

These would be the last words voiced by the veteran pilot. Soon the Zeroes flying cover for the aggressor force would prove base commander Marine Colonel Skyler right. The protecting F4Fs and Buffaloes were blown out of the sky. Only 3 Wildcats returned to Midway, while the crew of 3 Zeroes and 2 Vals would meet their maker.

§§

"Let's get those TBFs and B26s into the air and on their way before Nagumo's birds hit the island and catch 'em on the ground," ordered the concerned C.O.

The TBF, the new Grumman Avenger, was to see its first action. It was 70 miles an hour faster than the TBD and could carry twice the payload. Previous action against the enemy had shown the U.S. torpedo plane inferior to its Japanese counterpart.

§§

Out-to-sea things began to happen. As Yorktown was recovering her scouts, Spruance, known for his aggressiveness, wasted no time closing on Nagumo's reported position at top speed. He must not let Halsey down. The Admiral had recommended him as his replacement. Why? Because like the Bull, Ray was a go-getter.

§§

"Wow," shouted the excited corporal as he climbed down from his 25 ft. high observation tower, heading for a nearby foxhole. "They're comin' in from all directions, and I think those bright flashes are machine gun bullets! They're strafing already."

First the Zeroes, then the Vals, finally the Kates, each about 50 ft. above the runways, each with their guns blazing, then as they found specific targets would drop their bombs of various capacity. The island's anti-aircraft guns, mainly 30 and 50 caliber old-fashioned, water-cooled machine guns tried their best, gun barrels red hot with the heat generated by the constant firing, causing minor damage to the enemy's in-flight armada, acts of heroism in most every foxhole or bunker unnoticed because they were so common.

§§

As Lt. Commander Nemora, sporting several bullet holes in the wings of his Val, surveyed the island's damage from a safe distance above, he knew that his mission would require a second strike. This first strike had caused little damage on the ground, and Nagumo would demand total destruction of the island's defenses as well as its ability to raise havoc with the ships of his fleet, this before committing the 5000 invasion troops waiting closeby. Nagumo thought preparing a second strike would not be of great importance as he did not suspect the presence of the American carriers.

§§

Spruance knew that all of the Japanese aircraft had left Midway by 06.50. He would launch TF16 strike after 07.00, timing it to arrive at the time when Nagumo's flight decks would be cluttered with recovered aircraft, fuel tanks and bomb racks empty, as well as guns unarmed. Fletcher would launch TF17's might about an hour later, as soon as all scouts were aboard and Yorktown's flight deck reset for launch.

§§

"Admiral, at 07.10 our CAP has reported Grumman Avengers and B26 Marauders coming in," shouted Nagumo's air officer, Captain Kimimora, "but they have the situation well in hand. In fact, shot down 7 of the enemy."

"Have Kaga's combat-ready aircraft exchange their anti-ship weapons for high-explosive bombs," ordered the Admiral. "These twin engine aircraft have to be coming from Midway. A second strike is imperative. We have no information of any enemy surface fleet in the vicinity."

"Admiral, at 07.25 one of our cruiser float planes has reported that an American surface force is approaching," exclaimed the slightly confused Kimimora.

"Stop the rearming of the aircraft," demanded a disturbed Nagumo, "especially the Kates still armed with torpedoes."

But then between 08.00 and 08.30 came three heavy raids, from obviously shore-based aircraft and although they were repulsed, Nagumo was concerned which target needed neutralizing first.

§§

Nagumo had every right to be concerned. Before leaving Japan on its mission to Midway, a high level meeting had been held by Yamamoto and his top admirals at which time Nagumo voiced his distrust with the intelligence information on hand. The Japanese admirals had been told that, although it had not actually been sighted recently, last reports indicated the American fleet safely in Pearl Harbor.

Prior to the fleet leaving Japan, a group of submarines would be stationed in such a pattern as to allow it to scout and report any movement of Halsey's fleet in or out of Hawaii. This did not satisfy Nagumo who asked that an actual sighting of the fleet in the harbor be arranged. When one of Nagumo's compatriots implied that the Admiral was becoming soft, he angrily replied that he had taken his carriers within a few hundred miles of Pearl and that his aircraft devestated the American fleet, this a much more dangerous mission, and he would do the same at Midway.

Although the Admiral had voiced confidence in the presence of his men, he took the extra precaution just this morning to have four of his cruiser's float planes launched, each to patrol a ninety degree sector of the area around Midway, and it was one of the float planes which reported a sighting at 07.25.

§§

At 06.30 aboard Yorktown, the last SBD touched down picking up number one wire, and after receiving a sign from Lt. Shingleton to cut engines, the pilot and radioman stepped down from the Scout onto the flight deck and headed for #2 ready room. Six yellow-shirted plane handlers rushed back to push the plane into an area that would correspond with the eventual take-off position for the air group's dive bombers while its plane captain, red-shirted ordinance men, and gasoline crews went about the duties of readying the aircraft for the upcoming strike along with every other plane aboard certified airworthy.

The grim, serious flight deck officer faced the responsibility of seeing that these potent weapons of destruction, parked forward of the barriers as well as below on the hangar deck while landings were taking place, now be brought into position or spotted for takeoff. The torpedo planes were parked back aft, then the dive bombers, and up forward the fighters, the aircraft that required minimum distance to become airborne.

§§

The Yorktown had been at flight quarters since early in the day. The flight crews had had the traditional breakfast of steak and eggs, and soon after assembled in one or more of the ship's ready rooms, were briefed on weather conditions, enemy position, the situation at Midway as well as the goings-on aboard its sister task force TF16.

While Admiral Jack Fletcher sat in his leather sea chair on the austere bridge of Yorktown, receiving data, digesting it, and deciding the fate of this hungry, bare-bones fleet, Captain Fielder, along with the air officer and air group commander, stood on the open catwalk of the air bridge overlooking the take-off position of the aircraft warming up on the flight deck below.

Then the order, "pilots, man your planes," followed by, "let's get this ship headed into the wind," as the airmen raced from the ready rooms, through the island hatch onto the flight deck, up onto the wings of their respective aircraft, into the cockpits of the fighting machines soon to engage the enemy. Plane captains helped with chute packs, seat belts and shoulder harnesses; radiomen and gunners checked weapons; pilots surveyed the instruments which would be some indication of success or failure of the mission.

Then at 0700 the flight deck officer's arm and white flag came down indicating the engines of the first F4F in line of fighting squadron #3 had revved up to a pitch that satisfied the trained ear of the khaki-clad lieutenant and that the leader of Yorktown's protectors could push his throttle full forward, release his brakes, and head for the ever-shortening end of the flight deck, then hard over and back stick and rudder, wheels up, and the agile little Wildcat in the hands of an experienced master seemed to leap from its home aboard, bank to starboard, and head into the wild blue yonder, only to cruise in time while the balance of the squadron formed up.

Second position on deck fell to Ensign Lopez, designated LCdr. Mullen's wing man. Lopez had not drawn a flight assignment since his run-in with Lt. Crantz after the earlier near-fatal landing aboard Yorktown, but now, not only would he have a chance to vindicate himself when he returned, but the opportunity to get one or more Jap kills.

Takeoffs continued like a well-oiled watch until, with only three more TBDs to take to the air, the engine of 1stLt. Caker and his radioman gunner Willie Smaltz sputtered as it neared the end of the runway, veered to port, and seemed to glide into the angry ocean below.

Pilot and gunner could be seen evacuating the plane, May Wests inflated, looking longingly up toward the bow of the great ship as it began to pass them by. No sooner had the ill-fated torpedo plane begun its voyage into the deep when Captain Bill Fielder's order rang out loud and clear to the helmsman on duty "stop all engines," and to maneuver the ship's fan tail in the direction of starboard, making every effort not to suck the floating airmen into the ten foot diameter screws that could chew them up and spit them out like hamburger.

Captain Fielder had a standing order aboard all carriers he skippered that the helmsmen be drilled and drilled again in executing the order just given. Again he would remember the day aboard the old Langley when he and his flight instructor had lost a tail hook on the biplane they were taking off in, had dropped into the water below, breaking both his ankles, and sucking the unsuspecting trainer into the whirling blades of the ship's propulsion system, causing Bill Fielder to have nightmares to this day.

Then there was the recent incident as Yorktown was steaming home to Pearl after Coral Sea. A long-time flying chief Ronney Heller had been drummed back into a combat F4F squadron because of a lack of available experienced commissioned pilots at the time. He had performed admirably during the skirmish, shooting down a Kate and a possible Zero. When only 200 miles out from his home base and while taking off on an anti-sub patrol carrying two depth charges, his little Wildcat's engine sputtered and died when halfway down the deck. Ronney made every effort to brake the cramming aircraft and almost succeeded.

But as the end of the flight deck loomed up and just before a full stop could be made, the two front wheels of the landing gear eased over the edge. The plane somersaulted forward of the massive ship's bow, hitting the water at the same time the vessel passed over it.

There was complete silence for what seemed like an eternity. Then the ping-ping sounds of the depth charges going off when they reached their set depth, this as the pressure exploded against the giant hull of the carrier, the fusilage of the aircraft, and the body of Chief Heller.

But this was another day, thought the Captain, and we have munitions to deliver to an unsuspecting enemy. Let's get on with the launching. No time for reminiscing.

§§

"Captain, any report from our air groups?" asked an anxious Ray Spruance as he stood, bent over, hanging his chin on the steel shrapnel guard protecting the catwalk of the air bridge.

"No, Admiral, the groups are still at radio silence. I can report that our TF16 strike got off 20 fighters, 68 dive bombers, and 29 torpedo planes and when fully formed up had 200 miles to go before engaging the enemy."

§§

Aboard Nagumo's carriers, confusion reigned. Kates recently stripped of torpedoes and anti-personnel bombs to take on bombs normally used against land-based targets started to have the operation reversed. These planes could not be positioned on the carriers' flight decks for take-off due to the first aircraft starting to return from the strike on Midway, low on fuel, some with damage both to crewman and machine. It would not be until 09.15 that the Japanese carriers would be able to turn to face the enemy. Admiral Spruance's TF16 strike group was only ten minutes away.

"Admiral, fire control reports 15 TBDs coming in low on the water," voiced Nagumo's aide. "Damn," exclaimed the Admiral, "these planes must be coming from an enemy carrier."

§§

"Form up, Ensign Gay," ordered the skipper of Hornet's torpedo eight.

"But where's our air cover, Commander?" asked the young pilot.

"We must have lost 'em in the layered clouds above. Let's not worry about our fighters. Let's concentrate on those three big beautiful bastards ahead."

§§

Nagumo's carrier force at the time found Akagi, Soryu and Kaga in a formation about 20 miles from Hiryu. Between them, the Japanese carriers had 80 or more Zeroes scrambled, and they eagerly hit a badly fragmented American force which at that range had no fuel to spare for reforming.

As Nagumo stood on Akagi's bridge, he witnessed the slaughter his ship's guns performed as they put up a wall of fire against the slow, lumbering outdated TBDs of first air group 8 followed by 14 TBDs from the Enterprise. When the smoke had cleared, all 15 of Hornet's aircraft and 10 from the Enterprise contingent had been splashed, mostly outside of range to drop torpedoes, and the Japanese force continued to bore on, still unscathed.

"More torpedo bombers! That can't be," said the surprised commander of the Japanese striking force.

"Yes, Admiral, our air cover is reporting 12 more Devastators coming in both from port and starboard being covered by a few F4Fs."

At about the same time, the guns of the entire invading fleet opened fire, and within minutes ten of the twelve Yorktown TDBs would be sent to a watery grave.

§§

"What the hell's goin' on, Captain?" asked an excited Jack Fletcher, as all transmission from the planes of his striking force seemed to go dead.

"I don't know, Admiral, but the last information we had indicated of the 41 Devastators that found and attacked the Japanese fleet 35 had been lost, for no result."

"That can't be, Captain. These were experienced squadrons. Over four years with the carriers. God, when Nimitz hears this, he'll have a heart attack!"

"We're not through yet, Skipper. We still have those SBDs ready to attack."

§§

Aboard Akagi, Nagumo and his aides were feeling better. His attackers had been virtually wiped out, and by superhuman efforts his own strike was ready to be launched. The order was given to have the carriers turned into the wind, and at 10.24 precisely, Akagi gave the executive order launch. Even as they did so, there was seen far above the glint of other wings as the American SBDs began their dives.

Ensign Gay was one of those privileged spectators who would see those dark specks forming about the mighty enemy's imperial fleet. Perched atop his yellow-colored rubber life raft, it seemed almost a dream. In shallows the ocean seemed tropical, shoaling from pale green to deep blue, and clean, clear, yet in sight in broad daylight he had witnessed the devastating massacre of 34 of his fellow crew, brave men going to their slaughter, asking no quarter and getting none.

He had followed his squadron commander in as they each made their torpedo run on Akagi. It seemed like a run on hell. LCdr. Craton was within torpedo release distance when a large caliber shell exploded just behind the rear gunner's compartment, blowing the aircraft and its occupants into smithereens, the young ensign having to bank sharply to port in order to avoid being hit by pieces of the wreckage.

Then after what seemed an eternity, the Akagi came closer and closer. Ensign Gay reached for the torpedo release lever when wham, bang, hot metal, then pain shot through his right arm, sparks emanated from the side of the aircraft. It seemed as though mighty external forces lifted the TBD high into the air, then dropped it dangerously close to the ocean below, lifted it up again, hurling it over the bow of the mighty carrier and slamming it in a cartwheel manner into the waters presently occupied by the wounded aviator.

Dazed, he could feel the plane slowly sinking into the blue waters below. He climbed out on the wing, yelled back to his radioman-gunner slumped over the 30 caliber machine gun ring, blood flowing from beneath his summer flight helmet, not moving.

"Red, let's get outa here before this sucker takes us with it!" No answer.

Gay had walked back on the wing and with one good arm and hand, released the gunner's shoulder harness and seat belt, only to have the radioman slump to the floor of the aircraft exposing massive, massive stomach and back wounds. This man was dead.

There had been time to release the inflatable raft, climb aboard and paddle away, just as the aircraft's tail rose high in the air as the gallant machine slipped silently into the waters below. Now he could apply what little first aid was available, then hope that Nagumo's screening vessels wouldn't spot him, while taking in the firey show unfolding before him.

§§

"Let's form up with Yorktown's SBDs, men," shouted LCdr. Spider Maxwell, squadron commander of Enterprise's dive bomber group. "We'll go in together."

The Enterprise aircraft had overshot but had the luck to sight a lone Japanese destroyer and realized it was heading for the main body of the Japanese fleet. Following its projected course, they arrived over the Japanese carriers at the same time as Yorktown's group. All of the Zeroes were low down, low on fuel and ammunition after the destruction of the TBDs and the 55 Dauntlesses formed up without interference.

The Hornet's SBDs had missed its target altogether. Low on fuel, most of them either returned to home base or flew on to Midway for safe haven.

"Check those electronic bomb release switches, and if they're not working properly use manual release," ordered Clint Herker, veteran skipper of the Yorktown contingent as he winged over and pointed the nose of his sturdy, proven SBD into a power glide mode heading for the deck of Nagumo's flagship, Akagi, below.

"We're with you, Clint," voiced the Enterprise leader over the intercom, following suit, his group focusing on the closeby Kaga. Vengeance for the destruction of the TBDs was about to begin.

"Look at that bugger burn, Commander," yelled Harry Blitzstein, Herker's radioman, as the bomber pulled out of its power dive, this only after releasing two 500 pound bombs that smashed into the Japanese aircraft warming up on deck, armed and ready for takeoff.

Flames and explosions erupted above and below decks; men and machine could be seen being catapulted over the side, against each other, into the air, all of which caused a continuous chain reaction as SBD after SBD completed its dive, releasing the weapons of mass destruction on the inferno below.

Conditions aboard Kaga were no different. Cdr. Maxwell's brave, mostly unopposed warriors were having the same success, so much so that both squadron commanders ordered the balance of their combined assault force to focus on Soryu which was shocked to a standstill by three bomb hits, two of which wrecked the hangar deck, their explosions forcing out the forward elevator. Within minutes, like the Akagi and Kaga, Soryu was an inferno both above and below deck.

"Let's go home, men. That's a job well done," cried a jubilant Herker as he viewed the firey destruction.

"Yeah, let's hightail it back before our luck runs out," agreed an equally happy Spider Maxwell. "My fuel gauge shows less than half and that's not good. What the devil happened to the Zeroes our TBDs reported earlier?"

Commander Maxwell was commenting on the 80 odd Japanese fighters, most of which had been in the air above and beyond their normal fuel capability, had been pulled down low to help destroy the American torpedo bombers, now shocked to see their home base a mass of flames.

Remnants of the fighter protection in air groups of the Yorktown, Hornet and Enterprise bored in on the unsuspecting Zeroes as they maneuvered toward landing space either in the ocean or off at the distance, the unmolested Hiryu.

"You got one, Commander!" yelled the excited Lopez as his wingman hot on the tail of a speedy maneuverable meatball pressed the trigger on the stick of his F4F. The Jap Zero seemed to disintegrate before his eyes.

"Chalk up another" could be heard over the intercom, then a frantic "watch out behind, Ensign," as incendiary bullets tore at the plastic canopy housing the young Hispanic pilot. Then another yell "get out, Lopez" as the cockpit of the F4F went up in a blaze of fire.

Two Zeroes, one from the side and one from above, had penetrated the American defenses and poured 50 caliber bullets into the little fighter as it rolled over on its back, glided to starboard, then as its blazing canopy tore off, an on-fire bundle seemed to fall away from it, plummeting alongside the screaming plane, both hitting the ocean below at about the same time.

Then all was silent. Ensign Lopez's chute never opened. He would worry no more about Lt. Crantz or that next landing aboard Yorktown.

§§

Aboard the flaming Akagi, Nagumo was forced to transfer his flag to a cruiser, soon after abandoned by her crew, but undamaged below the water line, had to be put down by one of her escorts. Kaga was also abandoned and eventually blew up and sank, as did the Soryu.

Aboard Hiryu, all landings had been curtailed. Nagumo's second in command, Admiral Sakota, was preparing to launch the 18 Val dive bombers available, escorted by a handful of Zeroes. He saw the chance of reversing the fortunes by hitting the American carriers during the delicate recovery phase.

§§

"I can't believe we caught Nagumo with his pants down," shouted the jubilant TF17 leader aboard Yorktown. "Three great big, juicy carriers! I'd sure like to be in Pearl when Nimitz gets this report."

Both Spruance and Fletcher had turned their fleet into the wind and begun to take on the returning victorious flight crews, and in some cases, their battered, low on fuel, aircraft. Both admirals were pleased but puzzled as to why there had been no retaliation to their strikes. Had the SBDs caught the unsuspecting Nagumo with full deck loads of planes, not having gotten any of their dive bombers or torpedo planes into the air before the attack? Nagumo must have had information on the whereabouts of the American fleet. Where was his intelligence? He had annihilated three brave TBD squadrons. He must have known they came from American carriers, not Midway.

§§

Jack Fletcher's TF17 was being shadowed by a Japanese cruiser float plane. Sakota knew exactly where the American devils were. With his pursuing dive bombers in the air and on their way, all he could do now was contemplate. The remaining sons of heaven would sell their lives dearly. The Emperor would be avenged.

§§

"When we once get all our flock aboard, Captain, let's prepare another strike. Could be that some of Nagumo's cruisers and tin cans are still around with the idea of softening up Midway for troop landings."

"Admiral ordered another strike, fellows, so let's get with it as time allows."

Captain Bill Fielder was in his usual spot during landings, on the open flight catwalk above the busy flight deck, in a position to communicate both with the bridge and at the same time partake in the landings of his returning birds.

"Captain, LCdr. Mullens just reported that the engine oil line on one of his F4Fs must have been hit. It's smeared oil over Lt(jg) Possos' windshield cutting visibility in front of him. He's presently flying beside Lt. Redford's wing, taking open canopy hand signals and queues from Redford. Crantz asks if we should try to land Possos, Redford taking the landing signal officer's commands and passing them on to the visually impaired pilot, or should he order Possos to ditch. He does have an injured leg."

"Tell Crantz to bring 'm in. That injured leg could keep Possos from leaving the plane once it hits the water."

It was not uncommon for members of the black gang to line the catwalks during flight quarters, assuming they were off duty below and, of course, that the ship was not at general quarters. This day they were to be entertained as they had never been entertained before.

Off in the distance, two Grumman fighters, wing tip to wing tip, could be seen approaching aft and to starboard. They flew past the island at about 200 feet above the water when several thousand feet ahead of Yorktown, they made a 180 degree turn, flying back to the portside of the vessel.

Then when several thousand feet back aft of the ship, they made another 180 degree turn and headed toward Lt. Crantz and his waving paddles. Redford was on Possos' portside, the tip of his starboard wing no more than three feet from the wounded lieutenant's port wing tip.

As Crantz performed his ballet of movement, Redford obeyed, first centering the vigilant Possos over the bobbing flight deck, then as Crantz gave the signal to cut, Redford, facing Possos, drew his right hand across his throat and at the same time gunned his throttle forward, the little radial engine leaping to the command as the fighter rose above the signal officer and to port while Lt(jg) Possos throttled back, his arresting gear hook dangling for number two wire, and another miracle landing.

"Let's bring those wounded SBDs aboard next," shouted the air officer as the yellow-shirted plane handlers quickly moved the incapacitated j.g. and his aircraft forward of the #5 barrier.

None too soon, as the first returning Dauntless was already in the pattern, heading down the groove waiting for Lt. Crantz to swing the arm and flag across his chest, indicating a "welcome home" to a weary warrior.

§§

About the same time, "general quarters, general quarters, clang, clang, clang, man your battle stations, man your battle stations, all hands on deck, man your battle stations," loudly voiced the call over Yorktown's bullhorn. Radar had picked up 25 boggies about 30 miles out, closing fast.

Captain Fielder quickly headed for the bridge, yelling to the air officer as he left, "Keep landing our aircraft until you hear otherwise. Then if we're actually attacked, vector the remaining ships to the Enterprise and Hornet. We don't want our boys to end up in the drink."

As the well-trained crew moved to their battle stations, guns poised ready for the enemy, ready for anything, Ed Hill, although relieved of his everyday duties to participate in Fred Daukins' murder investigation, would now refute that order and quickly clamor to his previously assigned battle station, as would Marine Lt. Craiger forestall all thoughts of his investigation and take control of the all-important duty of Yorktown's fire gun control.

Then off in the distance the ship's bullhorn loudly sounded, Boggies 25 miles out, closing fast, then 15 miles, now 2 miles. All flight operations halted. Yorktown's ten 5 inch mounts answered with a deafening roar along with many guns aboard her screening vessels.

Distant flyspecks in the sky came closer and closer. Hard to distinguish the enemy planes from the everbursting shells in a clear blue sky. As the enemy closed in, their outline as Vals or Zeroes could be defined, and the forty millimeter gun tubs began their rapid fire, pom, pom type action.

Instructions went out to the fighters flying Yorktown's CAP, to break off contact with the enemy as the air battle approached the ring of hot, deadly steel Task Force 17 was putting up to protect it from the potentially dangerous enemy approaching fast.

Over the deafening roar, the ship's bosuns could be heard yelling instructions into the bullhorn. Shut down the inert-gas system, close all hatches, repair crews to the forward hold. A Val had penetrated the ring of steel being put up, had snuck in on the starboard side forward of the island, dropping a 500 lb. bomb, hitting the flight deck, penetrating the 4-inch thick wooden planks and exploding on the hangar deck among many of Yorktown's fighter, bomber, and their few remaining torpedo planes stored in the area, being readied for further action against the enemy.

Flames and smoke belched from the exploding aircraft. Screams could be heard above the roar of the fire and exploding ammunition, ship's guns, and diving enemy aircraft.

Chief Stewards mate Jim Caffrey's all negro 20 millimeter gun crew had joined the fracas adding to the excitement aboard. It was well-known that when the 20s were in action, the enemy was close enough to define easily the identifying red glossy meatballs on the sides and wings of the enemy aircraft.

It was time for all personnel not directly manning guns or firehoses to dive for shelter. Seconds later, another whoom - an odd sound, not a bang but a whoom, like all the oxygen around had been taken out of the air.

Another bomb hit, this time through #3 elevator, 50 feet from where Bosun 2nd Class Harry Canter had been standing, the concussion, shrapnel and flying debris sending the young Jewish boy smashing head first against a nearby red hot bulkhead, rendering his lifeless body prone on the wet, pungent, slippery deck below.

More fires, more exploding ammunition, gasoline and airplanes, more roaring guns. Then a Val, hit by shell fire, plummeted flaming over Yorktown's fantail into the edge of the flight deck, slithering into the 20 millimeter gun tub below, killing Chief Caffrey and ten of his negro stewards mates serving as gunners and starting more fires in the arresting gear crew quarters.

There was frantic activity aboard the wounded warrior. A third bomb had gone deep, causing severe fires below and a loss of steam power.

Then what seemed like an eternity, the guns stopped, the bullhorn roared repair parties to the hangar deck aft, corpsmen, man your stations, arresting gear officer report your damage, order after order until the chilling order - bosuns, man your boats. That could mean abandon ship.

But wait, all hands helped fire and damage control crews put out fires and were ready to work around the clock in order to get the damaged carrier back in operation so that Yorktown could continue to do battle along with her sister carriers who hadn't been touched.

TF17's CAP and ship's guns had downed half of the attacking Vals and Zeroes, but great damage had been done to the fighting lady, and at 12.30 a cruiser came alongside ready to prepare lines for a tow. Now it was Fletcher's turn to shift his flag to another vessel. Within an hour, the cruiser was dispatched, although, still blazing, Yorktown's black gang working at super-human speed and under ungodly conditions had gotten #2 boiler lit and she was sailing at half speed.

At the same time, Lt. Commander Billy Blake, aircraft engineering officer, drenched from head to foot and covered with soot, had his plane captains and engineering personnel preparing the few undamaged aircraft for action. The Yorktown was not giving up.

§§

Nor was Admiral Sakota aboard Hiryu. His aircraft ordinance men, mechanics and flight crews had been working at a feverish pitch to prepare her remaining 10 Kate torpedo bombers to follow two hours behind the Vals, and they were now in the air, an hour's flight time from the struggling, gasping Yorktown.

§§

Captain Fielder had just had his crew stand-down from General Quarters to give them a well-earned rest and maybe some chow, when off in the distance 30 miles away the ship's radar picked up unidentified aircraft, 14 blips in all, heading straight for the badly damaged carrier. Clang, clang, clang, General Quarters, General Quarters, all hands man your battle stations, the familiar eerie call coming over the loud speaker system would strike fear into the bones of even the bravest men, and cause massive heart palpitations in those of ordinary courage.

Herb Andrews had just taken five from his duties of helping in sick bay, bandaging, treating and overseeing some of the earlier injured, and had dropped down to the mess hall to grab an ever-ready horse-cock sandwich and a cup of Joe. Gee, he thought, that piece of bologna between two slices of white bread sure hit the spot when you were hungry.

"Let's get those fighters up topside, onto the catapults and into the air," bellowed the air officer as all hands took to their duties. "Radar is reporting problems vectoring the CAP, Captain. Claims that the air direction radar is out."

"Well, have the fighters spread out using visual tracking. Where there's a will, there's a way."

"Captain, latest report from our CAP has 4 Zeroes attacking our F4Fs and that's leaving a whole mess of Japanese torpedo bombers coming in fast about 5 miles out."

Humphrey Craiger had gun turrets not damaged ready, the crews straining their eyes for a glimpse of the oncoming enemy, while the most forward destroyers providing screening protection could be seen opening fire with twin 5 inch guns.

Admiral Sakota's foxy pilots weren't interested in the tin cans; the formation split, half to port, half to starboard, and took up offensive positions which would allow a torpedo run on the big, lumbering, smoking hulk of a carrier listing slightly to port. Now all guns of Task Force 17 opened fire, putting up a wall of fire and flack that would have discouraged the most courageous pilots. But the Japs with the usual disregard for losses, kept coming.

"Boy, those guys got guts," commented LCdr. Mullens, still dressed in his tailored flight coveralls, standing on the air bridge viewing the action played out before him, like he did just a few years ago in the bleachers at Wrigley Field, watching his beloved Cubs play the Brooklyn Dodgers, only this time it was for keeps.

In turning to comb one group of torpedoes, Yorktown exposed her flanks to the rest. Two struck the gallant ship on the portside and an immediate major list occurred.

"Engine room reporting all power lost, Captain, and major casualties below the water line. All watertight hatches in place, but without pumps those compartments are filling fast."

"Let's make preparations to abandon ship," ordered a scowling Bill Fielder. "Let's get a cruiser alongside to take off the wounded and whatever men not needed to fight remaining fires. Let's get another cruiser to prepare a tow. We'll keep close tabs on the skeleton crew. If it looks hopeless, we'll scuttle the old lady."

§§

"Damn, there has to be that fourth carrier out there," mused the unsettled TF16 skipper as, head hung low, he listened to reports coming in from Fletcher's group, reports of destruction none of which his task force had experienced. All of Sakota's wrath had come down on the Yorktown, the same carrier which had experienced such devastating wounds during the battle of the Coral Sea, but had come back to fight again.

Scouting reports had begun to trickle in from American submarines stationed in and around the Midway battle area, reports that indicated the aircraft that had attacked TF17 were coming from the deck of a healthy Nagumo participant, not from the ghosts of Hiryu, Soryu or Kaga.

"I want that sucker, and I want him before he does more damage!" scoffed the wary Ray Spruance as he met with his air officer.

"Spider, I want you to lead this attack, and I want those bastards at the bottom of the sea when you finish."

"You can be sure we'll give it our best try, Captain," echoed a fatigued lieutenant commander as he faced Enterprise's veteran air officer. "We have 40 SBDs ready for launch, a conglomerate from Yorktown, Hornet and your group."

"How come Yorktown's planes are aboard our carrier?" asked Maxwell.

"They had no other place to land, low on fuel, their ship was being attacked, so Enterprise and Hornet were safe havens."

"I want you to fly the group navigator in your ship. He's been briefed on the likely location of the fourth carrier. The rest of the squadron will follow on your wing."

Another big responsibility, thought the squadron leader. He had just flown through a maze of steel, this before releasing a bomb that would help send one of Hirohito's sons of heaven to its maker. His sturdy SBD had taken flack through its main control surfaces, just barely holding together before expiring as it touched down for a safe landing, not a good landing but a safe landing. Well, any carrier landing you can walk away from is a good landing, thought the tired Spider as he climbed into the office of his spanking new bomber.

With the help of his plane captain, he buckled up his shoulder harness, fastened his seat belt, checked the gauges, then signaled the flight deck officer that he was ready, a quick glance at his watch indicating the time was 15.50, not that much light remaining, he thought. Let's get on with the show.

§§

When the command was given to abandon ship, aboard Yorktown LCdr. Hilton Chamer was making preparations to transfer his last patient from sick bay. He had been in surgery since first flight quarters early this morning, long before he would be working with the other ship doctors to help relieve pain and suffering of the many casualties caused by the two Japanese raids.

As the air group was warming up prepared to launch its first aircraft, one of the plane handlers had walked into the whirling blades of an F4Fs three-bladed propeller, causing a slashing blow to the young seaman's skull, throwing his almost lifeless body against the nearby island. Only a stroke of luck or a miracle saved him from almost certain instant death. Dr. Chamer, along with a quickly assembled surgical team, spent two hours in an effort to save the young man but to no avail.

Later, with casualties coming into surgery at a steady rate, less time could be allotted to treatment, stop the bleeding, relieve the pain, further preparation when time came available.

§§

Herb Andrews and Ed Hill had met at the designated rendezvous along with the sealed watertight container holding evidence accumulated for the Fred Daukins' case. They would receive priority evacuation as the breeches buoy transported the trio from the flaming, listing Yorktown to the safety of the deck of the cruiser alongside.

"Well, Ed, this new job has its advantages," commented the smiling, relieved yeoman.

"Yeah, but we might be sorry," retorted the muscular bosun. "Maybe from the frying-pan into the fire! Time will tell. We're not in Pearl yet."

§§

The air officer had been killed so Billy Blake assumed responsibility for the entire airedale contingent. As many aircraft as possible had been catapulted off before total power failure. No need for the officers and men of the remaining air groups, maintenance, aircraft ordinance, arresting gear, catapult, plane handlers and such, no skeleton crew needed here. Nor was there a need for cooks, black gang, stewards or the office force. A skeleton crew would be staying aboard, led by Captain Bill Fielder. The exec had also been killed in the second attack.

Marine Lt. Humphrey Craiger had been ordered to leave with men and officers of his gun crews but talked Captain Fielder into letting him remain to oversee the few free standing 40s, plus the 20 millimeters and crews should another air attack occur.

All the powered 5 inch turrets and 40 millimeter gun tubs were worthless. The wheelhouse had been manned along with the skeleton crew of bosun mates responsible for maintaining the lines being used in the tow now in progress. Several communication people and their mentor did what they could to establish and maintain contact with the other ships of TF17 as well as Spruance's sister force.

What was most important was Commander Jim Ryan's fire fighters. Several major blazes were still in progress. Every available firehose, hand pump and CO2 bottle were being applied with little result. Should the fires continue after dark, Yorktown would be a flaming torch in the night, a signal for any and all lurking enemy submarines or marauding cruisers to attack not only the near-helpless carrier but its supporting destroyers and cruisers.

§§

No better man than Jim Ryan could have been in charge of the situation. Jim had been fire chief of the massive Chicago, Illinois, fire department for a number of years, holder of many citations for his leadership and bravery over and above the call of duty.

On December 8, 1941, Jim resigned his Chicago appointment and applied for a Navy commission. Although older than most, he passed the physical and was given three full stripes, silver leaves, as well as scrambled eggs to be worn on his cap visor.

Commander Ryan would first earn the respect and admiration of his damage control people while serving aboard Yorktown at Coral Sea. His quick thinking, expert advice, and high degree of bravery not only played a big part in the ship staying afloat, but earned him a Navy Cross, the second highest medal awarded men of the sea.

§§

The few remaining pharmacist mates were busy preparing the mound of dead sailors and marines for a quick burial at sea. The overworked clergy aboard continued to make rounds, lest just one brave crewmember not be given last rights.

§§

It was 16.02 when all of Spider Maxwell's dive bombers had formed up and headed toward the latitude and longitude given his navigator. "This is where you should find the enemy." In fact, one of Midway's PBY scouts had just verified the readings previously reported by Nimitz's submarines. Flying time would be short.

The two fleets had been on a closing course, in fact a course that had concerned both Spruance and Admiral Fletcher. Neither one wanted to engage in a surface battle, especially when further submarine scouting reports had indicated a large fleet of enemy battleships, cruisers, along with one carrier about 300 miles behind Nagumo's fleet. This could be deadly, especially at night, where the American aircraft would be of no value while the 14 or 16 inch guns of the enemy had an overwhelming advantage. They could stand off miles away and just pepper the outgunned U.S. ships at will.

§§

"Admiral, our cover is reporting a massive strike heading directly for Hiryu."

"How many fighters do we have in the air?" asked a concerned Sakota.

"Only three, Admiral."

"Well, let's head into the wind and launch the two we have standing by. Five Zeroes will surely give us much-needed protection."

Admiral Sakota's gun crews had not been tested at this point. All enemy action had been directed at Nagumo's three carriers and their escorts, but tested they would be and now was the time.

§§

Lt. Commander Maxwell had split his invading SBDs into two groups. The lower group and its few protective fighters would absorb the brunt of the attack of Sakota's five Zeroes, while Spider would take the remaining birds high above the zigzagging, frantically turning enemy carrier, lead off, tip over, and with 30 and 50 caliber machine guns blazing, head for a spot at the center of the flight deck of the massive enemy carrier, not cognizant of the wall of steel being put up against them, the SBDs would one after the other release their 1000 pound bombs, four of which pierced Hiryu's flight deck, causing massive explosions and uncontrollable fires.

Hiryu, like Akagi, Soryu and Kaga, was doomed. It would be 05.00 the next morning, June 6, that the few weary survivors would be taken off and the defiant vessel sent to her watery grave by torpedoes fired from an escorting destroyer.

§§

Nimitz was pleased, very pleased, as he continued to receive messages sent not only by Task Forces 16 and 17 but from the still-staggering forces on Midway.

"Four big carriers, Admiral," shouted his aide, and although Yorktown was hit and hit hard, she was still afloat and on her way back home.

§§

The 5000 invading troops Nagumo had waiting in the wings had made no attempt to land, although several of supporting cruisers and destroyers had made vague, half-hearted attempts at shelling the island, causing little or no damage.

§§

Once the returning SBDs were back aboard Enterprise and Hornet and LCdr. Maxwell had given his damage report, it was decided that TF16 should follow Jack Fletcher's decision to break-off and head south for Hawaii.

More and more information verifying the massive strength of a battleship-led fleet coming out of some dirty weather from the north continued to reach the ears of Jack Fletcher and Ray Spruance. Rumors were that Yamamoto himself was leading these reinforcements.

"Let's get out of here," ordered the Admiral. "We could get hurt, hurt bad. We've done our job. The fleet's low on fuel. No time to take unnecessary chances. Our submarine and PBY scouts will comb the battle area when the time is right not only continuing to report on the enemy, but pick up any of our flight crews that might have ditched."

"I'll sleep better tonight, Admiral," smiled an unshaven Spider Maxwell. "Two of my crews had to ditch coming back from the Hiryu job and that's a big ocean out there, even if you have people looking for you."

§§

Back aboard the maimed Yorktown, listing but far from sinking, the retreat was going exceedingly well. All fires had been put out by a hard-working Cdr. Ryan and his dedicated damage control crew. Although she was not able to generate power, she was under tow and under the circumstances making good speed toward eventual drydock at Pearl Harbor.

Captain Fielder and his skeleton crew had spent a relatively peaceful night of June 6 aboard, although several of Yorktown's screening destroyers had reported submarine contacts. Unable to get into depth charge range, they eventually lost all contact with the predator.

What the protectors did not know was that the shadowing enemy had been given a course by a Nagumo float plane scout that would allow it to intercept and hopefully sink the badly-damaged warrior.

Each time the deadly undersea craft would get into range, set its sights and prepare its tubes for launch, one or more of Fielder's destroyers would pick up the familiar ping-ping-ping on its sonar, scatter in the direction of contact, deploy its deadly depth charges and hope for results, but to no avail.

It was not until 04.30 on the morning of June 7 that the marauder would finally get a clear, unobstructed shot at the Yorktown. A four-torpedo salvo directed at its broadside, two of which would actually hit, caused the vessel to rise out of the water like a playful whale wallowing in the sun, then slamming back with such force that most all members of its dedicated skeleton crew would be tossed about like bowling pins in an overcrowded bowling alley.

Once back on their feet, paying little attention to the wounds they should have been nursing, the gallant men would begin a desperate rear guard action to save CV-5, but to no avail. She had taken too much. Captain Bill Fielder would order all remaining crew members to abandon and at 0500 she rolled over.

She had fought a gallant fight, but her days of battle were over. And so was the battle of Midway.

§§

Yamamoto's supporting battleships, cruisers and carriers reached the battle area only to find a sea empty but for Japanese wreckage and survivors. The triumphant, retreating American fleet was long gone, not anxious to do battle with the superior forces of its hated enemy.

Nor would Yamamoto commit his fleet or landing forces to further attack of Midway itself. It was time to head for Tokyo, time to present himself to the Japanese Emperor, time to apologize for the devestating defeat of his forces, time to apologize for the loss of four large first line carriers and their full aircraft complement of 256 as well as over half of their air crews.

§§

In Hawaii, Admiral Nimitz, his staff and a welcoming band waited at the dock to greet the jubilant, triumphant Ray Spruance and Jack Fletcher as they disembarked from their respective vessels.

Included in the welcoming committee dockside were many factions of relieved crewmembers' families and friends. News of the triumph had been headlines in most American newspapers, newsreels, and had been trumpeted on radio.

Americans needed a victory to shore up their psyche. Very little good news had trickled in since the attack at Pearl. There had been Doolittle's nuisance raid on Tokyo and the standoff at Coral Sea, but four big Japanese carriers with only the loss of Yorktown at Midway, that was news, good news. Maybe now we were ready to start taking back the Pacific. Maybe now we were ready to show the world that the United States was a super power, not only a super power but the super power.

§§

Bosun Hill and Yeoman Andrews were following Marine Lt. Humphrey Craiger's instructions to deliver the container of murder evidence accumulated while aboard Yorktown to JAG headquarters on Ford Island.

Nimitz had been forewarned of the non-publicized atrocity and had one of his staff cars waiting to wing the two couriers and their bounty to the offices of the ever-waiting Admiral Stephen Ernest, commandant of the very capable legal arm of the Navy on Hawaii.

Captain Bill Fielder had not been happy about losing jurisdiction in the case, but these were the people who not only had the know-how but the tools, the trained investigators, lawyers, legal scholars plus the backing of the supreme U. S. Justice system in Washington. This is where Fred Daukins' case would find the people to solve his murder and bring the culprit to justice.

"You say Lt. Humphrey Craiger was provost marshall aboard Yorktown and that he was in charge of the investigation into the murder of AM3 Fred Daukins?" asked the probing Stephen Ernest.

"Yes, sir," answered the erect, at-attention Ed Hill, wondering just why this case had come before such a high level member of the Judge Advocate General's office. Daukins was only a 3rd class Joe. He'd expected some lieutenant would be handling it.

Although Herb Andrews was thinking much the same, he had not controlled his facial expression which brought on a further question from the Admiral.

"Yeoman, you look surprised or confused. Do you have anything to say that I might want to hear, something pertaining to the case?" he asked.

"No, sir," stammered the stuttering pen-pusher, better known as feather merchant. "I was just surprised to see the head of JAG conducting this investigation."

"Well, sir," barked the grinning Admiral, "I'm interested in any and all cases that come before my office, especially cases where I get a personal phone call from our gallant leader, Admiral Nimitz, asking that my special attention be given this case due to its extenuating circumstances. Not many murders in this man's navy, especially out to sea while in the battle zone."

"But rest easy, Yeoman. I don't plan on investigating this case personally. My understanding is that Lt. Craiger is a well-trained, capable former prosecutor who has gathered around him a team of men also capable and already familiar with the case. Lt. Craiger and his team will continue to head up the investigation, with all the backing and tools my office can afford him. I'll just be looking over his shoulder to watch the progress."

"By the way, one more thing. You can tell the lieutenant I'm going to assign one of my men to help, more or less act as liaison, show him the ropes, how our office operates. I'm meeting with the lieutenant as soon as he comes ashore and gets some clean, dry clothes. I'll pass this information on to him personally."

"And thanks, fellows. I think you've both done an excellent job of getting this container ashore and to our office. Keep up the good work. Also, how about that Midway operation? You sure whipped their ass this time! Congratulations. I'd have liked to been out there with you instead of riding this desk, but there's a time for everything."

§§

Yeah, thought the relieved bosun and yeoman as they saluted, did an about face, and headed down the hall and out the door of the impressive, stone Hall of Justice.

"You can bet your ass he'd have liked to be out there. Bullshit! Most likely been behind a desk since Annapolis and loves it," yapped the cocky yeoman.

"Yeah, grass is always greener on the other side of the pasture," commented the thoughtful bosun. "Bet he's never even been out to sea, let alone combat."

What the two non-coms didn't know was that the aging Admiral was one of the few living naval personnel eligible to wear the Medal of Honor, the congressional Medal of Honor, the highest tribute given out by a grateful nation, only to men who had served above and beyond the call of duty.

Admiral Stephen Ernest, at the time a full lieutenant, was serving as skipper aboard a four stacker destroyer back in 1917. His ship, along with other destroyers, was shepherding a convoy of men and material to England when several German undersea raiders attacked the group. A salvo of German torpedoes was seen off in the distance heading for a ship loaded with American doughboys. Only by a miraculous, unselfish maneuver initiated by Ernest, his destroyer positioned itself between the in-coming torpedoes and the slow, lumbering and helpless troop transport, taking the full impact of the three deadly tubes of dynamite, throwing the shielding ship into the air, tearing it apart at the seams, then over on its side, only to sink below the cold, wave-trodden waters of the Atlantic.

Lt. Ernest, though badly wounded, was thrown from the bridge of the doomed vessel, still conscious, credited with pulling four of his crew, two unconscious, aboard a nearby adrift raft, and providing what little first aid available until help arrived to take aboard the cold and wounded, almost frozen, survivors. The lieutenant did not leave the raft for safety until he had surveyed the surrounding waters, making sure there were no other bobbing heads or above surface alive floating bodies.

Nor did the two seamen see the Admiral get up from his desk and walk across the room or they would have noticed the distinct limp caused by the ever-painful artificial limb he had worn so gallantly since leaving the London Naval Hospital that had been his home for so many months after the incident.

§§

Also on the dock waiting with the many other eager family members was a short, slightly pregnant Hawaiian lady, straining to get a look at the faces of the officers exiting the whaleboats transporting crewmen from the destroyers and cruisers anchored just off shore.

Liddy Lopez had heard about Yorktown's misfortune. She was also aware of the fact that her husband's air group had been assigned to the unlucky vessel and assumed he most likely had to be evacuated and would be coming ashore with this group.

"Cdr. Mullens," screamed the excited, dark-eyed, olive-skinned lady as she observed her husband's mentor, his friend, his squadron commander, disembark from the water taxi and head up the gangplank toward waiting surface transportation. Oh, please, let him hear me, she thought.

"Commander, please wait," she called out. Just for a second the victorious warrior bent down and started to enter the waiting vehicle, when that voice, those pleading words, brought him to a standstill. I know that voice, he thought. That's Liddy's and she's spotted me.

Mullens and Lopez had been more than skipper and wingman. The lieutenant commander had liked the raw, smiling, friendly ensign from the day he had first been introduced into fighting 3 squadron. He had stood up for the happy bridegroom and his bride only three months ago. Mullens, a bachelor, would spend many evenings in the company of Lopez, Liddy, and Liddy's family, a family that had more or less adopted not only Liddy's husband but his idle, fighter group 3's capable skipper, Cdr. Mullens.

The surprised ace backed out, straightened up and surveyed the dock area where the voice had come from. "Take off, guys. I've got a job to do," the commander's voice trailing off as he headed in a trot toward the waving, smiling young lady.

"Oh, Commander, it's so good to see you," as she threw her arms around him. "Is Petro still aboard ship?"

What now, thought the man who had just been so warmly welcomed, how do I tell this excited, mother-to-be that her husband was killed in action, killed in action protecting my butt?

"Well, Liddy, I have some bad news. Well not so bad," lied the squadron leader. "Petro's fighter had some battle damage and he had to ditch, but there's a good chance he was picked up by one of our scouting submarines or PBYs."

God forgive me, Mullens mumbled to himself. He just didn't have the strength to tell the truth. The stressed procrastinator hailed a cab, helped Liddy into the back seat and set about explaining his distorted version of the young ensign's demise. Mullens knew the day would come when he'd have to face Lopez's wife.

That's why when he made his squadron's report, he listed Petro as an MIA, not a KIA. After all, he told his conscience, am I really sure this man is dead? Of course, by the same token, how many flaming bodies will fall thousands of feet, then into the ocean, and live to tell about it?

And if Ensign Petro Lopez was listed as missing, not dead, his wife and child would continue to receive his pay, flight skins and allotment, instead of just a one shot lump sum $10,000 insurance settlement. And after seven years she would most likely get that insurance money anyway. No, he told himself. I did the right thing. I gave her hope and security.

§§

The lieutenant commander was glad to get this off his chest. Just yesterday while still out to sea, he was notified that he was being made a full commander, given that third full stripe and scrambled eggs.

He was to head for Alameda, California, on the first available B17 to form a new air group. The group would consist of fighters, bombers, and torpedo planes, not F4Fs, but F6F, not SBDs but that new big monster, the SB2C, and of course, the TBD was out. His group would fly the faster, more maneuverable TBM or TBF, and this group was to go aboard that new Essex class carrier CV-10, presently being outfitted down in Norfolk, Virginia. Only yesterday her name was changed. Guess what? CV-10 would be known as the Yorktown. That should confuse those Jap bastards.

§§

Lt. Craiger had also talked with Bill Fielder just before both men left ship for their immediate tasks on the beautiful island of Hawaii. Humphrey had continued on to a meeting with the head of JAG and left pleased with the man who had become his new boss. He would continue the duty as head of the murder investigation of Fred Daukins. That's great, he thought, let's get with it.

"Okay, men. The time has come for some results. We don't have any more room for excuses. We're on the beach, we have all the necessary tools and, by-God, any fellow who doesn't give it 100% will find himself back in the fleet pool scratching for sea duty. Do I make myself clear?"

"You bet, Lieutenant," chorused the gathered group of Yorktown veterans.

Humphrey's team had been billeted at the Pearl Harbor Naval Base, given office space at JAG headquarters, told that they had only to ask and their wishes would be granted, and yes, been assigned a new member, a Lt. Greenberg, a representative of JAG. He was to lead the group through the maze of rules and regulations, the detailed procedures that governed the legal arm of this great institution.

Lt. Greenberg would not be on board until tomorrow. He was still on leave, had had a heavy schedule the past month or so, needed some R & R resulting in ten days at the Royal Hawaiian Hotel on Waikiki beach.

"Boy," commented 2ndLt. Herb Shacter. "That's rough duty. Those rooms at the Royal Hawaiian had been renting for twenty-five bucks a pop, just before the war, and look at it now, swabby skivvies hanging out the hotel windows to dry! Sad, sad situation. What's this world coming to."

"Let's not worry about Greenberg. Anything since our last meeting on the 2nd aboard Yorktown?"

All three Marines shook their heads, "Nothing but a lot of Japs," commented Shacter.

"Hill?"

"Nothing, Lieutenant, but I'm ready to go now. I might have something. Had a little time on the morning of the 3rd, Skipper, and did some checking on the serial numbers and names of the men taken into custody with Fred Daukins in that Ford Island gambling raid, you know, his second Captain's Mast?"

"What did you find, Yeoman?" asked an excited Humphrey Craiger.

"Well, we might have gotten lucky. Records show that one of the names, serial numbers, etc. checks with Yorktown's Midway roster. It's a Seaman 2nd by the name of Jim (Rusty) Pattern. Been up for gambling many times, has 7 years in the service and is only a S2. We don't know if there was a game going on the morning of the stabbing, but if there was, this guy could very well have been a part of it."

"Do we know where to find this Rusty fellow? This could be the lead we're looking for," Craiger said.

"No, sir. As you know, Ed and I just came ashore with the evidence container, had our meeting with Admiral Ernest and really haven't settled into our barracks yet. Still trying to get some new dungarees, skivvies and shoes. Lost everything when we went over the side."

"I understand, Herb. You fellas have done one hell of a good job. Get settled, then see if you can locate Mr. Pattern. Stick with 'm, Ed. You two make a great team."

"How about Daukins' previous workplace, the sheetmetal shop on Ford Island? I s'pose you haven't been able to get any dope on that yet, Lieutenant?"

"No, sir," he replied, "I haven't been over to the air base yet. Like Ed and Andrews still trying to settle in, but plan on making this #1 priority this afternoon."

"Sergeant, I want you to work with Herb Shacter and if you find time with Corporal Spies to break down the address book found in Daukins' locker. The way I look at it, three ways, those names with a Chicago address, next the Columbus, Ohio, contacts, and last but not least, who did he know right here in Hawaii. And if you really get lucky, who aboard Yorktown on the last cruise? Also go through his high school yearbook, any written comments. You know how kids write those anecdotes, any names that might tie into the Navy, and especially Pearl and/or Yorktown. What about his family back in Columbus? See what you fellas can find out from a distance. If we feel it warrants a trip later, we'll do it."

§§

"Can I come in, Lieutenant?" asked the small, boyish, somewhat unkempt-looking Navy lieutenant, sporting two full gold stripes on the cuffs of his blue uniform.

"Yes, Lieutenant, how can I help you?" asked Craiger.

"Well, I'm Isaac Greenberg, from JAG. Admiral Ernest has assigned me to your investigating team."

Humphrey Craiger moved quickly from his chair to a standing position, offering his hand to this would-be bearer of information. This would close the loop on his team. This man would be the needed catalyst to jell any and all data, such that if and when a murderer was found, he could and would be swiftly prosecuted and given the sentence so rightly deserved for such a dastardly crime.

"Welcome, Isaac. Can I call you Isaac?"

With a smile the officer assured him he could, adjusting as he spoke the heavy, black Navy-issue eyeglass frame that housed the minus three diopter lenses he needed so badly in order to function at distance, a correction that had become progressively worse the last few years, so much more that the Navy would not have allowed him to enlist years back should his uncorrected visual acuity been such as it was today.

"Call me anything, sir, but late for chow," quipped the friendly newcomer. "I don't stand on formality, and I hope you feel the same way."

No, the Marine lieutenant was not one to insist that his troops follow all the rules and regulations set forth in the Marine manual, but he did feel there should be a certain amount of spit and polish, that commissioned personnel present themselves as officers and gentlemen, shoes shined, uniforms pressed, close shaven hair in that traditional Marine crew cut, and above all, respectful language, especially when in the company of the female gender, be they service or civilian ladies. This the lieutenant had not necessarily learned being in the Corps, but from a hard-working, much loved, much respected mother. When in the company of a lady, watch your language.

"Well, Isaac, I know you're just off R&R. Why not take the day to get your feet on the ground. Tomorrow I'll assemble the team, introduce you and make an effort to fill in the cracks outlined in my latest report to the Admiral. You should have a copy within the hour."

"Thanks, Humphrey. I'm happy to be part of the investigation. See you in the morning."

§§

"Good morning, Miss. Bosun Hill and myself would like to check your roster to see if a former member of our crew is in your manpower pool."

"By what authority, and by the way, it's Yeoman Kite, not Miss."

"Sorry, Yeoman, guess I still haven't gotten used to having Waves in this man's navy, but I'm Y2 Andrews, and as I mentioned my partner is BM1 Ed Hill, former members of the Yorktown."

"And your authority to check our roster, Yeoman?" she asked again.

"We are presently assigned to JAG, working on a case requiring this information."

"Have a seat, gentlemen. Let me do some checking. Will be back in a jiffy."

"Lt. Commander Mary Wilkens will see you now, gentlemen. Please follow me."

This gal sure took no guff and seemed very capable, commented the bosun to a ruffled Herb Andrews.

"Always thought feather merchants could be replaced by the female gender," a smiling Hill said good-naturedly.

§§

"Sit down, men. I've checked with JAG and was told to cooperate with any request you might have, so what can the pool do for you?" asked LCdr. Wilkens.

"We're looking for a seaman 2nd class named Jim (Rusty) Pattern, ma'm. He had been aboard Yorktown during the Midway skirmish. Believe he acted as a plane handler. We don't have a list of MIA or KIA, but thought your office would be a good place to start looking for him."

"We have a Jim Pattern billeted in Barracks 231," said the lieutenant commander. "The Yorktown group has not been given liberty yet so if he's not on a working party, he should be available. Let me check and if he's in, I'll have him brought over. Suppose you'd like to talk to him in private so will assign you one of the conference rooms."

§§

"Your name, Seaman?"

"I'm Rusty Pattern, Boats. What do you want with me? Gee,

I hope I'm not being sent back out to sea already!"

"No, Rusty. Yeoman Andrews and I have a few questions for you. Sit down and relax. Want a cigarette or a coke?"

"Sure, why not. Lost all my dough going over the side at Midway. Don't have enough to buy a carton of sea stores and haven't seen a pay chit or paymaster come aboard the base, and that God-dam Red Cross, they give nothing!"

"Keep the pack. Now how about some answers. First, we know about you being busted a few months ago for gambling here on the island."

"So that's what it's about," grouched the stocky six-footer. "Here I'm a war hero and you guys are needlin' me about something that happened months ago. I had my court martial and served my time for that. What's this? Double Jeopardy?"

"Sit down and settle down, seaman. We'll ask the questions and you give the answers."

Gee, I'm glad Hill is along, thought the mild-mannered pencil pusher as Ed Hill, gently grabbing the seaman's arm, firmly pushed him back into the chair he'd jumped out of when confronted with the previous charge.

"And you know damn well you didn't serve your time," Hill continued, "You served 5 days in the brig, 5 days of a 6 month sentence. The only thing that saved you from serving the balance of your time was that the Yorktown needed bodies, and you were given a reprieve. But believe me, Rusty, one, you're no hero. You broke your butt getting off Yorktown with the first group of evacuees, and two, if either the Yeoman or myself think you're not giving your full undivided attention to the matter in hand, we'll be in contact with the judicial panel that sentenced you and you'll be serving, not six months, but a year at hard labor in a federal pen."

Herb Andrews and Rusty Pattern were experiencing the real Ed Hill, toughened by his years as a bosun mate, brought up on the wrong side of the tracks, and of course that stint assigned to the Honolulu Shore Patrol.

"Now, once again, seaman. Let's be clear. We know you're a gambler, but that's really not what we're interested in. We're looking for some other information that we feel you can furnish, and believe me, if you cooperate and we get the right kind of answers, we can make that impending federal prison sentence go away. Do you know a Fred Daukins?"

The confronted seaman looked away for a minute, dropped his eyes, paused, then asked, "What if I do, or should I say did? Ya know, Bosun, it was all over the ship, at least we airedales knew, Daukins had been planted. We didn't know exactly what happened, but pretty boy had met his maker."

"You have anything to do with that, Rusty?"

"No, sir, might like to throw dice or play cards, but I'm really a gentle guy. I hate violence," he replied.

"You knew Fred before the two of you boarded Yorktown?"

"You know I did. If you read my sheet you know that Daukins was one of the fellas busted along with me at that Ford Island fiasco. Yeah, I knew Fred."

"OK, Rusty. You've been truthful so far. Let's continue. You and Fred were a part of a game aboard Yorktown the morning he was found dead."

"Come on, guys, you're asking me to incriminate myself. Do you think I'm some kind of a dam fool?

"Rusty, we gave you our word, JAG's word, that we weren't interested in prosecuting you for gambling. We're interested in names, names of people who sat in on the morning poker game."

"I didn't say I was in any game aboard Yorktown with Daukins or anyone else, at least not for money."

"Are those your last words on the subject, Seaman?"

"Yeah, those are my last words," he answered.

"OK, Yeoman, let's draw up the paperwork to have S2. Pattern released from the naval manpower pool and transported over to the brig at JAG headquarters."

"Now, that's a hell of a thing, guys. I cooperated!"

§§

"Where can we find Lt. Commander Billy Blake, fellas?" asked a friendly Herb Shacter as he approached a group of dungaree-clad mechanics on a coffee break.

"Don't know any lieutenant commander by that name, Lieutenant, but at the far end of the hangar is our office. They'd know."

§§

"Commander Blake? Yes, he just came aboard yesterday from Air Group 3, you know, the Yorktown. Don't know his assignment yet. In fact, he was in earlier this morning. You might see Commander Ricker. He heads up our operation. I'll see if the Commander is in and if he'll see you. Who should I say is calling?"

§§

"You say you're from JAG, Lieutenant."

"Yes, sir, I am, actually investigating a case which has something to do with the Yorktown."

"Oh, yes, the Yorktown. Tough luck. We were pretty involved with Yorktown's air group several weeks ago, getting it ready for that Midway job. You wanted to talk with Billy? Well, you just missed him. He was heading to officers quarters. No, wait. Said he had an appointment with a tailor first. Guess he's been wearing some hand-me-downs, lost everything. Suppose it was much the case for most guys aboard, both officers and men."

"Yes, sir, it was. I'd been aboard and am pretty much in the same boat."

"You look no worse for wear. How come a Marine officer from JAG was aboard a fighting vessel?"

"Well, sir, first off, I'm lucky I had a roomy about my size. Hence, the first class duds, and second, I wasn't assigned to JAG until after returning from the sinking of the Gallant Lady."

"Commander, since Blake isn't available, maybe you or your people can help me."

"Would like to try. Shoot. What do you need?"

"Well, I'm interested in two men from your aviation sheet metal shop assigned to Yorktown just prior to her leaving for Midway."

"What do you want to know about these men?"

"Their duties while under your command here on the island and also why they were sent aboard the carrier, who requested them, and so forth."

"I don't have that information at my fingertips, Herb, but I'll put you in touch with Mrs. Klein. She can get our personnel files. I'll let her know she is to give you everything you need."

"Commander Ricker, did you say a Mrs. Klein?"

"Yes, I did. Marilyn has been with us a good number of months."

"Would she have a husband named Jeffery, a 1st class aviation metalsmith assigned to Yorktown?"

"She sure has. We here at CQTU were mighty happy to hear Jeff got off safe and sound. Should I have her come in with the files you want?"

"No, sir, please. For now for security reasons, forget we had this conversation. I'll be back to you later, sir, and thank you. By the way, who heads up your personnel department? I sure would like to talk with him?"

"It's not a him, it's a Wave, Ensign Betty Brandon."

"Thanks again, Commander, and please say nothing about this visit to Mrs. Klein.

"Oh, Lieutenant, if you want to talk to Ensign Brandon, you'll have to come back tomorrow. She's off on the main island today, some conference. You can be sure that our office will let her know you want to talk. Have a good day."

§§

Herb Shacter's head was in the clouds. Finally, some meat. Those two bastards lied to me. Said they didn't know each other, and the one guy's wife worked in the same area as Daukins and Tarry. That's no coincidence. There's more here than meets the eye, he thought. Humphrey's going to eat this up. Those bastards and Commander Ricker called Klein by his first name. This was just one happy family, or was it?

§§

"Chief Ankerman, I understand a 2nd class aviation metalsmith named Milt Tarry and a 3rd class aviation metalsmith named Fred Daukins both worked directly under you. Is that correct?"

"Yes, it is, Sarg, you're right. They did work for me but lost them to Yorktown a few weeks ago. Why do you ask? Hope you're not gonna tell me they went down with the ship."

"I'm not here to tell you anything of the sort, Chief, just want to ask you a few questions."

"Why should a Marine sergeant be asking me questions? Who in the hell are you?"

"I'm Staff Sergeant Ron Milkusky, attached to the Hawaiian office of the Judge Advocate, and it's your prerogative to check with my superior before you answer questions."

"No, you look pretty authentic. What can I help you with?"

"Let's take Tarry first. Good worker?"

"Yes, he was. Handy with the tools, knew his rate, in fact, is or was up for first class."

"How did he get along with the rest of the fellas in the shop?"

"Great, minded his own business and as I said before, did his job."

"Why did you send him out to sea?"

"I didn't send him. Hell, ever since December 7th we've had twice as much work as we can handle, and good metalsmiths are hard to find. Keep sending me new kids but they're all on a learning curve. No, Sarg, both men you're asking about were asked for. I don't know by whom. You'd have to check with personnel on that."

"Let's talk about Daukins."

"Now, that's another case. Almost worthless in the shop, or maybe I should clarify that. I really didn't miss him as far as repairing the skin on an F4U wing or rudder on a PBY, but he did have some merit or value to our organization. The kid had personality, knew how to get the job done, especially if he was dealing with the ladies. Good looking, had a good line, a good gift of gab, smooth, never got in my way but might have rubbed the male element the wrong way. Get what I mean? I used him to push papers, forge a link between the guys out here in the shop and the office staff, mostly ladies."

"Know anything about his off-duty doings?"

"Not really. I know about his Captain's mast several months ago, know he liked to gamble, never when I was around. He always seemed to respect me. I hate to spread rumors but there was talk that he was having affairs with several of the gals in the office, which ones I don't know, but knowing the kid, I would guess the rumors could be true."

"Who passed on those rumors, Chief?"

"Gee, I don't remember. Never seemed that important. Maybe I shouldn't have mentioned it."

"I'm going to give you my name and a telephone number where you can reach me, Fred. If by chance you should jog your memory and come up with anything more on either of the two fellows, give me a call. Sure would appreciate your help."

"OK, Sarg, stop up at personnel. They can tell you who asked to have the fellows transferred and why."

"Say, Chief, ever know a Jeffery Klein?"

"Jeff? Sure, he worked for me before being transferred several months ago. Good worker, really knew his stuff, a little hard to handle, but I'll take a hothead like Jeff any day compared to the Daukins' type. And then there's his wife Marilyn working in our office, sort of assistant to our skipper, Commander Ricker. Wouldn't have wanted to step on any toes in that area. No, Jeff and I got along great."

§§

Jeffery Klein worked for Ankerman here at the base, and he didn't know Daukins or Tarry before coming aboard Yorktown. Bullshit! Why did those fellas commit perjury, wondered the slightly balding former New Jersey policeman. And Klein's wife works in the office. Please, Jeffery, how can you be so damn dumb. How could you think we wouldn't find out? I've got to get over to the personnel office to pass this on to Herb. Boy, he thought, this should create a bombshell when it hits the JAG offices.

§§

Gene Spies wasn't having such a good day. He had checked to make sure that a telegram had been delivered to Fred Daukins' folks. The telegram noted that the petty officer had been killed in action but didn't say how or where.

After getting up courage to pick up the telephone and place a call to the Ohio number, he was relieved when Fred's younger brother answered. Didn't sound like the hyper type, didn't slobber all over, just a kid asking what happened to his big brother. No, his mother and dad weren't home. They had taken a trip up to their mountain cabin, a way to grieve away from the rest of the family and friends. He didn't know when his parents would be back home, but he would take the corporal's number should they have questions or want to talk with the Navy.

§§

"Good morning, fellows. Want you to meet our new member, Navy Lt. Isaac Greenberg, JAG's representative."

Humphrey Craiger had assembled the troops in an informal way, 0600, early yes, but there was plenty of hot Joe and some freshly baked rolls, all the elements to start what would be a very eventful day in the lives of the seven men present.

"Herb, will you take notes, or should we say minutes?"

"You bet," quipped the more or less excited yeoman. He couldn't wait until the lieutenant would ask Hill or himself to report on yesterday's events.

By the time the two had arrived back at JAG headquarters with the prisoner, the lieutenant had left for an appointment in Honolulu and it would be the next day before the good news could be delivered.

As Isaac moved from member to member shaking hands as he went, you could see the more or less stunned looks he was given, especially by the Marines. This fellow a lawyer? A full lieutenant? Looked so young, so boyish, and how could they say it, unkempt.

Ed Hill got up, shook the lieutenant's hand, then sank back into his chair. Ed was doping off again. I know this officer, but where, where did I meet him?

Gee, that bothers me, thought the bosun. He had the name, he had the face, that unkempt hair, that voice. Was it during his hospital stay? No, that wasn't it. Shore Patrol? Was he our attorney for the prosecution or defense? No, that doesn't ring a bell. He really never got to know the legal arm down at headquarters. Maybe aboard the cruiser? Most likely not. Didn't get into officer's quarters. Couldn't have been in boots. This guy's an officer. Maybe he had a brother, cousin, one of those look-alikes.

"Pardon me, Lieutenant. Could I have a minute of your time?"

Isaac had settled into a chair next to the inquisitive Hill, cup of Joe in one hand, jelly donut in the other, jelly leaking down the outside over the powdered sugar and onto the wrinkled dress blue jacket of the unsuspecting, friendly, legal-eagle.

"Sure, Ed, anytime. That's what I'm here for."

"It's not about the case, sir."

"Ed, call me Isaac."

"Well, Isaac, since meeting you, I feel as though we might have met before and I can't figure where. Thought you might have a brother or cousin or some relative that might have been from Oklahoma or maybe an enlisted Navy man?"

"Gosh, I'm leaking this donut all over my uniform."

"Here, Isaac, take my napkin."

"Well, I'm an only child. Mother is a surgeon. Never could take time out to have another baby. Both mother and dad are only children in their families, no aunts, uncles, or cousins."

"My guess is that our paths might have crossed while I was an enlisted man. Not for long. Enlisted, went to boot camp at the Great Lakes Naval Training Station in North Chicago, Illinois. Given some placement tests while going through the process and ended up in the Navy V12 program in Evanston at Northwestern University. Great program, but I really didn't want to become an officer. Liked the enlisted ranks, had been around bookworms all my life, time for a change."

§§

"Alright, fellows, fill up your cups and let's get down to business. You can reminisce later," interjected the lieutenant.

Ed was shocked into reality, but as Humphrey said, it was time to go to work, time to let the man on top know progress was being made. There might be some light at the end of the tunnel after all.

"Andrews, you mentioned that you might have some good news. You and Ed brought in a potential suspect yesterday?"

"Sure did, Rusty Pattern, long time seaman, worked the tables at Vegas and Reno before enlisting in the Navy, might have been just a little bit involved with the mob, we're not sure. Rusty had been picked up with Daukins on the Ford Island raid, and he was aboard Yorktown for the Midway trip."

"What did this Rusty have to say?"

"Admitted to being with Daukins on gambling bust several months ago, but we couldn't get him to talk or admit there might have been a game aboard Yorktown."

"So we really don't have anything here."

"I think we do, Lieutenant," cut in the hard-nosed bosun. I think this Pattern guy is lying through his teeth. I sensed there was a game, both Daukins and Rusty participated, but Rusty doesn't want to involve himself anymore. He's already in up to his teeth, facing a six month sentence. If he doesn't shape up, we told him it could be twelve if he didn't cooperate. Think he has to be leaned on to come clean."

"I don't think this man is capable of murder," chimed in the yeoman, "but I agree with Ed. He loves to gamble and his whole attitude during our interrogation smelled of involvement."

"There is a weakness. Now, how do we attack it? Has he asked for a lawyer?" asked the Marine.

"No, sir, he hasn't. In fact, Rusty shied away from the subject when I read him his rights."

"Good. That means we have time on our side, no 72 hour problem. Let the three of us get him in the box this afternoon, see if we can't sweat some names or other information that can help."

"And, Sergeant, you said you had some hot dope?"

"Yes, sir, I have. Both Tarry and Daukins were asked for by someone involved with the Yorktown."

"Who on Yorktown?" asked the stunned Craiger.

"I don't know as yet. Head of aircraft maintenance personnel was away yesterday, but you can bet Herb Shacter and I will be pounding on her door early this morning. Also, until several months ago Jeffery Klein, head of aircraft sheetmetal shop aboard Yorktown, had worked in the aircraft maintenance shop on Ford Island."

"Well, wouldn't that crack your balls, fellas? Klein said he didn't know either Daukins or Tarry and that the two were sent aboard ship on a random basis, he assumed through the Pearl pool. Something really smells here."

"One other thing, Humphrey, Klein's wife Marilyn works in the shop office, sorta secretary to Commander Ricker, overall head of the maintenance program."

"I can corroborate Ron's tale," broke in Herb Shacter. "I talked with the old poochie heading up maintenance, and as Ron mentioned, Klein had been a fixture around the shop up until several months ago when he went aboard ship."

"Klein was referred to as Jeff and his wife as Marilyn. Like Ron, I wasn't able to get into the records, but that comes this morning, and I agree with Humphrey, something's going on that smells to high heaven. We may have this case in the palm of our hands."

"Well, Corporal, I suppose it would be asking too much to expect that you also picked up some leads."

"Yes, sir, it would. I really haven't laid any ground work either in Columbus, Chicago, or here in Hawaii, but after listening to the rest of the team this morning, I wonder if maybe this case is on its way to being cracked real soon, without my help."

"Keep plugging, Gene. Every little bit helps. We're far from anything positive, but yes, its heartening finally to be getting a few leads."

"And say, bosun, you can earn your keep by asking whoever is responsible for the services of a yeoman to sit in whenever we have these meetings. Herb Andrews has his hands full with other duties."

"By the way, Ron, when you and Herb talk with maintenance personnel people this morning, see if Jeffery Klein has been reassigned to their shop and if not, check with the pool, see if he is there. Whatever or wherever, slap a warrant on him for perjury and have him sent to JAG lockup. By the way, same goes for Milt Tarry. Find him and charge him. He had to know Klein before going aboard Yorktown."

"OK, Skipper, but I have a feeling this isn't going to set well with Ricker."

"The hell with Ricker. He's small potatoes."

§§

Ed Hill couldn't get Isaac Greenberg out of his mind. As the meeting broke up, Ed cornered his new partner, told him he would meet him and Humphrey at the JAG lockup in time to interrogate Rusty, then on the double caught up with the slight Jewish person, apologizing for asking, but would he continue with the story he began unfolding before they were so rudely interrupted with the business at hand.

"Lieutenant, you said you'd gone into the Navy as an enlisted man, took boots at Great Lakes. What Camp?"

"Dewey," smiled the gentle man, happy to see someone finally interested in his career.

"You know, Isaac, I think I finally know where we might have met in the past. I went through boot camp at Great Lakes, and pardon the expression, there was a young man in our company who seemed to have two left feet."

"That's me, Ed. Left Foot Greenberg, they called me, billeted in Barracks 2304, member of Zebra Company, and had a chief petty officer by the name of Larson. How about your boot C.O? Was he a big, good-natured Polak?"

"He sure was. A great guy. Sure helped me over the hump when I needed it. Well, Lieutenant, welcome to this man's navy."

A happy, smiling Ed Hill stuck out his burly hand, took the somewhat slighter hand of his comrade-in-arms. Here's a guy who made it the hard way, didn't ask to be coddled, a 90 day wonder, yes, but he earned that braid by first seeing how the enlisted man lived, took his lumps, but in his own way, came back fighting.

§§

Ed had taken the same tests Isaac Greenberg had taken while in boot camp. They were called placement tests. Just before graduation, a list was posted on the barracks' bulletin board, scores were given, and men placed by grade they received. Ed's name was near the bottom.

He never did look to see whose name was at the top, but had he done so, he would have found that Isaac had aced it and alongside his score was noted he would be sent to yeoman school. Next to Ed's name was a big sea duty, in other words, the Navy wasn't going to waste time sending a guy barely capable of reading and writing to a service school. They not only needed electricians, machinists, pharmacists, aviation personnel, radiomen, etc. but men who could tote that box, ladle that chow, peel those potatoes, swab those decks, and in Ed's case, clean those heads.

When Isaac Greenberg arrived at the university in Columbia, Missouri, to begin his sixteen weeks of training in order to become a feather merchant, a counselor finally took the time to review his records. When it was found that the student had a B.A. in Biology as well as a degree in law from Columbia University, things began to happen.

This conscientious lady contacted the appropriate people in Washington, D.C., and Isaac was soon on his way to Evanston, Illinois, and a place in the next officers' training class, then soon after to become part of the proud JAG organization.

§§

And now after those days at Great Lakes, the two would meet again, not boys any more, but men, each with a different job, but in many ways the same job--to catch a killer and bring him to justice.

But if he was to do his part, thought the ever-conscientious bosun, he'd better get over to the lockup and help Humphrey and Herb.

§§

"Nice to meet you, Seaman. My men have told me a lot about you. Told me you were honest with them about the bust earlier in the year, you know, the one Daukins and you were part of. I don't know if they told you what happened to Fred, but I want to be on the up and up with you. He was murdered around 0400 on the morning Yorktown left for Midway."

"Well, thanks for being straight with me, sir, but scuttlebutt had it that someone put a shiv between the metalsmith's shoulder blades, so I knew."

"Can you remember who passed that information on, Rusty?"

"No, sir, I can't. Guess it was one of those things. You know, one person to another."

"Where were you that night, Rusty?"

"Oh, I was in the sack, had a 0400 watch coming up, didn't want to be caught sleeping on watch."

"What was your watch that night, Seaman?"

"Well, it was aft on the flight deck. Had to make the rounds through the night checking on aircraft tie-downs."

"And who did you report to that night?"

"Well, it was that fellow who stands just behind the island when airplanes are landing, that lieutenant, don't remember his name."

"Was that Lieutenant Shingleton?"

"Yeah, that's it. Lieutenant Shingleton."

"Can I ask the lieutenant about you that night? Would that be alright?"

"Yes, sir. I did a good job. Was on duty until 0800."

"So you say you were sleeping prior to going on watch. Where did you sleep? Where were your quarters?"

"Back aft, portside one deck below the hangar deck, compartment C4."

"What time did you get up to go on watch?"

"Oh, about 0330."

"Seaman, what would you say if I told you that I checked with the Bosun who had the midnight to 0400 watch in C4 compartment the night in question and he told me your sack was empty, not slept in."

"Well, that can't be true, sir. He must have got my sack mixed up with someone else's, or I made a mistake, came in, was dark, and crawled into another empty sack by mistake."

"Seaman, you know you're under oath. Do you know what perjury is?"

"Yes, sir, I do."

"And do you know what the penalty for murder is in this man's navy?"

"No, sir, I suppose twenty years or somethin' like that."

"No, Rusty, first degree murder carries the death penalty, no ifs ands or buts about it."

"Lt. Craiger, I didn't have anything to do with Daukins' murder. Why are you tellin' me those things?"

"I'm explaining or trying to explain the difference in charging you with gambling for money aboard a ship at sea and taking a man's life. Think about it. I have to go to the head. Be back in 5 minutes. I'm asking you to come clean, tell us about your little game, who was there, the time frame, etc. Be honest with me and the bosun, give us some names, that will allow us to check with the other fellows who also played, this will allow me to check your story against theirs."

"What fellas, Lieutenant? They're lying. There was no game."

"That's your story, Rusty. Looks to me like you're trying to cover up and maybe for good reason. Instead of being charged for a little game, a charge I could brush under the rug if given the straight dope, the charge could very well be murder, firing squad. Think about it. We'll be back in a few minutes. Here, have a Chesterfield."

§§

"Looks like you have him thinking. Your cool, calm approach this past ten minutes probably did more good than my hour of badgering yesterday," admitted the bosun who'd been standing and listening outside the room.

"Yeah, Herb and I think you're doing one hell of a good job. When did you get names from another source?"

"Just bullshit, guys. There are no other informants. My overall gut feeling is that there was a game that morning and that Rusty was a part of it, and being a part of it, he could implicate others, maybe even the killer. Well, it's imperative we get him to confess. Maybe the only way to do that is to scare the hell out of him. Do I think he's the killer? No, he doesn't have the guts for anything like that. Let him stew for awhile, make him think we're talking with the other players, then Ed, you and I'll go in and if he still doesn't respond, we'll play "good cop/bad cop." If he isn't guttsy, that could work."

§§

"Wow, wait 'til the group gets a load of this. Marilyn Klein's name in Fred Daukins' address book, and this Jeffery claims he didn't know the metalsmith before coming aboard Yorktown. This could be the straw that broke the camel's back. Maybe Jeff didn't know the fair haired boy, but it sure as hell looks like his wife or sister did."

Gene Spies wasn't happy with his attempts to add to the investigation by contacting Columbus. All there was on that end was heartache. He could do without that. Last night after the latest meeting he started to look into the murdered man's little black book, a book that if handled properly could tell an awful lot about the person who had owned it.

As suggested, the corporal began listing names under three categories, names of people living in Chicago where Fred did boots and attended aviation metalsmith school, names of people living in Columbus, Fred's hometown, he went to school there, grew up in the burg. Then there were the locals, names, addresses, and telephone numbers of more recent acquaintances here in Hawaii.

As Gene got to the "Ks" in that address book, he started to enter the name Klein under the Hawaiian category, when it hit him like a ton of bricks. Marilyn Klein, 214 Okua Street, Paradise Trailer Park, Ford Island, Hawaii, telephone #Naomi 1747. But Klein is a fairly common name, he thought.

Yes, but when his eyes dropped to the line below, the work phone was Navy 3241. Here was the lady Marine Sgt. Ron Milkusky and Lt. Shacter were talking about, the lady Commander Ricker praised so highly, his right hand at the aircraft maintenance facility, Jeff's wife, and her name and telephone number listed in the dead man's little black book. Seemed too good to be true. Another piece to the ever-increasing evidence accumulating in a bizarre turn of events pointing a suspicious finger at a man who had lied to the group.

§§

"Commander Ricker talked to me about AM2 Milt Tarry and AM3 Fred William Daukins. I had pulled both of their sheets. Our records show that both men went aboard Yorktown the day she left Pearl for Midway. Records also show that the request for services of both men came from the head of the ship's metalshop, AM1 Jeffery Klein."

"Ensign, do you usually transfer people on the authority of a 1st class non-commissioned person?"

"No, Lieutenant, I would have had to have permission from my boss, Commander Ricker."

"And did you have that permission for the two men in question?"

"Yes, I did. In fact, we had an open policy 48 hours before the ship left Pearl. Admiral Nimitz had contacted our Chief, leaving a standing order to give any and all requests from Yorktown #1 priority."

"How about this fellow, Jeffery Klein? Do you have his jacket available? I understand he worked for your shop before leaving for Yorktown sometime before the battle of Coral Sea."

"I'm one step ahead of you, Sergeant Milkusky. I have his sheet and it shows that he worked under the supervision of Chief Ankerman."

"Does that sheet tell you anything else, Ensign?"

"Not too much more, good worker, capable, maybe headstrong,

temperamental, go off the handle at a drop of a hat. Oh, yes, one other point. His wife is a civilian employee, works in our office, secretary to Commander Ricker."

"We're aware of that, Betty. Now tell us about this lady."

"Not much to tell. Capable, almost perfect attendance. Only one gap in her timesheet. Seems like she fell down some stairs, badly bruised face, black and blue arm, damage to rib cage, off work for two weeks."

"When was she off work?"

"That would be starting the day Yorktown came into Pearl from Coral Sea. She was so anxious to get over to drydock to see her husband that she tripped coming out of her house, causing the damage."

"Was she treated for the bruises, etc?"

"Yes, she was. Base hospital took X-Rays. Followed up a week later to make sure she was OK."

"Who was her doctor?"

"Commander Siegal. He gave her a clean bill and sent her back to work."

"Ensign Brandon, do your records show where Jeffery Klein and Milt Tarry have been assigned?"

"My records do not show them as part of our group, but I put in a call to the base pool. Both men are on stand-down at their facility."

"We have warrants for their arrests. Will you be kind enough to have them served and have both men brought to the lockup at JAG headquarters?"

"Arrests? Why would you want to arrest these two fellows?" asked the surprised personnel director.

"We're not at liberty to say, ma'm. Please have your Shore Patrol carry out our orders, and we ask that you keep this in strictest confidence, not a word to Commander Ricker or Klein's wife, let alone to anyone else on the base. If you find you're being pressured, give us a call. Thanks for your help, Ensign. We may be calling you later."

§§

Lt. Greenberg had been involved with the base manpower pool also. He had talked to Wave Yeoman Kite about sending a temporary secretary to JAG headquarters to act as recorder for the group investigating the metalsmith's murder, but this person must have top secret clearance, not that many young ladies around with those credentials. Kathy Kite had talked to LCdr. Mary Wilkens about such a person, but neither of the feather merchants could come up with a name.

"Well, Kathy, we know Nimitz has given JAG top priority for this case, and as much as I'd hate to lose you even for a short time, you're going to have to be it. Pack your typewriter and shorthand pad and head for the stone columns of our Justice Department."

§§

Greenberg was as surprised to see the pretty young yeoman as she was to have been given this top level assignment. He had admired her from a distance whenever visiting the offices of LCdr. Wilkens. Maybe one or two of his visits really were not necessary, but what the heck. Who would know.

Isaac could remember dreaming about those long, shapely legs, about her not too large firm breasts, that pretty face, dark hair and sort of slightly swinging rear as she walked from desk to desk assigning work to the many people in the department.

Kathy Kite reminded Isaac of his cousin, Julie, of Rupholding. It had been seven or eight years since Isaac's parents had sent him to Germany, thought he might meet a nice Jewish girl, maybe eventually get married. Julie's dad, Isaac's uncle, was a surgeon in the area, in fact, had more or less a world-renowned reputation for taking on cases other doctors had given up on, most of the time seeing them through successfully.

Julie was beautiful, same tall, slender body as Kathy, lighter hair with a beautiful face and great personality. Isaac didn't find a Jewish girl to fall in love with other than his cousin. In fact, it would be several years before the lieutenant could keep her out of his thoughts and dreams.

§§

Three months before Isaac Greenberg would join the Navy and head for Great Lakes, his dad, a very successful corporate lawyer, would travel to Rupholding for a visit with this same family. He would return to the States devastated, telling stories, horror stories about conditions in his brother's homeland. How his brother had been forced to close his office, denied privileges at the Rupholding Hospital he had helped to build, forbidden to leave Germany; his daughter Julie now a prominent movie star, taken from the country, where nobody knew; Morrie Greenberg lucky to get out of Germany and to book passage back to America.

Isaac pondered the situation for several months, what to do, how could he help his uncle and family, what better way than to join the service, to fight back with all the might this great country could muster. He would be a part of that fight.

§§

"Ed, let's give it a try. I think the kid has stewed long enough. It's now or never."

"Humphrey, if it gets down to good cop/bad cop, which do you want me to play?"

"You be the bad guy, Ed. That's the way it's played so far."

"You remember Bosun Hill, don't you, Rusty?"

"Yes, he worked me over yesterday, Lieutenant. I'd just as soon talk with you. I don't like the rough stuff."

"Are you ready to talk about the game?"

"There was no game, Lieutenant. I told both you and the bosun there was no game for money the night Fred was croaked."

"Well, guess I'm wasting my time trying to be nice to you, giving you a way out if you give me names. I have more important things to do than listen to your lies. Ok, Ed, take over, but remember, no blood or broken bones."

"Why don't you leave, Lieutenant? Rusty and I can get on with it alone."

"No, Lieutenant, stick around. I told you I don't want to deal with the Bosun. What did those other guys tell you about me?"

"Well, Rusty, they named names and what I want is you to give me your list of names to see if it checks. If it does, I'll feel this is an honest confession, you'll go free, and as promised, I will not press charges on the gambling situation."

"Send the Bosun out, Lieutenant. I'll give names."

"You heard the man, Ed. Send in Yeoman Kathy Kite with her pad and pencil. You can take a walk."

"Here, have a cigarette, Jim, while we wait for the yeoman to come in. You're doing the right thing."

"I hope so, sir, and I don't care what those other guys tell you, what you're going to get from me is the truth, the whole truth and nothing but the truth."

"OK, shoot."

"There was a game the morning Fred was whacked. We got a few guys together that had the coin and like me, loved to gamble. You know, Lieutenant, I sorta grew up on the tables before joining up. Worked at Vegas, Reno and a few jobs in joints along State Street in Chicago. Never made a bundle, but had three squares and a roof over my head until I made one big mistake. I crossed Fat Eddie and he came lookin'. Next thing I know I'm at an enlistment station. The rest is history."

"Well, the Navy can be a good home, Seaman, that's if you keep your nose clean. Now what about the game."

"We found a spot in one of the paint lockers up on the forward part of the ship. Had a few flashlights. The locker had no port holes, the hatch could be battened so as long as we made zero noise, it was a good place to play. Game started about 0130, ended 0330 because several of us had 0400 watches. We played blackjack and seven card dealer's choice. I wouldn't deal 'cause of my background at the tables."

"OK, Rusty, now who played?"

"Well, there was Daukins, you know about him. There was me. Then three other guys I'd played with before and two that I didn't know. Fred brought 'em into the game."

"And who were the fellas you knew?"

"First was Binky Heins. I don't know his first name. We always called him Binky. Don't know his rate or anything but he worked down in the black gang, never had a lot of mola. Brought along Pete Omar, prince of a guy. Now he had the scratch. Guess the reason being he was a 1st class machinist. The third guy I also knew. He used to pass out the sulfa when I'd go down to sick bay with the clap. His name was Roger Bertron, a pharmacist 2nd, another good guy, always had the jack. I tell you, Lt. Craiger, I'd vouch for the three fellas, the names I just gave you."

"How about the two fellas you didn't know?"

"Daukins didn't introduce us. Funny, he was a sorta hep guy, seemed to know all about the etiquette. One fellow was tall, slender, sorta gangly, sorta good-lookin', knew his way around the table, seemed to have the bucks. Had a drawl or talked like he might've been from the hills, can't say I ever saw him before."

"Now the second guy, he was a piece of cake. Short, slender, ugly, I mean ugly. Not the kind of kisser you'd forget. I've seen him around somewhere but can't remember where. They called him by some kinda nickname, prune stone, orange peel, somethin' like that. He didn't seem to be well-healed, kept borrowing from his big friend in order to stay in the game."

"We'd set a time limit. When that rolled around each person picked up their marbles and after checking to make sure there wasn't any watch in the area, we took off our separate ways. That's the last we saw of each other, at least last I saw of any of the players."

"You did good, Rusty. Now one other favor to ask you. If you see any of the men you talked about just now, don't, do not tell them that you gave out their names or that we talked. If you see the two fellas you didn't know names of, get in touch with me or Yeoman Herb Andrews right away. Again, you did a good job. We'll keep our end of the bargain. All gambling charges will be dropped, and if you need any help in the future, see me. By the way, was there a big winner or loser in the game?"

"No, sir, other than the redneck who kept borrowing. I'd say there was no loser. I won a few bucks, maybe a sawbuck or two, others seemed to break even."

§§

"Miss, when will I find the Commander at the base hospital?"

"He has hours there right now. Will be there for another hour, twenty minutes, but you'll need an appointment."

"Thanks. I'm sure the good doctor will see me."

§§

"You're from the JAG office, Corporal?"

"Yes, sir, I am."

"Well, why do you want to see me, especially without an appointment? If it's an emergency, we have a procedure for that and people who normally provide care in that area."

"Commander Siegal, I want to talk to you about a patient you took care of, an emergency, this was a month or so ago."

"Who is or was that patient, Corporal?"

"A Mrs. Marilyn Klein. Had a bad fall, facial bruises, rib cage and arm injury, and if you don't handle emergencies, why did you treat her?"

"Corporal, you're aware of the patient/doctor confidentiality code?"

"Yes, sir, I am, but we're investigating a murder. The information you have or provide could very well help solve that murder."

"And I suppose if I fail to cooperate, you'll come back with a warrant."

"Yes, sir. Don't make me do that. It gets messy, time consuming, all the time putting pressure on you and giving the hospital a bad name."

"First of all, I treated the lady as a favor for a good friend of mine. Don't ask for a name. The patient was badly bruised and emotionally stressed, didn't want to release her, planned on having her stay overnight, let her gather her thoughts, but she insisted that her husband was about to leave for sea duty, she needed to be home to help get him ready for the trip."

"She had another lady with her. Claimed to be the person who drove to the hospital. This person had been a nurse in the past, felt she could take care of Marilyn."

"Do you know who this lady was, Doctor?"

"No, claimed to be her next-door neighbor, referred to her by first name only, believe it was Rhonda."

"Could Mrs. Klein's injuries have been from a source other than falling?"

"Yes. When I first viewed the patient, I assumed she had been battered."

"Did you confront her with your initial thoughts?"

"I did and was told both by Marilyn and Rhonda that it was a nasty fall. In fact, Rhonda claimed to have seen the accident happen, helped Marilyn to her feet, then drove directly to the hospital."

"Thanks, Doctor, you were very helpful. By the way, might your friend be Commander Ricker?"

§§

"This information is unbelievable, Gene. Tie this in with what Shacter and Milkusky came up with and we could be 75% on the way to solving the case. We want to keep Tarry and Klein apart. We don't want them to talk to their wives."

"We want to bring both Rhonda Tarry and Marilyn Klein in for questioning, not together, again keep them apart. We can bring them in on the pretense of questions regarding their husbands, keeping in mind that we want to know most of all, what was going on between Marilyn and Daukins, if anything, and if there was any hanky-panky, what did the two sailor-boys know about it."

§§

Humphrey Craiger was riding high. This case had started out as almost a sure loser, man murdered in the middle of the night, out to sea aboard ship in the war zone, no witnesses. Then the very ship the event happens on is sunk by enemy action, the murderer either killed or scattered to the four winds, yet now there seemed hope.

The team the Marine had gathered around him was intact, functioning with all cylinders firing, plus there was the added outside help from Admiral Nimitz, Admiral Ernest, Lt. Isaac Greenberg, and a whole raft of people here on Ford Island, Pearl Harbor, Hawaii.

§§

"Craiger, I have some good news. A B-24 heading for Moffett Field this afternoon has room for two more passengers. You'd asked when and if a flight became available, you'd like to send one or two of your team to the Columbus area, maybe Chicago. Now's your chance."

"Admiral, Moffett is around San Jose, California. Chicago or Columbus is at least a two day, three night train trip away."

"Don't worry. Our Frisco office will have air transport the rest of the way, might be on the floor of a DC3, but it will be transportation, good fast reliable transportation. Have your guys ready by 16.40. Will send a jeep around to pick 'em up."

"Thanks, Admiral Ernest, and by the way, should have some results for you real soon."

§§

"That's the fastest I've ever packed a parachute bag, Ed," commented the smiling Corporal.

"Yeah, Gene, it's going to be great to get back to the States, snow should all be melted, weather something like here in Pearl."

The two happy campers were excited about the latest assignments. The bosun would work Chicago, talk with the construction company that built the Great Lakes addition, maybe a few people listed in Daukins' little black book. Chicago! Lots of memories.

The corporal would take over the job Ron Milkusky started working on with people in Columbus, Ohio. Talk with Daukins' family, get over to the high school, maybe interview some of the ill-fated sailor's friends or enemies. This was to be a whirlwind trip.

§§

The jeep stopped in front of a busy group of airedales climbing all over a monstrous four-engine aircraft parked in front of a hangar. Ed and Gene were used to seeing single-seater fighters and two-place bombers. This big fellow would normally carry a crew of nine with plenty of room to spare for bombs, guns, ammunition, and aviation gasoline.

"They're waiting for you in the hangar, fellows, doling out flight gear and parachutes. We leave in ten minutes."

One very young-looking Army Air Force 1st lieutenant and his 2nd lieutenant co-pilot were going over a flight plan, while another 2nd lewy climbed into his navigation office readying the instruments of trade. The radioman and flight engineer stood outside the starboard waist directing the odd conglomerate of passengers as they boarded the big bird.

There would be no need for tail, waist or turret gunners, nor would the flying limousine carry a bombardier. All machine guns had been removed. Individual, lightly-padded chairs or seats had taken the place of what was normally the rear business end of this highly modern fighting machine, starting to make a name for itself, especially over Europe.

Most passengers were already aboard. Ed was asked to sit up front in the bombardier's seat, while Gene Spies was placed next to an older Navy 1st lieutenant introducing himself as Bert Robinson. He was on his way back to the States to form several motor torpedo boat squadrons.

Gene would learn later that he'd been sitting next to the unpretentious skipper of Motor Torpedo Boat Squadron 3, stationed in the Philippines at the start of World War II, his squadron or the remaining three boats of his squadron responsible for ferrying General MacArthur and his entourage from the Philippines to a remote island in the South Pacific where a DC3 would complete the retreat to Australia.

Just forward of the quiet lieutenant sat a young pilot named Gay. This Navy flyer had been picked out of the sea around the remains of the flaming Battle of Midway by a scouting PBY.

The ensign's right arm in a sling, he was deep into preparations for what was to be a lavish tour of the States, paired up with those hard-working Hollywood movie stars, all striving toward selling the necessary war bonds. Ensign Gay was billed as a Navy war hero, the only member of torpedo eight to survive the horrendous wall of steel put up by Nagumo's forces.

One empty chair remained. Then just outside the open hatch a small Navy ambulance pulled up, stopped, and with the help of several corpsmen removed an older gentleman who seemed to be weighted down with a beautiful pair of gold Navy wings on the left breast of his blue tunic, complemented by row after row of campaign ribbons. The gold stripes on his cuffs as well as the scrambled eggs and two stars introduced this distinguished man as a rear admiral, requiring all hands to rise and salute as he was helped aboard.

Gee, the Admiral looked familiar, thought the Marine corporal. From the time he walked from the ambulance to the plane with the help of crutches, he seemed to roll, sort of a bow-legged gate, just like our skipper aboard Yorktown, our skipper with the two badly-healed ankles. Last we heard Captain Bill Fielder was in the base hospital in Pearl.

Bill Fielder wasn't the kind to linger. Just as soon as he was able to get out of bed and move around, he convinced his doctors to release him. Voila! He was now on his way to Moffett Field, soon to be reunited with his twin sons. Mike and Bob Fielder were finishing advanced training with a fighter squadron waiting to be assigned either to one of the new carriers coming on line or to a remote island strip somewhere in the hot, humid, malaria-infested South Pacific.

Once the newly-appointed admiral had completed his fatherly duties, he would be on his way south to visit the son of his friend and confidant, the late Chief Jim Caffrey. Jim's death weighed heavily on the shoulders of this aging warrior. Until he could explain in person why a grateful country had bestowed the Navy Cross, the nation's second highest honor, posthumously, upon his dad, well his work on this earth would not be complete.

As the flight engineer climbed aboard "Hail Mary" locking the waist hatch after him, announcing takeoff would be momentary, be sure all seat belts are in place, Ed Hill perched in the most forward part of the aircraft, could not help wonder why Humphrey Craiger was sending him and the corporal on this VIP flight. Gee, it looked like evidence against Klein, or possibly one of the players in that midnight card game, would eventually lead to a bust and conviction of the culprit who murdered Daukins.

§§

Maybe not. It could be Craiger knew something the other members didn't. Greenberg let it slip yesterday evening during dinner that it would be hard to convict without witnesses, and from the information presently available, the killing looked like a one-man job.

Isaac had invited Ed to spend the evening at the restaurant of the Royal Hawaiian Hotel located on celebrated Waikiki beach, quite a plush place, too rich for a bosun first's blood, or should we say, bankroll.

The Jewish lawyer and Oklahoma sailor had struck up a friendship, mutual friends at the Great Lakes Naval Training Station often the center of the conversation. Isaac would tell how the tall, pugnosed, broad-shouldered, deepvoiced boot C.O. had come to his rescue on more than one occasion. How the husky Polak warded off threats made toward the awkward, not too street-smart nerd by a couple of rednecked southerners out to get their jollies at the expense of what they considered an easy target, a no-good kike. How he spent some of his free time drilling the left footed apprentice seaman, always patient, never critical.

Greenberg, in turn, had tutored Ed Corshane in subjects known to come up on Navy placement tests. Corshane, an early high school dropout, was not the brighest pupil in math, science and English. Sure he was a very capable leader of men, but this art failed to show up on scores that would eventually determine the direction a fledgling seaman would take once he had completed basic training.

Apprentice Seaman Corshane had found his name two-thirds of the way down on the placement list posted on the company bulletin board. Chief Larson had gone to bat for the hard-working Stosch, had intervened at the training center's education office, had gotten him a place in gunnery school. Stosch was happy.

Happy until several months ago, while gun captain of a five

inch gun turret aboard DD476, an explosion occurred, killing two of the turret's gun crew, injuring several others including the gun captain. An inquiry into the incident pointed a finger at Ed. He had failed in his duty. He was to be court-martialed.

Isaac Greenberg had heard of the charge, gone to Admiral Stephen Ernest, explained his friendship, and given leave to represent the bedraggled Corshane. This was the big case the Admiral had mentioned earlier when explaining why the lieutenant would not be available immediately.

Greenberg had taken on one of JAG's super-star prosecutors, and whipped his ass. The big Polak would go free without a blemish on his already perfect record. Good job for good friends.

§§

No. Humphrey really wasn't at all that confident he had this case licked. What did he have? Names of three men other than Rusty who had a midnight card game with the deceased. That meant nothing. Gambling, although frowned on in the service, had been going on since the beginning of time, perfectly innocent way to pass the time of day on a job that left healthy, eager individuals with nothing to do much of the day or night, a lot of free time.

Then there was Klein and Tarry. They had lied about knowing each other, and in Klein's case, asking that Daukins and Tarry be brought aboard as replacements. Yes, this sounded a little fishy, but by the same token it could be argued that the two metalsmiths were capable, Klein found this out one way or other, and because he needed help in a hurry, requested the transfer. Still no real reason to suspect Klein of murder.

Finding Klein's wife Marilyn listed in Daukins' little black book could be another story, although Fred worked with Marilyn. Again, it could be argued that this was just a work-related platonic relationship.

What made this whole Klein situation interesting and suspicious was Klein's lying, asking that Daukins be brought aboard Yorktown, and his wife's name appearing in that little black book. Add the three ingredients together and you could have the makings of, maybe not a murder, but at least a scandal.

So when Stephen Ernest offered a trip to the States for several of the men on the team, the lieutenant snapped up the offer, a way to gather more evidence, knowledge about a man though young in years seemed old and experienced in breaking the hearts of fair maidens and maybe, just maybe, crossing one too many boyfriend or husband, or even banking the money that should have gone into weekly funds needed to buy groceries or shoes for a growing family.

§§

The investigating team had been reassigned: Hill to Chicago, Spies to Columbus, Andrews would work on locating the three gamblers, while Shacter and Milkusky interrogated the Klein faction, Craiger and Greenberg coordinating and advising as necessary.

§§

Klein and Tarry were adamant. Why had they been brought in for questioning? What was the charge? Should they seek counsel? Both men were read their rights, both told that at any time during the questioning they felt a need for counsel, such would be provided. Shacter then took Klein into one room and Milkusky and Tarry occupied the space next door.

"Jeffery, why did you tell the investigating team that you didn't know Fred Daukins or Milton Tarry before they came aboard Yorktown?"

"I don't know. Did I say that? I didn't know Daukins."

"But you did know Milt?"

"Sure, I knew Milt. Don't believe I ever said I didn't."

"Let's stop right here, metalsmith. You're under oath. Remember, under oath. You're also suspect in a murder investigation, the murder of 3rd class Fred Daukins. Any lies will be held against you. We call that perjury. That can get you big time in the federal pen. Now do I make myself clear?"

"Yes, sir, Lieutenant. I got nothing to hide. Maybe I did say I didn't know Daukins or Tarry back aboard ship. Maybe I didn't think it was important or any of your business."

"Well, do you realize it is my business now, sailor?"

"Yes, sir, I do."

"You also said you hadn't specifically asked that both Daukins and Tarry be brought aboard as replacements for the two men killed at Coral Sea. You claimed the pool sent them at random, true or false?"

"That's true, but again, I didn't want to get involved."

"Well, you are involved, fella, whether you like it or not. Now tell me why you requested Fred and Milt."

"Well, I had worked with Milt at the base shop, knew he was a good worker, knew his stuff, and I needed competent men."

"Why Daukins?"

"Well, Milt suggested he might be the best available at the time."

"Don't lie to me, sailor."

"I'm not lying, didn't have a big choice, and time was of the essence."

"Ever beat your wife, Jeffery?"

"Now that's one hell of a question to ask, Lieutenant. What does that have to do with the metalsmith's death?"

"Thought I'd ask. You said you didn't know Daukins before he came aboard ship, but did you know of him?"

"No, sir, I said I didn't know anything about him. Just took him on by Milt's recommendation."

"Did your wife know Fred?"

"She may have. They worked in the same building."

"Did she ever talk to you about Fred?"

"Hell, no, why would she talk about him?"

"They may have been friends. As you said, they worked in the same building."

"Let's get one thing straight, Lieutenant. Anything my wife had to do with the guys in the shop was business. You can talk to Commander Ricker about her. She was an all-business employee."

"Would you consider the Commander a friend of your wife's?"

"That's it. I don't like your insinuations. I want a lawyer before I answer another question."

"All right, Jeffery. That will be arranged but in the meantime you're still under arrest. We'll have counsel assigned before the day is over."

§§

Things were going much the same in the room next door. Milt Tarry claimed he didn't think that the conversation aboard Yorktown regarding who knew who or when was anyone's business but the two metalsmiths being questioned at the time. He did change his tune after being warned of perjuring himself, admitted to knowing Klein and suggesting that Daukins be an adequate replacement.

Asked if he knew Klein's wife outside of work, Tarry said hell no, why would he? Did he know if Klein and his wife had marital problems? How could he, he said, he really didn't know either one on a social basis.

What neither Tarry or Klein knew was that their wives had been asked to come into JAG headquarters to answer questions, not together, but Rhonda in one room, Marilyn in another.

Tarry was told he was being held for further questioning and at his request, was being furnished counsel.

§§

"Tell me, Mrs. Klein. Do you know a 3rd class aviation metalsmith named Fred William Daukins?"

"Yes, Lieutenant, I do. He worked at our hangar."

"How well do you know this man?"

"Well, first off, I heard he'd been killed at Midway."

"OK. Before going aboard the carrier, how well did you know him?"

"He would bring work orders from the shop into the office quite often. That's how I knew him."

"Did you know him socially?"

"I don't know what you mean, socially, officer."

"Did you ever meet with him outside of the shop?"

"No, I didn't. Oh, maybe we might bump into each other at the bowling alley or shopping at the grocery store. That's all. Yes, that's all."

"Mrs. Klein, did your husband ever beat you?"

"Why, no. He never laid a hand on me."

"Any other man ever beat you?"

"No, sir, why do you ask?"

"You reported into the hospital some weeks ago, at the time Yorktown was in for repairs after Coral Sea. The hospital records show that you were covered with bruises, black and blue marks, all typical of physical trauma associated with a beating."

"That's a mistake, Lt. Shacter. I fell coming out of my trailer."

"Marilyn, why would Fred Daukins have your home telephone number and address in what we call his little black book?"

"I don't have the slightest idea. I never gave my number to him. Maybe he got it out of the phone book."

"Why would he take those numbers out of the telephone book?"

"I told you, officer, I don't know. Maybe he thought he might have to call me regarding a work order. Ask him. Oh, no, you can't ask him. I'm sorry."

"Sgt. Milkusky is talking with your neighbor Rhonda Tarry. When they're finished, we'll ask Rhonda to drive you home. We are holding both Jeffery and Milton for further questioning. If you should want to change any of your answers, the answers you gave today, call me. Thanks for coming in and give my regards to Commander Ricker."

§§

"Rhonda, I understand you're neighbors with the Kleins. Is that right?"

"Yes, Sergeant. We live next door in a trailer home."

"Do the Kleins live in a trailer?"

"Yes, they do. Same kind as we have."

"Have you known the Kleins for a long time?"

"Pretty long. They lived in their home when we moved into ours. Think Jeffery helped Milton find our place."

"Do you and your husband ever go out with the Kleins, you know, bowling, dinner, maybe for a few drinks?"

"Oh, sure, especially while Jeff was away out to sea. We sorta looked after Marilyn, and, of course, while both of the guys were at Midway, Marilyn and I would go to the movies and things."

"Would those things ever be a few drinks at the "Bucket of Blood?"

"My God, no. I wouldn't get caught dead in that place, and if Milt would have found out, he'd have killed me."

"Would he really, Mrs. Tarry?"

"Well, I'm exaggerating, but he wouldn't have liked it."

"Is Milt a violent man?"

"No, but he is a church-going person. Doesn't like what goes on in places like you mentioned."

"Let's change the subject. Did you take Mrs. Klein to the base hospital about a month ago?"

"Yes, Marilyn fell coming out of her house."

"Wasn't her husband home at the time?"

"I guess so."

"Why didn't he take her? Wouldn't you think he would be concerned?"

"I don't know. Maybe they were on the outs or something."

"That's odd. Jeff had been gone for awhile. You would think they would sorta be lovey-dovey."

"I don't know anything about that, Sergeant."

"Didn't Marilyn ever confide in you, Rhonda?"

"Well, we were best friends. I guess she did some."

"Did Jeff and Marilyn ever argue?"

"I suppose so."

"Well, you live right next door. Did you ever hear them argue?"

"Yes."

"Did Jeff and Marilyn ever fight? Did he ever beat her?"

"Don't ask me that kind of question, Mr. Milkusky. These people are my neighbors, my friends."

"Well, Rhonda, what would you say if I told you that I have talked with other neighbors in the trailer park, and they claim Jeff Klein beat his wife."

"I don't know who would tell you those kinds of stories. Who said that?"

"Never mind who. You're under oath, Rhonda. Lie to me and your next stop will be the base lockup. Let's start over. Did Jeff Klein ever hit his wife?"

"Well, yes. I don't want to tell on my friends, but I don't want to go to jail either."

"Did he hit his wife the day you took her to the base hospital?"

"Yes, he did. Beat her bad. Marilyn made me promise I would say she fell. She didn't want him to come after her."

"What do you mean, come after her, beat her some more?"

"He is a very jealous man. Can't stand even to see some guy look at her, you know, give her the eye."

"Why was Klein jealous that particular day?"

"Well, from what Milt tells me, this Fred Daukins guy sorta cuddled-up to Marilyn on the job."

"What do you mean, cuddled-up?"

"Well, he would spend more time talking with her than the job really took."

"And how did Jeff find out about this?"

"Well, you see, Milt and Jeff are pals. Guess Milt didn't want some other guy to tell his friend that Fred was sniffing around his woman."

"Tell me, Rhonda. You're good friends with Marilyn."

"Yes."

"Did Marilyn ever talk to you about Fred?"

"Well, yes, sorta. She said he had asked her out."

"Did Fred and Marilyn ever go out? Did they ever have a date?

"Come on, Sergeant. Please don't make me tell you things like that."

"Rhonda, there was a man killed, murdered. We're beyond telling stories out of school. We need facts and as I told you earlier, you're under oath. Lie and you could go to jail."

"I don't know for sure but I think they may have gone bowling together."

"Did Fred come to the trailer to pick up Marilyn?"

"I don't know. Think they just met at the alley. All Fred did was drive her home."

"Did Fred go into the trailer with Marilyn?"

"Yes, he had to use the bathroom."

"How long did Daukins stay that night?"

"I don't know. Marilyn didn't say, and Milton was sleeping. I didn't want him to wake up and see a car next door, so I went back to bed."

"So Milt didn't know about Fred's visit?"

"No."

"Let me ask you another question. How often did Fred Daukins visit your neighbor?"

"I only know about two times."

"Did Marilyn ever tell you that she slept with Daukins?"

"No, she never said that."

"And your husband never knew about those visits?"

"Oh, no. I wouldn't dare tell him. He would have been furious."

"Ever see any other person go into the Klein's home while Jeffrey was away?"

"Only one time. An older man one evening. Marilyn told me it was an uncle from out of town."

"What did this uncle look like?"

"It was too dark to tell. Nicely dressed man, had a package under his arm. Marilyn said her uncle brought her a present. He was from out of town so he stayed over for the night. He had a train to catch next morning so he had to leave early. Otherwise Marilyn said she would have introduced me. Please don't tell Milton or Jeffrey that I told you about that Fred Daukins or that Jeff beat his wife. I wouldn't have, but I don't want to end up in jail."

"You did real good, Rhonda. Will do my best to keep you out of this mess. Your friend is waiting for you to take her home. Can't say when your husband will be released. Depends on what our boss has to say about our interviews. We'll keep you posted."

"Rhonda, one thing bothers me, before you leave. Did Marilyn tell Jeffery about her uncle's visit?"

"Oh, no. This uncle and Jeff didn't get along very well. Marilyn swore me to secrecy. I was not to tell either Jeff or Milton about his coming and staying with her."

"Did she show you the present he brought?"

"Yes. Marilyn said her uncle knew Jeff was a cheapskate, hardly ever bought her anything nice, so when he, the uncle, was in Paris, France, he bought Marilyn a pretty nightgown, pink silk with bows, lace and ribbons. Marilyn said she hid the present. Didn't want her husband to find it. Guess they weren't having the best marriage."

The balding, former New Jersey desk sergeant thought he had heard it all. The years spent as a policeman on the beat as well as behind the desk in a district that catered to prostitutes, drug pushers, thieves, molesters, even murderers, had prepared him for the type of detective work he was presently doing.

This gal Marilyn was skating on thin ice, a very jealous husband with an eager-to-help co-worker as a neighbor and a wife who gambled on extra-marital relationships. Had she been shacking up with Daukins? Most likely. And this uncle guy. Could this just be her boss, the fellow who couldn't praise her enough, the dirty old man who most likely wanted to get into her pants and maybe did? Well, Marine Sgt. Milkusky would take the whole ball of wax back to the team. Let's see how this piece of the puzzle fits.

§§

"I have the information you requested, Mr. Andrews. Why don't you sit down and we can review it." Once again LCdr. Mary Wilkens had come to the aid of the group of men investigating the murder of Fred Daukins.

She continued. "You're a little late in the case of F2 Heins. He went to sea three days ago aboard DD396."

Although classified, the destroyer was part of a task group headed toward the Solomon Islands.

"It seems we've lost a number of experienced black gang people lately. A man with Binky's background doesn't linger in our pool for long. I can tell you his record is clean, the kind of serviceman who will leave the Navy with a good conduct medal."

"You also asked about MM1 Peter Omar. Again, spotless sheet, still in our pool. I've put a hold an any possible transfer, at least until you give me the all-clear. Keep in mind, should you exonerate Peter, let me know. The fleet can use him."

"The record on your third suspect reads a little different. Again, he's still in our pool, still under my jurisdiction, but I have loaned him to the base walk-in clinic. Seems there has been a rash of German Measles just this past week, especially in the case of men in two of the base barracks. Very contagious. Clinic personnel have camped out in those barracks, thus the need for temporary replacements. Just say the word and PhM2 Roger Bertron will be at your service."

"Now to his sheet. Bertron's jacket shows one Captain's mast, and he was AWOL for six days back in the States. Nothing regarding gambling. Roger came up before the courts for drunk and disorderly conduct. Served a week in the brig here in Hawaii."

"Regarding the six days away without leave, it seems he received a 'dear John' letter from a high school sweetheart. He had sent money to buy an engagement ring. The lady bought a dinner ring instead. Then went on to marry his best friend, another sailor. Guess the corpsman went to pieces, couldn't convince his C.O. that he needed emergency leave, so just took off. Shore Patrol picked him up just in time. He had a gun, claimed he would have used it when and if he ran into this good buddy."

"Roger went to trial, a very serious offense, yet in the eyes of the men judging the case, they saw just cause. This young man had been taken advantage of. Instead of a year in Leavenworth, he was given 30 days in the local brig, then a suspended sentence, to serve the balance of the war overseas, thus Hawaii and eventually aboard Yorktown."

"Sounds like he could commit murder, Commander. I'm sure Craiger will want to talk with Roger Bertron."

"How is Yeoman Kite handling JAG?"

"Great. What a help she's been to me. Taken over all my paperwork, sits in on meetings, takes minutes, has asked to participate in the investigation should a female be needed."

"And how is Lt. Greenberg holding up being around her day after day?" asked the smiling commander.

"Well, I don't know," countered a surprised Herb Andrews, "don't quote me, but I think he has stars in his eyes."

§§

Starry-eyed or not, it had been decided that Greenberg would continue the interrogation of Tarry and Klein who at this point had been assigned counsel.

"Send in Jeffery Klein, please. His lawyer is with him in the lockup. Have her come in also."

"Nice to meet you, Lt. Burns. I've been assigned by the prosecution to get a final deposition from metalsmith Klein regarding the Daukins' murder, and how are you this afternoon, Mr. Klein?"

"Not good," barked the unshaven suspect, "damn mad about having a woman represent me and what's this murder crap! You think I killed a guy I didn't really know?"

"You are a suspect. What you tell us today could go a long way toward determining whether you will be held over for trial. As far as a woman representing you, 1st Lt. Hilda Burns is a highly qualified member of the bar, top JAG lawyer. Feel lucky she's on your side and if you're smart, you'll cooperate with her."

Hilda smiled over at the youthful-looking legal-eagle. "Thanks, but I can handle Mr. Klein."

"You are going to cooperate, aren't you, Jeffery?"

"I didn't do nothin, what's there to cooperate," grumbled the airedale as he looked down at his folded hands clasped together in a squeezing motion, "I just want to get the hell outa here."

"Well, let's talk. You told Marine Lt. Shacter that you brought Milton Tarry aboard Yorktown as a replacement because you had worked with him at the Ford Island metal shop before you were aboard ship, is that right?"

"Yes, that's right. Milt knows his stuff. Should be a first class instead of second. I'd hoped to help him go up another rate."

"You told the Lieutenant that you brought AM3 Fred William Daukins aboard as a replacement at the request of Milton Tarry, is that right?"

"Yeah."

"Why bring a man who was more or less a go-between, a paper pusher, aboard a ship badly undermanned. You needed people who could repair aircraft, not write or transfer work orders."

"Well, there just wasn't any good metalsmiths other than Milt around."

"What would you say, Mr. Klein, if I told you that I talked with the Ford Island supervisory force, the men who not only oversee personnel but are responsible for getting work done at the metal shop, and they told me that they were very suprised that you picked Daukins for the type of work normally done on a fighting ship out to sea."

"Lt. Greenberg, I'd say those guys don't know what they're talkin' about."

"Mr. Klein, you're saying that Chief Aviation Metalsmith Fred Ankerman, a 25 year veteran, a man who heads up the metalshop on Ford Island, doesn't know what he's talking about when it comes to assigning men to jobs they are capable of handling?"

"No, I didn't say that."

"Well, Mr. Klein, he's the person I was referring to when I said the choice you made was a poor one."

"Well, I really didn't make the choice. Milt did."

"Mr. Klein, could it be that you picked Fred Daukins because you wanted to get him off the island, away from your wife?"

"Why would I want to do that? What's my wife got to do with it? Let's keep her out of it."

"Mr. Klein, what would you say if I told you that Fred Daukins had your wife's telephone number, her home phone number, in his little black address book."

Klein's face flushed at this news, his temples pulsed, restraint became a real problem.

"Calm down, Mr. Klein," voiced the defendant counsel as she reached over and placed a hand on Jeffery's shoulder, at the same time asking Isaac if the allegation was true.

"Yes, it's true. Further, we have a witness who will testify that your client knew that Fred Daukins had been overly friendly with Marilyn Klein and that's the reason the murder victim was brought aboard Yorktown and assigned to the aviation metalsmith shop."

Klein straightened up in his chair, rose to his feet, gripped the edge of the table with one hand, balling his fist with the other in a move toward striking the slight interrogator who had moved back just enough to stay out of the reach of the enraged man's lashing blow.

"None of that," yelled a burly Marine guard as he moved with the grace of a gazelle to pin Jeff's arms behind him, wrestling the suspected killer to the floor, while a second Marine guard also stationed at the back of the interrogation room, clamped a pair of handcuffs on the prone man's wrists.

Once restrained, calmed by words of compassion from Hilda Burns, the defendant again faced questioning from a slightly ruffled but ever-pressing Lt. Greenberg.

"Your attorney will tell you, Mr. Klein, that outbursts like the one we just witnessed will only hurt your case, only show that you are a violent man, maybe violent enough to stick a knife in the back of a fellow seaman."

"That's enough, Mr.Greenberg. That's supposition. You have no evidence, no hard evidence that my client murdered the deceased. Please don't muddy the waters with innuendoes, let's stay with the facts."

Hilda Burns had not taken a liking to the man she was to defend, but like him or not, it was her sworn duty to protect him to the best of her ability. A capable, experienced trial lawyer she was, not in cases of murder, this was her first, no Miss Burns had spent ten plus years defending goons, strikers, union people, fighting for working-man's rights, in most cases against major companies, and in most cases, coming out on top.

She was new to the Navy, new to JAG, came aboard just six months ago, wanted to do her part to defend this great country.

"I think we've covered enough for today. Lt. Greenberg, I'd like Jeffery Klein sent back to his cell, after which you and I should talk."

"Talk about what?" asked the shaking, sweating metalsmith. "I didn't murder no Fred Daukins! I hardly knew him. I might have if what you said is true, he was flirting with my wife."

"That's enough, Jeffery," commanded the defendant's counsel. "Guard, take Mr. Klein back to his cell. I'll be in to see you shortly. Shut-up for your own good."

"You were trying to bluff Jeffery Klein, weren't you, Isaac?"

"No, I wasn't, Miss Burns. Let me tell you what we know at this point."

§§

The defendant had been returned to the JAG lockup while Isaac Greenberg and Hilda Burns huddled over coffee in the small JAG tea room located in the lower level of this navy's hall of justice.

"Although we still don't have Milton Tarry's sworn deposition at this time, that will be taken this afternoon, we do have witnesses who will swear to the following: Jeffery Klein asked that Fred Daukins be brought aboard Yorktown, we believe the reason being both Jeff and Milt thought he was getting too friendly with Marilyn Klein."

"Klein beat his wife to within an inch of her life the day after he returned home from the Battle of Coral Sea. We believe Milt Tarry told his friend about the advances of the deceased, and it was decided to remove the threat, that Marilyn just might not be capable of resisting the temptations of this good-looking kid."

"We know that Klein was an exceptionally jealous man when it came to his wife. We have at least one witness who will testify to that."

"We also have a witness who will testify to the fact that Marilyn Klein had at least two dates with Fred Daukins, and that upon the couple returning home to the Klein's trailer, Fred was invited in, how long or late he stayed, at this point we don't know."

"We also have a witness who will testify that another man, Marilyn claims was her uncle, an uncle her husband hates, spent the night in the Klein's trailer, bearing gifts, not leaving until almost daybreak."

"We don't feel that Jeff or Milt know about the stayovers. That would have been icing on the cake. What we do know is that Marilyn most likely was sleeping around, that both of the fellows had violent tempers, were capable of doing great bodily harm, maybe murder, to anyone they considered a preditor."

"So where does this leave Jeffery Klein, Isaac?"

"This leaves Jeffery a #1 suspect, Hilda. I'd suggest that you review the evidence with Jeff because we'll most likely be bringing him up before an inquiry board in the not-too-distant future."

"Who's representing Milton Tarry?"

"A Marine captain by the name of Roger Pastnu, new with JAG, just came down from the States."

"Well, you fellows have your work cut out for you," commented the pretty Hilda Burns. "I ran up against him several times while he defended big business against union grievances, a ruthless, well-prepared, high-class individual. I'm surprised he would be assigned to a case of this level."

"What do you mean, Lieutenant, a case of this level?" asked a slightly perturbed Isaac Greenberg. "JAG considers the murder of one of their flock, a murder out to sea in the war zone, a number one priority."

"Isaac, don't get your balls in an uproar," smiled the taunting barrister. "Sure, it's a big case, but this fellow Pastnu had been paid big bucks to represent companies like Ford Motors against people like Jimmy Hoffa. Just trying to put it in perspective."

"Well, Hilda, he puts his pants on one leg at a time just like me. We'll really see how good he is this afternoon when I get him and Tarry in the box, and speaking of legs, neither Tarry nor Klein really have a leg to stand on."

§§

Ed Hill had pulled priority at Moffett Field to board a flight heading for the naval air base at Alameda, California. The modified JM1, known as B26 by the Army Air Force, was on the tarmac, warming up ready to go. Ed had drawn a standard issue chestpack from the local parachute loft, snapped it into the already in-place body harness before entering the aircraft through the access opening just aft of the nose wheel.

Once in the aircraft, the Navy bosun was waved back through the narrow walkway of the bomb bay and told to make himself comfortable on the deck looking out what in combat would be the waist gunner's hatch. As Ed moved through the cramped quarters of the bomb bay, the handle of his parachute ripcord caught the hooked end of a bomb rack, causing the release of a massive amount of silk, carefully packed by some rigger, the purpose of course to save the life of a distressed airman, should the need arise.

Sheepishly, the shocked investigator gathered the many yards of lightweight material into a ball, pressed it into his chest, engulfed by straining arms, and proceeded to his place for takeoff.

"Don't worry, boats," laughed an Air Force sergeant, attaching a long sausage-like silk sleeve to the cable of a bolted-in-place winch. "These guys are straight shooters, at least most of 'em are. Seldom do they miss the target, and if they do, they usually hit thin air, not our tail surfaces."

Ed Hill had signed on to a flight headed for Frisco but didn't know that on the way his transportation was to pull double duty, along with the ride, tow a target for the guns of the training ship Wyoming, patiently waiting in the blue waters of the Pacific below.

§§

"We heard about your adventure," laughed the Alameda chief rigger, as he signed in Ed's bundle of silk. "They radioed-in your predicament. You won't need a replacement. The DC3 that's to take you to Chicago doesn't warrant chutes for its passengers."

This was great. Finally, a commercially-rigged aircraft, normal seats, no more floor, and only two stop-overs before landing at the Glenview Naval Air Station just outside Chicago.

As the twin engine aircraft neared the training field and requested clearance to land, Ed, looking out over the massive operation, could feel a tingle of excitement at the hustle and bustle going on below.

Off to the right was the large round asphalt mat with dozens and dozens of N2Ss, the well-known yellow perils taking off and landing. This was the single engine two-seater bi-plane the Navy was using so successfully for primary training, taking fledgling pilots after three months of classroom training and introducing them to the real world of flying.

To the left was a massive cement block and concrete building housing the SNJs, TBFs, F6Fs and SB2Cs, the aircraft making up CQTU, the Carrier Qualification Training Unit. This was the final phase of Navy and Marine Corps training necessary to prepare airmen for operation out in the fleet either aboard carriers or distant land-based jungle outposts.

Each day the aircraft with the eager pilots would leave the hangar, move out onto the miles of concrete runways, then on the way south and east to a spot in the often rough, dangerous Lake Michigan, the lake bordering on the eastern shores of the great city of Chicago.

Plying these waters were the training carriers Wolverine and Sable. In earlier life the converted side-paddlers hauled passengers and coal. Now they would make or break the life of many a young man striving to wear the coveted gold wings so vividly portrayed on the many full-size, lifelike posters hanging from the walls of postoffice and recruitment centers around the country.

Many of these young pilots would take one waveoff too many, bounce over the protective barriers provided forward, fail to pick up a deck pendant, or maybe land in a catwalk, toppling over the side into the cold, icy waters below, lucky to be picked up before hyperthermia took effect, or going to a watery grave trapped inside a jammed cockpit canopy.

Ed could remember back at Great Lakes while taking boots, a working party had been organized to transport furniture to this same air station. He had been a member of that party and was amazed to see the change in what was once a farmer's field, cows grazing in the distance, grapes hanging from the vine, now a magnificent and efficient naval air station producing the well-trained Navy pilots so badly needed to stem the progress of Hirohito's warriors in the Pacific.

§§

The training station bus would transport Ed to Navy Pier where he could pick up a streetcar to the 1400 block of West Harrison Street to the offices of the Ellis Brothers construction company.

A well-dressed, midddle-aged secretary escorted the Navy bosun into Tom Ellis' office, introduced him, then quietly closed the door.

"You've come a long way, officer," voiced the paunchy, balding, half-smiling vice president of the company that had built the structures now gracing those former farmer's fields, the buildings known as Camp Moffett.

"Yes, sir, I have, and with a purpose. The Navy is trying to gather information that might help in the case of one Fred William Daukins, a man picked up along with five of your carpenters several years ago for gambling on Navy property."

"Oh, yes, I remember that situation, Mr. Hill. We turned it over to our company lawyer, Jim Heller. He in turn dealt with the base commander at the time, can't remember his name, but all charges against our workmen were dropped."

Yes, sir, I know," commented the Navy representative. "We thought you might have the names of the five men. Just could be that they might shed some light on the situation."

"No, Mr. Hill, I have nothing. I'll give you Mr. Heller's address and telephone number. Maybe he can help. By the way, it's lunchtime. Let me treat you to some excellent food at the Club. We members are always eager to wine-and-dine our war heroes."

§§

Ed hadn't had anything but Navy chow for months. Never complained about the food, in fact, thought it was pretty good. Most civilians inducted into the various branches of the service complained bitterly about many things, but mostly the food. Ed always figured those guys came from families where the mother coddled their babies, spoiled them rotten. Not Ed. He ate what was put on the table before him.

In the Navy you got up, had grapefruit, eggs, shit-on-a-shingle, oatmeal, maybe a steak when in the battle zone, all the Joe you could drink. Real man's breakfast.

Lunch saw soup each and every day, maybe bean, pea, vegetable, potato, chowder, all kinds. There were sandwiches, especially those great horse-cock sandwiches, mixed fruit, salads, hamburgers, pork and beans, what more could you ask for.

Suppers always had potatoes, fried, mashed, sweet, all kinds, and always plenty of gravy. Tonight might feature pork chops, veal steak, fish, chicken, turkey, spaghetti, sauerkraut, always plenty of homemade bread, pie and cakes. If Ed had one complaint when aboard ship, it was the milk. They had what was called a mechanical cow, and it put out a product that tasted like chalk water, not good, but better than nothing. What Ed could never figure out was why the Giddunk Stand could put out a fairly decent ice cream cone, but not milk.

§§

Tom Ellis made the most of introducing BM1 Ed Hill to each and every member of the Chicago Athletic Club present at this day's luncheon. He didn't make lightly of Ed's duty aboard the now-famous Yorktown. In the eyes of Chicago's elite, this man was a real hero.

It would be several hours into these introductions before Ed would sit down to the most magnificent lunch of his life. Only after many manhattans and a number of toasts would the happy sailor feast on Caesar salad, cream of brocolli soup, shrimp cocktail, baked salmon, braised filet mignon, green beans almondine, twice-whipped potatoes, crescent rolls, all topped off with chocolate-covered cheesecake, coffee and after-dinner cordials. Navy food was good, but this was really living.

Where was this ration situation our poor civilians were supposed to be going through, Ed thought. Surely not here at this exclusive men's club.

It would be well into the evening before Tom Ellis, hat in hand, would leave the weary, tipsy hero of the day, and then only after he had arranged and paid for a suite of rooms at this exclusive palatial palace, rooms that were to serve the needs of Ed Hill for as long as his Chicago stay warranted.

§§

That can't be, 10.30 hours, sighed a sleepy-eyed, groggy hero of the elite Chicago Athletic Club, this as he slowly withdrew his aching body from under the satin sheets and silky covers, trying hard to remember what day this was.

Ed was not a teetotaler, nor was he a drunk. Maybe a shot and a beer occasionally at the non-commissioned officers club on the base, maybe a hi-ball or manhattan at the "Bucket of Blood" when off-duty, but last night they came fast and furious, too fast for a man with a mission, a mission he better get with. Shave, shower, some good strong black java, maybe an alka-seltzer or two, and he'd be good as new, able to tackle that Ellis Brothers' lawyer. That is if Ed could find him at his office.

§§

The Michigan Avenue bus ran right in front of the Club, but Ed figured walking would help clear the cobwebs from a not-too active brain. Heller's LaSalle Street office was only five blocks away, the sun was shining, causing both shadows and shafts of light to appear in a more or less twinkling, dancing manner as the bosun moved along the warm concrete sidewalks in an area of Chicago better known to natives as the Loop.

Large steel structures hovered over streets named Van Buren, Wabash, Lake, etc., structures that supported the rails allowing the electric trains to pass mostly uninhibited even during rush hour, the dreaded hour when Loop street traffic would be backed up for blocks, in some cases for miles at a time. The pattern taken by the structures actually was a continuous, irregular circle, thus the term "loop."

Embodied in the area surrounded by the mass of steel were the better shops, hotels, movie theatres, restaurants, and business offices of all kinds and types. Lawyer Heller served an elite clientele.

§§

"Tom Ellis called this morning, said I could expect a visit, asked that I cooperate to the fullest. Those Ellis Brothers are real gentlemen, clients who appreciate what you do for them and aren't afraid to show it."

Jim Heller was a little man with a deep voice, mustache, grey wavey hair, sorta distinguished-looking, just a slight twinkle in his eyes. When he arose from his plush swivel chair, moved forward to put out his hand, a slight limp was noticeable in the left leg. Sensing Ed's reaction to the limp, he smiled, "just an old football injury, sailor, kept me out of WWI."

Ed remembered Tom Ellis talking about his friend and lawyer yesterday, how Jim Heller had quarterbacked the Notre Dame eleven back in 1915 and 1916. This little man, a former football player? Hard to believe, but then again, in the days of soft leather helmets and no shoulder pads, they'd toss the backs over the line, the lighter the better.

"Do I understand that you want to reopen the Daukins' case where five of the Ellis Brothers carpenters were caught in Barracks #10 gambling with Mr. Daukins on government property?"

"No, sir, Mr. Heller. I'm investigating the murder of Fred Daukins, a murder that took place recently, out to sea. Really has no bearing on the gambling incident. What I would like to know is what the status of the five workmen is today, where are they, and what are they doing?"

"Well, you understand there is client/lawyer privacy privilege I could invoke, Mr. Hill, and will to a point. I will not give you the names or put you in contact with any of the men involved, but will tell you that all the people continue to work for Ellis Construction. They all work on projects in the States, and have had no further illegal gambling problems. Believe what I'm saying is if this incident, the murder, happened out to sea on a naval vessel, it couldn't have been one or more of my clients because they have continued to work close to home on the beach."

"Now, Mr. Hill, if I can't be of any further service regarding the investigation, how about lunch? You Navy people look slim and trim, look like you might enjoy a good rich civilian meal and I know just the place. How about the main dining room of the Chicago Athletic Club?"

Oh, no, thought the still woozie bosun. Another afternoon like yesterday would kill him!

§§

The trip to Columbus by Marine Corporal Gene Spies was much less harrowing than that of fellow-investigator, Ed Hill. Once the Army Air Force plane traveling from Hawaii had landed at Moffett Field, Gene decided he had had enough flying for awhile. Administration at Moffett made Pullman reservations for him on one of the better steam-driven trains of the time.

§§

It was not uncommon to expect the average rail trip between the San Francisco area and Chicago to take three nights and two days, or three days and two nights. Then it would take another eighteen to twenty-four hours to get to Columbus, but Gene was in no hurry. Humphrey Craiger had set no time limit on the trip nor the investigation, so why not enjoy the time back in the States. There had been no leave after the Yorktown sinking. Let's consider this trip not only business but maybe a little R&R, he thought.

Gene thought back to the last time he traveled between Chicago and Frisco, coming from leave, just before being sent overseas to Hawaii, only months before that fateful day at Pearl Harobr. No Pullman cars on his train then, in fact, you were lucky to get a seat. Many passengers stood in the aisles through the three day ordeal. Servicemen desperate for sleep would try to crawl up into the steel luggage racks mounted near the ceilings of the coach. It was not uncommon to find one or more guys crowded into the small lavatory stalls, seated on the pot or standing against the walls or bulkheads of the compartment, sound asleep.

What was really sad, he remembered, was the wife or girlfriend traveling to some camp or ship to visit a husband, fiance or boyfriend. How undignified, thought the corporal. Not all seated servicemen would get up and offer a seat to the fairer sex, not all gentlemen, that's for sure. For these ladies to experience the indignities provided was in poor taste. Yes, Gene could thank his lucky stars he was on his own, no attachments to worry about. But raised in an atmosphere where the fellow was expected to open a car door for a lady or help her on and off with her coat, this bothered him.

And chow. This was an experience. Lines of people to the dining car would begin to form around 0300 hours, extend through four, five, six passenger cars, lines coming in both from the front and rear ends of such cars, diners that wouldn't open or begin to serve before 0600 hours. No sooner was breakfast finished, the lines would again begin to form for lunch, then dinner. What a mess.

The fellows who really made out were the colored dining stewards. Tips were generous, service was good. Bourbon whiskey came in small one or two shot bottles that would usually run out after the second day of the trip. Then came the Scotch, like taking medicine, but a taste would usually be cultivated by the time the train pulled into Union Station, part of that great rail hub of that great city of Chicago.

§§

No, this Pullman was a different story, thought the reminiscing Marine, as he pulled up the soft sheets and woolen covers over a relaxed body while digesting a meal of cream of chicken soup, crisp duck, mashed potatoes and gravy, finished off with a plum pudding, rich coffee, a cognac and Cuban cigar. This is the life. Wonder how Ed's doin' in Chicago.

§§

Corporal Spies was now the keeper of Fred Daukins' little black address book as well as his high school yearbook. Spies had made a list of all the Chicago numbers for Ed Hill as well as a separate list of names and addresses that might be of interest back in Hawaii.

He had decided that approaching the Daukins family at this time was not a good idea. There had been the telegram and telephone call; mother, dad and brother knew of the death, but of course at this time, not the cause. Why add to the family's grief.

§§

Principal Fran Hawkins of John B. Sawyer High School greeted Corporal Spies with open arms. A war hero, especially a shipmate of an alumnus, was a rare treat in this part of a most patriotic city and country. Could the corporal stay on until the third of next month? There was to be a war bond rally in the high school auditorium, several movie stars were slated to appear, but a man just back from sinking four large first line Japanese carriers, that man would really sell bonds.

It took a good part of the next hour for the much-praised and respected Marine to explain that he had played only a small part in the demise of the enemy ships, and that he would hope to be back with his investigative team long before the rally occurred.

Gene insisted that this visit to the principal's office be kept a secret. Any information Fran Hawkins might be able to furnish regarding Daukins and friends would be kept confidential, and what Spies would divulge to the principal would also be of a secret nature. The nature of Daukins' death was not to get out to the press or to any member of the Daukins family.

The principal was shocked. For what seemed an eternity, he sat with his mouth wide open, blood drained from his face, and his thin, wrinkled hands began to tremble.

"Murdered out to sea! How could anybody, your own people, do such a thing?"

"Yes, sir, it was gross. Our own people are asking the same question and, of course, that's why I'm here, to see if you or any of his friends can shed light on the matter."

"How can we shed light on the subject? We weren't there."

"Yes, sir, we think we know that, but we'd like to know if any of the people Fred went to school with could have been members of the Yorktown crew. Any of the girls he dated have brothers, cousins, aboard? Any of the girls or fellows have an axe to grind with the metalsmith?"

"That's hard to say, Corporal. I've been principal at this school for twenty-three years. As you can see, it's not a large school. Think I know just about everything there is to know about each and every child that's come through, not only the student but in most cases, their parents. How can I help?"

"All right, sir. Let's start with Fred. What kind of kid was he?"

"Good, or should I say, fair student. Never in any real trouble as he moved through the grades. Maybe better looking than he should have been, good personality, the girls loved him."

"How about the fellows?" Gene asked.

"Never played sports. Liked the guitar, seemed to have male friends. Suppose some of the guys were a little jealous because of his way with the ladies. No real incident I can think of off the top of my head. He comes from a nice family, brother a student, father works for the County, drives a truck, mother works part-time in a local gift shop. A real quiet, hard-working family."

"There was one incident though, soon after Fred graduated. It was rumored that his steady girlfriend, Mary Lou Hopkins, was pregnant, that the Daukins boy was the father, and that was the reason he joined the Navy. Talk was he didn't want to take the responsibility for a child, you know, get married. This kind of talk got back to the Daukins family. Really hurt them, sorta made them withdraw from the town, crawl into a shell."

"What else can you tell me about Mary Lou and her family?" asked the interested Marine.

"Not too much. Mary graduated with Fred. As I mentioned earlier, they were best girl and boyfriend for the last several years of high school. Mary was an excellent student, pretty, in all the school clubs, popular, cheerleader, the kind of student that should have gone on to college."

"Why didn't she?" Gene asked.

"Don't know for sure. One reason might have been the Daukins boy. She didn't want to leave him, and he surely wasn't college timber. Might have been money. Her folks had been on and off welfare from time to time. Dad worked part-time for the local lumberyard, was sorta sickly, sure he didn't bring home a big paycheck. Mother cleaned houses several days a week. Believe they had a hard time meeting their bills. Fortunately, Mary Lou was an only child. She worked at the drug store soda fountain several afternoon a week after school, made enough money to pay her own way, I guess."

"Did Mary Lou have the child?"

"I don't know. She left town soon after the rumor circulated. Never did find out where she went, what she was doing, or if she had a baby."

"How about Mary's folks?"

"They're still in town. They never really participated in social or church functions. Suppose they also withdrew even more."

"Well, Mr. Hawkins, I'd like you to give me the home address of the Hopkins. You can be sure I won't let on that you were the one who filled me in on the daughter's situation. In other words, I won't betray your confidence."

"I'd also like several other favors from you. One, can you tell me who Mary Lou might have confided in, a girlfriend, relative, confidant of some form, close friend? Two, I have a list of names found in Fred Daukins' address book. Let's talk about them, and three, let's review the people Daukins might have been close to, people whose picture and comments are shown in the 1939 yearbook of John B. Sawyer."

"Corp. Spies, I'd be happy to help. First, to my knowledge Mary Lou had no special girlfriend. She was busy not only with schoolwork but as I mentioned earlier, working at the drugstore."

"As to the names in Fred's little black book, the four fellows mentioned were a group of boys who not only hung together here at school, but it is my understanding formed a sorta club or the nucleus of a club that took up much of their time out of school, evenings, weekends, and so forth. Soon after Pearl Harbor, this same group or club as a unit enlisted in the Army. Fine, patriotic young men, and again, the four boys mentioned were a part of the enlistment."

"Can you tell me where the four boys or group is today, Mr. Hawkins?"

"Yes, I can. They enlisted with the understanding they would be kept together as a unit. The Army kept its word. There was an article in our local newspaper just this past week.

They had been integrated into the 8th Army Air Force on its way to England."

"Now about the three young ladies, other than Mary Lou. Wanda Kirkmeyer is a cousin to the Daukins boys. She graduated with Fred. They seemed close. Her mother is a sister to Fred's mom. I'd be careful in talking with the Kirkmeyer family if you want to keep the Daukins family out of this investigation. The sisters always seemed close."

"Betty Miller and Viola Statke, the two other names you're asking about, might be another story. Their reputations have been questionable. Dropped out of school in the second year. Poor students, expelled in freshman year for drinking on school property. I remember the situation well. Both sets of parents fought very hard to have the young ladies reinstated and returned to class. Eventually they were, but it seemed downhill from that time on until, at one point, the girls just failed to come to class altogether. The girls and their families seemed to drift away from the community. I have no idea where they might have moved to, nor any additional information. I can't see why Fred would have their local addresses and phone numbers in his book. They didn't seem his type and, of course, then there was Mary Lou."

"Alright, sir, now the yearbook. First, let me say it's a fine publication, especially the fly page, that $8\frac{1}{2}$ x 11 blowup of the class ring. Beautiful. The detail is outstanding."

"Well, thank you, Mr. Spies. We here at Sawyer High School are proud of the design. It's been a symbol of success for the wearer for the past twenty-two years. Our governor and a senator proudly wear the ring to this day."

"Now as to pictures of the graduating students who might have been close to Mr. Daukins, well, I draw a blank. Other than the names already mentioned, I'd have to say that none were close or would have had a bearing on his life here in Columbus. As to the salutations, they seem typical of what you might expect to find in any 17 or 18 year old's vocabulary."

"Principal Hawkins, you've been a world of information, a great help to this ongoing investigation, a service to your country. Thanks very much. If the Navy department can ever be of service, please get in touch with me. I'm at your beck and call."

"It was my pleasure, Corporal. Sure wish you'd change your mind about the bond rally. Your presence would make a big difference. But thanks for your kind words and a safe trip back to Hawaii, for sure. I wish you Godspeed."

§§

What a fine man. What a great educator, thought the Marine as he headed for the Hopkins house just four blocks away. What bearing could a young lady, possible mother of Fred's child, have on his murder? Let's see.

The Hopkins house was small, one story, badly in need of a paint job. The front gate hung open, suspended by one hinge, moving ever so slightly as the afternoon breezes stirred the surrounding trees, with leaves bright green in sharp contrast to the lawn, unkept brown grass, so badly in need of cutting.

No answer or response to his attempts to ring the front doorbell, Spies thought maybe no one's home, maybe the bell doesn't work. Should he knock? Why not.

"Yes, officer, can I help you?" asked a heavy-set, middle-aged woman as she swung open the unpainted front door.

"Yes, ma'am, you can. Are you Mrs. Hopkins?"

"Yes, I am. Is there a problem?"

"Ma'am, I'm Corporal Gene Spies from the U. S. Marine Corps. I'd like to talk to you about your daughter, Mary Lou."

"What has Mary done? Have you found her?"

"Mrs. Hopkins, that's why I'm here. I'd like to talk with her about Fred Daukins. May I come in?"

"Please come in, Corporal, and have a seat."

In contrast to a poorly-kept outside, the inside of the house, although old and slightly tattered, was immaculately clean and in order.

"Is Mr. Hopkins home? It would be in all our best interests if we discussed what I have to ask with both of you, together."

"John, will you come in, please? This is Marine Corporal Gene Spies. He'd like to talk with us about Mary Lou and the Daukins boy."

"Pleased to meet you, Corporal. Welcome," this fron a thin, pale, greying man offering his hand to the robust Marine who sprung from his chair to recipricate.

"Mr. and Mrs. Hopkins, you may or may not be aware that Fred Daukins was recently killed in the Pacific battle for Midway Island."

"Yes, there was a piece in the local paper about Fred. Sure sorry to hear that."

"It is also the Navy's understanding that Fred may have been the father of your daughter's child. Is that true?"

"To the best of our recollection, that's true, Corporal. Mary never wanted to talk about that, said she would have the child and support it herself."

"Did she have the baby?"

"Yes, she did, a pretty little boy. Sends pictures every once in awhile, never asks for any help. Guess she knows we have trouble taking care of ourselves, let alone her and the child."

"Did Fred know about the baby?"

"Don't know, Mr. Spies. Mary never talked much, as I said before."

"How about the Daukins family, Fred's mother and father. Do they know about the child?"

"Can't say they do. We never told 'em and Mary left long before little Donald was born. There was talk around town that Mary was pregnant, could be the Daukins family put two and two together. Mary Lou and Fred were always together. If they heard the talk, they could've guessed it was Fred's baby."

"Mr. and Mrs. Hopkins, can you give me Mary Lou's address?"

"Wish we could, but she never sent it, no return address on her letters."

"Do you have the last letter, in fact, any of the letters she sent? The envelope should have a postmark to help us find her."

"Nope. All we kept were the pictures of little Donald. Sure is cute."

"Well, sir and ma'am, I'm going to leave you my address and telephone number. When and if you receive another letter or call from your daughter, please call me at my office, collect, and please save the envelope as well as the letter. It's very possible that if we can prove little Donald is Fred Daukins' son, Mary and the baby will be eligible for an allotment and possible insurance settlement, money that could help raise the boy all the way through college."

"Gee, if that's true, that would be a great help to our little girl. She never asks for any help, too proud, but raising a little guy and working to support him all on her own isn't easy, we're sure."

§§

After thanking Mary Lou's folks for their help, a heavyhearted Gene Spies headed for a downtown hotel. His work in this town was done. He'd get what little information he'd acquired on the teletype to Lt. Craiger. Glad he hadn't talked to the Daukins. There was no smoking gun in this town.

§§

Meanwhile, back in the Chicago area Ed Hill had talked with administrative sources at the Great Lakes Naval Training Center as well as the Naval Aviation Metalsmith School located at 87th and Anthony Streets. Fred Daukins had participated at each of the institutions, but neither could add to the information already listed in the jacket furnished to the investigative team by Y2 Herb Andrews.

Reviewing the list from Gene Spies of Chicago names, addresses, and telephone numbers from Daukins' little black book was another story. There were only two names of men on the list. One turned out to be an old friend of the Daukins family back in Columbus, actually a friend of Fred's dad. Young Daukins had had Thanksgiving dinner with the family one year. The second person had moved, no forwarding information. It drew a blank.

Five of the females remembered Fred as a handsome guy, lots of personality, all had met at the downtown Chicago USO. No real dates. Girls claimed they were not allowed to leave with servicemen, had given phone numbers to the sailor but never received a call back.

There were three other names and numbers where the individuals had moved, again no forwarding address or telephone number.

One call struck pay dirt. A Marge Dillon remembered a handsome sailor she had met at a southside bar. At first she was reluctant to talk about this man until Bosun Ed Hill identified himself as a member of the JAG organization on official business for the federal government. This lady was sharp. She asked for Ed's credentials, said she would check them out, and if credible, get back with him, which she did.

Marge Dillon worked for a large downtown law firm doing much business with the goverment. She would tell all she knew about Fred and his strange sailor friend. This struck Ed with pangs of hope. Maybe the Chicago trip wasn't a total failure after all.

"How about dinner at the Continental Room of the Palmer House, say 20.00 hours?" That wouldn't be too shabby, thought the recently upgraded, high-living swabby.

"Fine, it's a date."

§§

The person ushered to Ed Hill's table might have been a dream out of his past. Short, shapely, more of a round, robust figure, not really heavy, but not the long slender limbs of models of the time. A cute, pretty face, short dark hair, flashing blue eyes, Ed's type, the looks of a girl he once worshipped in high school, back in Oklahoma, a girl who wouldn't give him the time of day.

"It's a real pleasure meeting you, Miss Dillon. Thanks a million for taking the time to talk about Fred Daukins. First, how about a cocktail and dinner, and while we're at it, enjoy the music of Jimmy Stanton's orchestra. They're only here at the Continental Room for a two week engagement."

The young lady seemed easy to know, much more friendly than on the telephone. She was eager to know why JAG was interested in a seaman by the name of Daukins. What had he done? Where was he? How could she help?

Ed began at the beginning, ship out to sea, crew member murdered, investigation started, then the Yorktown sunk by the enemy. He explained that Humphrey Craiger's team had been put together to follow up on leads and one of the leads had been her name and telephone number listed in Fred's book.

As expected, the death came as a shock to the young lady, who paused just long enough to sip her martini.

"He was a real bastard, but didn't deserve to be killed. Who'd want to take another shipmate's life? That's hard to believe."

"Yes, it is, Marge, but it did happen. Tell me. How did you meet Fred?:

"Two of my girlfriends and I had stopped in at the Dutch Townhouse, a local west side bar, and while we were having a drink, this good-looking sailor came up to our table and asked me to dance. He kept putting nickels in the juke box and we continued to dance through most of the evening. Finally, my two girlfriends got up from the table, waved to me as if to leave. Well, I was enjoying myself but didn't want to be left behind, gave Fred my name and telephone number, and took off after my friends."

"He called me two days later, asked if I'd like to go to a movie, which was great. We had a real nice time. He was a gentleman, fun to be with. We had arranged to meet in front of the State & Lake Theatre. Fred had a curfew to meet, so after the movie, we went our separate ways."

"Two weeks later Fred called again, asked if I would like to go to Riverview and could I bring a girlfriend for one of his buddies. Eligible guys, you know, aren't plentiful in this day and age. Plenty of ladies on the lookout for a good time, so I agreed to fix up his friend with a blind date."

"Believing that because Fred was such a nice, good-looking, friendly guy, his shipmate would be the same, I took special pains to ask a young lady I recently met at a Red Cross bandage-rolling session, if she would like to have some fun at the amusement park while at the same time making new male friends. Virginia Koler just recently moved to the Chicago area from a small town in Iowa. Sorta pretty, very nice, seemed like a refined young lady, living at a Women's Club just off Clark Street in the Lincoln Park area. She seemed pleased to be asked, and we all agreed to meet in front of the entrance to Riverview Park on Western Avenue around five o'clock on a Saturday afternoon."

"Then came the shock. As Virginia and I patiently waited in front of the park entrance, no Fred or his friend. It got to be six o'clock when two white-uniformed figures approached at a distance. Could this be our dates, finally, an hour late? Sure enough, a waving, smiling Fred Daukins walked toward us along with a short, slender, rather ugly fellow in a wrinkled sailor suit. No, this couldn't be Virginia's date! Oh, no, please say it isn't true, but it was. How could I do this to her."

Marge stopped talking, took another sip of her martini. Ed could see remembering the incident was taking a toll on her, her expression had changed, one hand seemed to tremble.

"Miss Dillon, let's take a break. Let's order dinner, maybe have a dance if you'd do me the honor. Then we'll get back to the story."

§§

The lady ordered the petite filet mignon, Ed had the prime rib. The orchestra was playing Glen Miller's "Take the A Train." What a great tune to break the ice on the dance floor. Marge moved with grace both to the music and touch of the sailor's every signal, turn, twirl, close, what a great partner. No wonder Fred Daukins had fed nickels to the music machine the night he first met her.

After a gourmet dinner and much small talk, Marge Dillon seemed more herself, more relaxed, ready to continue her story about the murdered man and his shabby friend.

§§

"To make a long story short, it was a terrible evening. Fred never formally introduced his buddy, kept laughing and calling him 'Jack.' Fred had changed. He didn't seem the same likable fellow I remembered. His words were slurred from time to time, kept grabbing me around the waist and shoulders as we walked the park. Every time he came close I could smell rat gut alcohol on his breath."

"Virginia kept her distance from Jack. When he spoke, it was with a southern drawl, sorta hill-billy style, dese, dem, dos. Kept offering us all a drink from an unkempt flask or booze bottle, each time having one for himself. Fred would laugh, grab the bottle, take a few swigs, jump in the air, act like a real nut, 'dam that was good, baby, you orta try it,' were his comments, then back to grabbing and touching, real gross, constant pawing."

"After several hours, the disgust on Virginia's face and my own bad feelings about this evening made us excuse ourselves, to visit the powder room, but instead, we exited the rear door and kept right on going, through the park gate, into a cab, and never looked back."

"Although I tried apologizing and explaining to Virginia several times during the following week, each time she would say that it was all right, Marge, that it wasn't my fault, but in my book that just wasn't good enough. Found out later she had quit her job and returned to Iowa, just where I don't know."

"Never did hear from Daukins again. Often wondered what happened to him and his pal. Well, now at least I know what happened to Fred. What a sorry ending."

§§

Ed had listened to Marge's story with undivided attention and interest, especially the part about Fred's friend, Jack.

"Marge, can you tell me any more about this Jack fellow, maybe the insignia on his uniform, any campaign ribbons, and so forth?"

"He wore no campaign ribbons, and I know enough about a Navy sailor's outfit to designate Jack as an apprentice seaman. His hair was long so he wasn't a boot, although he wore his hat round, not squared. His most distinguishing mark was the unshined shoes, filthy, dingy whites, unshaven face, and dirty mouth. I'm sorry, Ed. I have nothing nice to say about this man."

"One more question, Marge. What was the relationship between the two fellows? Would you say it was friendly, standoffish, distant?"

"Ed, I would say that it was friendly from Fred's standpoint. As far as Jack was concerned, I don't know. In my opinion, he was the type of fellow you wouldn't turn your back on. What kind of relationship would you call that?"

"Marge, if I can call you Marge, you've been a big help. It's getting late, and I'd like to see you home. I'll have the doorman hail us a cab."

§§

The bosun had dropped Marge Dillon at the front door of her apartment and was on his way back to the Chicago Athletic Club. This would be the last night to stay in this lap of luxury, great town, great people, but there was a war to fight, a case to solve. Believe I'll write to that pretty lady, he thought, thank her again for her help, maybe start up a relationship, at least become penpals. Ed didn't have girlfriends, not even a girlfriend.

§§

Wonder what Humphrey will think about this Jack fellow. How can it help our investigation. Well, time will tell, maybe nothing at all, but it was worth the try.

§§

Shark City, Oklahoma, is on the way back to the West Coast, and a bus leaves for Tulsa at 0930 hours. Why not stop and spend a day with the folks? Been a long time. Maybe some word about Freddie Schumacher.

Ed had wired the information regarding the Jack person to his boss in Hawaii, said he was on his way back, would try to pick up a flight in San Diego at the Marine base, He was told a VIP flying boat left the base each morning around 0600 hours headed for Pearl. In fact, Corporal Spies had been on his way to San Diego, hoped to catch the same plane.

§§

"No, Freddie doesn't write very often," volunteered Mr. Schumacher, "and when he does, there isn't much in his letters other than asking about his girlfriend Charlotte. How was she, how does she look, does she miss me - all questions that go through the minds of most guys away from home, I'd guess."

"You know, Ed, the censors won't allow service people to name an overseas base, but we put two and two together and know that your buddy Freddie is somewhere in New Caledonia doing aircraft rescue work with a P.T. squadron, maybe not the most dangerous job, but much needed in a climate that's hot and humid, running around in a boat made of plywood. Your dad has made a point to fortify Freddie with his famous toilet paper novels, so you see, Ed, you aren't the only one beholden."

Where does he get that stuff Fred would ask? Nobody, nobody could have that much imagination. No, Freddie, Ed thought to himself, but he did have a lot of time on his hands. Maybe this was his way of making a contribution to the war effort.

§§

Mr. Hill had been more or less an invalid for the past three years. An automobile accident had precipitated a stroke rendering this once strong, active man helpless, in more ways than one. It was great to spend a few hours with him and mom, find out if that allotment he'd been sending home was enough to take the edge off everyday necessities, maybe cut down on the need to put in the number of hours mother had been working at the Shark City torpedo plant. Both had seemed to age. Why was that? Had he been away that long?

§§

Mr. Schumacher worked as a civilian aircraft mechanic at the Tulsa Army Air Base and had offered Ed a lift. A DC3 was leaving for San Diego and, although Ed hated to bump a young captain on his way home for leave, this was the way this man's navy worked in time of war; the higher your priority, the sooner you left. With luck he could catch the next 0600 hours flight to Hawaii and a reunion with his investigative team.

§§

The PB4Ys manifest showed that Corporal Spies had left two days earlier. With luck, barring a bump from some general or admiral, Ed would be on this morning's flight. What a beautiful morning, sun just coming up over the horizon, a band of red separating the blue/green of the Pacific from a sky that wasn't quite sure, should he call it grey, maybe grey with a slight tinge of purple, or was that more of an orange.

Waiting at the long wooden pier, the gull wings of the mammoth Mars flying boat glistened with dew as its four huge engines, propellers idling with protest, seemed to say 'let's get on with the day. We have a job to do, let's not waste precious time or fuel.' And so it was that Ed, along with a full complement of passengers and crew was soon racing along the calm waters of the harbor, the hull of the huge craft straining to break the frictioned forces between its shiplike characteristics and the sea, ever reaching for the sky, and finally once free, banking sharply to port and setting a southerly course for the islands of romance, beautiful Hawaii.

San Diego to Hawaii would have been a four day trip for the Yorktown, that's if Yorktown had been traveling full bore, wide open, the black gang giving it their all, twenty-four hours on end. This great winged machine would make short work of the travel times of the once-glamorous carriers. California today, Hawaii tomorrow.

§§

Ed was privileged to be seated just aft or behind the aircraft radioman's compartment and was being entertained by the constant exchange of messages going on between land, sea and air. There had been an earlier message regarding an S.O.S. received by a small convoy of merchant ships in an area of the Pacific half way between Pearl and Frisco. The message, sent on a very weak signal, indicated a Dutch tanker going down after being torpedoed by a Jap submarine, its crew in the water being shelled by the sub's 3" deck gun, all traffic in the whereabouts to keep a keen eye out for possible survivors.

The bosun could feel for those poor devils. His time in the waters around Ford Island were still fresh in his mind, but in his case help was near at hand. Those poor bastards, if by luck still alive, faced hundreds of miles of open ocean. Not a cheerful thought.

Rumors of the message filtered throughout the cabin and soon each and every porthole was occupied, in some cases not one but two eager pairs of eyes peering out, straining to reduce the myopic view of the ocean surface below. It seemed as though as soon as the crew in charge of guiding the magnificent aircraft to the isles of the gods got wind of the impending, almost sure, death of men left to fend for themselves out in the open seas, it dipped to a lower altitude and took on a more zigzag course, although all hands were awareof the fact that the chance of locating any of the men, if they survived, was like finding a needle in a haystack. But how could you not try. These were human beings, people like yourself, doing a job. God bless 'em.

And then, all of a sudden, a mighty cheer went up. Something was bobbing around about 10 o'clock, something flashing in or from the waters below. Could it be we lucked out? Could those bobbing, shining objects be survivors from that distressed Dutch tanker? Let's hope so.

The captain of the giant aircraft maneuvered his flying boat in an ever-circular pattern, continuing to drop down lower and lower with each pass until when a few hundred feet above the surface of the smooth, calm ocean, a half dozen jubilantly waving figures could be recognized, all hanging from one raft. The raft was so small that all that was sticking up out of the water were heads and a few waving arms with hands holding pieces of mirror, the life-saving articles that caught the rays of the sun causing the shining reflections to signal the looming angel of mercy of their plight.

Orders were given to prepare for an unscheduled landing as well as for both waist gunners to move into position and man the 50 caliber machine guns, should this be a trap, the Japanese submarine hovering just below the surface of the water, allowing the six merchant seamen to act as bait, drawing the flying boat down to the calm of the ocean, then surfacing and blasting it to smithereens with its deck gun. No, we will be vigilant. We know we'll be taking a chance, yet can't leave these poor souls to the sharks or ravages of the sea.

§§

The PB4Y floated to within a hundred feet of the survivors, dropped anchor, then inflated two rubber rafts, each manned by a member of the aircraft's crew, paddled up to the anxious, weakened, in some cases wounded men, tried helping them aboard the rafts, but in one case unable to free the legs of a sixth man, the last survivor, from being tangled in a maze of rope used initially to lash the raft to the bulkhead of the sunken tanker.

Ed Hill had been standing by the starboard hatch watching the rescue. When word was flashed from the rafts that the rescue party was unable to free this sixth man, Ed's uniform top, pants and shoes flew off, and placing a nearby sheath knife between his teeth, he dove into the warm, oily salt water. Within minutes his powerful strokes propelled him into position alongside the trapped man. He then dove under the raft and cut away the entangled lines, freeing a grateful youngster, hardly old enough to shave. After helping him into the second raft, Ed followed and picked up an oar, helping propel the rubber craft back to the waiting mother ship, ready to continue on the journey.

§§

The survivors would tell a harrowing story. A hush fell over the listeners as Darry Dykman went on quietly to say that everyone below deck had been killed. Many others were killed while trying to hang on the one raft afloat and many drowned because they were unable to swim. While a school of sharks circled hungrily around them, they told stories and sang raunchy songs until they were rescued 24 hours later by the flying boat, in the eyes of the survivors a flying machine from heaven.

Later, at a press conference in Hawaii, Darry Dykman said the thing he remembered most about the time was the diesel fuel which covered them. It was nearly impossible to wash off.

"What's really funny," Darry said, laughing, "is that most of the passengers on board the plane, waiting for us, had lit cigarettes. After all we'd been through, we came real close to being blown up all over again."

§§

"You lucked out, Hill," laughed a pleased Marine 1stLt. Humphrey Craiger as he greeted the returning sailor, a real hero. "Bet you didn't know that rescue incident you were part of was witnessed by a senator and two congressmen. They got to Nimitz and want a photo session this afternoon, want a picture taken with the man who is to receive the Silver Star. Their constituents back home will love the publicity. Sure to sell a lot of war bonds."

Bosun Hill thought it was great to be back. It would be some time before he would be able to cleanse the fuel oil from the pores of his skin or the roots of his hair. The pungent taste it left in his mouth seemed to add an unwanted flavor to any food or drink that passed his palate, but time would prevail.

Ed wasn't overly impressed with the medal, nor was he happy about the photo session until in a little corner of his brain a bell went off. Those photos will be distributed to newspapers back home in the States. Could it be that Marge might pick up a copy of the Chicago Tribune, see his picture, read his story? Now that would be the type of public relations he could go for. Ed Hill a hero, maybe Marge's hero.

§§

What Ed really was impressed with was what had been going on at the JAG offices while he and Gene were investigating in the States. Greenberg had confronted Captain Pastnu and his client Milton Tarry, explaining that both Tarry and Klein were considered prime suspects in the murder of AM3 Fred William Daukins, that both of the suspects had lied to the Yorktown investigative team, not once but several times, that both Klein and Tarry had violent tempers, jealous men, wife beaters, had lured the victim aboard ship so that at a convenient time could dispose of this threat to their women, at least to Klein's wife.

"You have actual evidence or witnesses to substantiate the alleged charges?" Tarry's counsel asked, "because if you don't, I'd like Milton released."

"Yes, we do, Roger. After your client's been sent back to the holding cell, I'd be happy to meet with you and Lt. Burns to review the witness list and evidence."

§§

Meantime, Yeoman Herb Andrews had a series of questions wired to the skipper of the destroyer on which F2. Binky Heins had been serving. It appeared that the suspect left his duties with the ship's black gang just long enough to answer Andrews' questions in a most satisfactory manner. At least for the time being, those answers, along with a spotless record, cleared Heins in the Daukins case.

§§

Despite LCdr. Mary Wilkens' glowing report on one of the men Rusty Pattern had implicated in the late night card game that first night out aboard Yorktown, Herb Andrews insisted on talking with Peter Omar. His sheet was clean, no previous mast, no gambling implication, not a troublemaker; the machinist mate, along with his friends, had been asked by Rusty to pass a few hours, maybe make a few bucks.

Did Peter know Fred Daukins before the game? No. Who did the 1st class machinist know? He knew S2. Jim Rusty Pattern, of course, and had struck up a previous friendship with Binky Heins and PhM. Roger Bertron, in fact, Roger had introduced Peter and Binky to Rusty. Omar continued to answer Andrews' questions.

"Anyone else at the game?" asked Yeoman Andrews.

"Yes," replied a calm, collected Omar, "two other fellas, one tall, one short, both talked with an accent, one borrowing from the other throughout the game."

"Do you know the names of these two fellas?"

"No, Yeoman, I don't. Heard the little guy call the taller fella Ray or Roy, sorta hard to understand. Never did get anything on the shorter fella."

"What time did the game break up?"

"About 0330. Several of us had watches at 0400 hours."

"Who had watches?" asked the shrewd pencil pusher.

"I'm not sure. I believe Rusty and I'm sure the pharmacist did. Said he was headin' for sick bay. I had the boiler watch. Binky walked down to the third deck with me, then headed for his rack."

"What about the two strangers?"

"Don't know. Last I saw of 'em, they were headin', along with Fred, aft on the hangar deck."

After talking with Peter Omar, Herb Andrews had to agree with the lieutenant commander. This guy was clean. His response to the yeoman's questions agreed with the answers given by Binky Heins and the story told by Rusty Pattern.

§§

Lt. Craiger had asked that PhM2. Roger Bertron be sent into JAG headquarters for interrogation. He wanted to talk with the shanker mechanic personally.

"I've gone through your records, Roger. Looks like you've had your share of problems with meeting the good conduct standards set by the Navy."

"Well, Lieutenant, other than a few card games and that AWOL charge, what have you got on me? Why do you want to see me? What have I done?"

"I, or we here at JAG, don't really know if you've done anything. Tell me about the card game you were in that first night away from Pearl, the game on the Yorktown."

The pecker checker looked surprised, wondered how the lieutenant knew about the game. He didn't deny being a part of it, just surprised that people other than the players knew anything about the escapade.

"Who let the cat out of the bag, Lieutenant?" asked the not too shy corpsman.

"Never mind, Roger. Just answer the question. Tell me about the game."

"Well, that was a little time ago. Let's see if I can remember. I hate to mention names, get others in trouble."

"Roger, name names. Others have told the story. Let's see if yours agrees."

"There was seven of us. Rusty Pattern got up the game. Then there was Binky Heins and Peter Omar, a fella by the name of Fred Daukins, you know about him. I worked with LCdr. Chamer during his autopsy, poor kid. There was me, as you said, I played, and then two other guys, funny-speaking guys who came into the room with Daukins. All three smelled of booze. Nobody introduced themselves. Got right down to business, set our rules, showed our bucks and began the game. Played until around 0330 hours. I remember that specifically because we set a quitting time before the game started. Some of us had the next watch, the 0400 to 0800 hours morning watch."

"Anything peculiar about any of the fellows at the game?" asked the investigator.

"I really don't know what you mean by peculiar, Lieutenant. I work down in sick bay or the clinic. I see all kinds of peculiar things and peculiar people. If you mean those two rebels with Daukins, yes, especially the little guy. Might have had a small scar on his chin. Always seemed to frown, didn't smell the best, and I don't only mean the booze. When he talked, he mumbled, usually only to his tall partner."

Bertron continued. "What seemed strange was not only their lingo, but they were an odd couple, sorta Mutt and Jeff, one guy tall, slender, sorta handsome, the other one short, dumpy. Neither talked to the third fella, Daukins. Yeah, Lieutenant, if you mean strange or peculiar, those three could be it."

"Did you all leave the paint locker together, Mr. Bertron, after the game closed down?"

"If you're asking if we all left the compartment at the same time, sir, I would say yes. It was dark. Once we opened the hatch the lights had to be out. As I remember it, the three strange ones headed aft down the hangar deck, the rest of us headed below decks. Other than myself I don't exactly know. I headed for sick bay, stopping off at the galley on the way for a cup of hot Joe."

"You never saw Daukins or his two friends before the game, Bertron?"

"No, sir, I just told you. I didn't know the three fellas. Oh, I'm not saying I might not have bandaged one or two of 'em at one time or 'nother, or maybe passed out some rubbers as they left the gangplank for liberty, maybe prescribed some black and white if they couldn't go, some cold tablets, you know, the million and one things the guys need to keep 'em healthy. That little shit did look familiar though, seems like our paths might've crossed somewhere along the way, most likely as I said before, in sick bay."

"Let me ask you one more question, Mr. Bertron."

"Shoot, Lieutenant, I've nothing to hide."

"Are you a violent man?"

The pharmacist looked surprised by the question. Took him aback. After pausing to think for a split second, he smiled.

"Do you really think I'd admit to that, sir? Do you really think any sane man being questioned in a murder investigation, violent or not, would admit to that potential? I don't think so."

"You can go, Mr. Bertron. I liked your story. You seem honest. That situation back home could have broken up most good men. By the way, if you run into either of those rednecks you talked about, give me a call. Here's my card, and by the way, if you run into Cdr. Chamer, give him my regards."

§§

The board of inquiry was being assembled, a date had been set for Tarry and Klein to appear before this prestigious body, while the Daukins' murder investigation had more or less stalled.

§§

Marine Capt. Roger Pastnu, Milton Tarry's lawyer, claimed that he had new evidence that would exonerate both his client and Jeffery Klein. Pastnu, along with Wave Lt. Hilda Burns, Klein's lawyer, had been working behind closed doors, working with their team of investigators, and the group had developed ironclad evidence that would show the two, Tarry and Klein, could not have committed the murder within the time frame or window of opportunity set down by Craiger and his team.

Both Pastnu and Burns were asking that a judge be appointed immediately to oversee the evidence, and that their clients be released pending an appearance before the once-assembled panel or board of inquiry.

Humphrey Craiger and Isaac Greenberg balked at the thought of sending the two potentially violent men back into their homes, into homes with frightened women, women whose safety was in danger, women whose testimony might stand these same men before a Navy or Marine firing squad.

Until a judge would be appointed, all four lawyers, Pastnu, Burns, Greenberg and Craiger would stand before the man in charge of JAG, Rear Admiral Stephen Ernest. He would make the decision as to the fate of the two men. Would they walk or not. But first, what was this ironclad evidence Pastnu possessed?

"Make it fast and make it good, Mr. Pastnu. You're not dealing with any of those sophisticated bureaucrats now. No bullshit, cut to the quick. Why should the two men in custody, suspected of murder, be released?"

"Well, Mr. Ernest, I have positive..."

"Hold it, let's hold it right there, counselor. When you come before me, when you address me, it's Admiral Ernest, not Stephen, not Ernest, but sir or Admiral or Rear Admiral Ernest. Is that clear, Lieutenant?"

A shaken Marine Capt. Roger Pastnu, face red as a beet, taken aback, embarrassed, not used to being talked to like this, voiced a mild, "Yes, sir, Admiral," and continued on with his evidence.

It seems that a third man billeted in one of the three bunks located inside and near the aft portside of the Yorktown aviation metalsmith shop could verify that both Tarry and Klein were in their sacks, sound asleep during the time frame the crime had been committed.

Who was this man assigned to the third shop rack? It was well-known that Klein and Tarry bunked in two of the three. The answer came as a bombshell to the intent group. A chief warrant officer with 38 years of naval service spent a few hours each night laid out in the lower bunk of this above deck bastion of safety.

He had elected to forego the comforts of the fixed, roomy wooden bunks located forward in the below deck officer's wardroom for what he considered the safer above hangar metal racks with paper thin mattresses and close quarters above. Just turn over quickly as you slept in the night, and you might rip the skin off your cheeks or forehead as you rubbed up against the metal wire acting as springs for the rack above.

§§

When the warrant officer said safer, he meant safety in the sense of the ship or vessel being torpedoed while the potential victims lie sleeping unaware they were in the path of destruction. Twice in his long career, Chief Warrant Officer Percy Kracklauer bunked in the wardrooms of wartime man-of-wars when they had been torpedoed, once during WW1 aboard a heavy U.S. cruiser, and the second time just before coming aboard Yorktown, assigned to a naval tanker that took two Japanese torpedoes from the tubes of a submarine, both times in the dead of night, both times without warning.

Percy could remember the first encounter. The torpedo didn't sink the cruiser but killed thirty-two officers in the below water-line compartment the fish penetrated. The culprit submarine, part of a German wolf pack, had shadowed his convoy since leaving New York, a group of ships headed for England with men and material needed to bolster a faltering allied defense.

Lucky for Percy he was only a chief storekeeper at the time, no gold braid, so his quarters were in another part of the vessel. He was safe. But those poor bastards up forward. If they weren't blown to bits by the explosion, they drowned in the sealed watertight confines of their tomb as the cold, icy salt water of the North Atlantic Ocean poured in from its new entrance, separating the men from what was once their home, their ship. They were now more part of an angry body of water, at least until the cruiser could reach port and drydock and its pumps could then return the brave seamen to their God-given world.

§§

Years later as the naval tanker Percy had been assigned to plowed the warm, blue waters of the Coral Sea, part of a different ocean this Pacific, the exotic sea so often portrayed with romance in American movies, movies of those South Sea islands, characters like Dorothy Lamour, Bob Hope, Bing Crosby, how they stimulated the imagination of viewers, the second incident occurred.

But this was another time, this was reality, this fat cow, this floating supermarket would provide the aviation gasoline, fuel oil, and in many cases the food supplies needed to sustain the Yorktown, Lexington and supporting screening vessels, the lifeblood needed to flow into and through the veins of fighting machines ever-hungry, ever-vigilant, in search of a cunning, capable enemy who up to this point in time had dominated the Pacific battlefield.

It was now 0020 hours, two days before the Battle of the Coral Sea. Percy had just come off watch, stopped by an out-of-the-way corner of the giant tanker, a small private compartment to which only he and a few close friends had access, containing what was called back home a distillery--or in the mountains of West Virginia better known as a still. It was a simple machine, a simple process, some copper tubing, a cooker along with the necessary food products, all items chief storekeepers aboard ship had access to, and, voila! fine booze, fine corn liquor, a product much in demand when out to sea. Sailors wanted to wet their whistles. Illegal, yes, that's if you got caught.

The storekeeper had just battened down and locked the hatch to the compartment housing his prized possession, started forward to the ladder that would lead him down to the officer's wardroom one deck below. The night was silent. All that could be heard was the lapping waves against the steel hull as its bow knifed through the warm blue waters, its wake leaving a fluorescent trail lighted by a clear full moon, then a deafening roar, more of a whoom than a boom.

The storekeeper had heard that sound before, many years ago in the North Atlantic: torpedoes, then seconds later, another whoom. The first blast had sent the bow of the vessel high out of the water. The second blast caught the giant fantail in a more depressed mode, the explosions together lifting the entire vessel up and out of the ocean, then what seemed like seconds later slamming it back down, straining each welded seam well beyond the stress points designed into the hapless vessel, in many cases causing them to fail, the hull opening up like a soup can being exposed to a can opener.

Explosions and fire racked its decks from one end of the ship to the other. Chief Warrant Officer Kracklauer had been tossed around like a rubber ball, finally being propelled against a previously strung lifeline on the portside of this dying vessel's catwalk. It had only been seconds since the invading torpedoes had created this hell, only seconds, but already she was sinking, rolling to port. Percy could feel the warm waters of the ocean rushing against his body as he hung perilously to the thin lifesaving cables. The waters around were taking on the light of the firey oil being expelled from the tanks of the wounded ship.

Off in the distance, the outline of a vessel silhouetted both by the light of the fires and a full moon, kept coming closer and closer, but not soon enough.

One more quick look around. Where was everybody? No one in sight. What were those screams and where were they coming from, screams that could be heard over the roar of the flames? It was time, if Percy was to save himself, it was now or never. The ship continued to roll until gently, ever so gently, it deposited the excited, aging old-timer into the sea. Releasing his grip on the lifeline, he dove under the flaming water and struck out in a path heading for the oncoming destroyer. Every twenty-five yards or so Percy would break water, look over the situation, keeping in mind he must clear the area around the sinking vessel or be sucked down alongside to a watery grave. Time was of the essence.

The DD387 had picked up Kracklauer and two other survivors from the burning tanker. It was assumed that the remaining crew members had gone down with the ship. What if he'd been in the below-deck crew's quarters, thought the grateful veteran. Just another example of the good life, living topside, above those containing steel decks, overheads, and bulkheads.

It would be on Yorktown's retreat from the Battle of the Coral Sea that Chief Warrant Officer Percy Kracklauer would be transferred from the close-quartered confines of this lifesaving tin can to the majestic comforts of a first line, although damaged, American carrier. And his request for topside berthing, although not conventional, would be granted.

§§

"Lieutenant, you say your witness was awake during the ungodly hours Daukins was thought to be murdered, and that he was in the darkened confines of the aviation metalsmith shop?"

"Yes, sir, he was, Admiral. The Warrant Officer suffered from insomnia, slept very little, was an avid reader with a shielded nightlight over his bunk. This particular night, not anxious to face thoughts of going into battle again, couldn't sleep, so spent the late evening and early morning hours reading."

"And you say he will swear to the fact that both Klein and Tarry were in their bunks well past the hours in question?"

"Yes, sir, Admiral, he will."

"Well, Lt. Craiger, what do you think of those apples?" asked the stern CEO of JAG.

"I don't know, Admiral. If it's true, we don't have a leg to stand on. The two suspects should be released, but by the same token, how do we know the warrant officer is telling the truth?

At this point, we know nothing about his character, we haven't reviewed his service record, we don't know what his relationship with the two defendants is or was. There is also the situation between Klein and his wife. Just how much does Klein or Tarry know about her sleeping around, just how violent a person is Klein, is her life in danger if he knows or finds out?"

Craiger continued. "We would ask that the Admiral consider giving my team a few more days to look into the points just mentioned, keep the two suspects under wraps just a little longer until we check the old timer's story, make sure no harm will come to our witnesses."

An angry Roger Pastnu interrupted Lt. Craiger, "you mean to tell me Kracklauer's 38 years of service to his country doesn't speak for itself! That's criminal. Here's an old salt, had three ships torpedoed out from under him and you're questioning his integrity, insinuating he might be lying. Get on with it, Craiger. That doesn't hold water."

"Now you hold on, Lt. Pastnu," interruped the grey-haired Admiral whose dislike for the recently-commissioned Marine lawyer was obvious. "The proposal Lt. Craiger has made is a good, sound one. We'll hold Klein and Tarry for 48 hours, after which if we can't dispel the chief warrant's story, they are to be released with the understanding the island Shore Patrol keeps an eye on them. Any sign of violence, in or out of their home-life, and bingo, into the brig for the duration. Is that agreed by all?"

"Yes, sir," chorused the group.

§§

The meeting that followed in Lt. Craiger's JAG office was a sullen one. After all those days and weeks of leg work, checking, rechecking, investigating, questioning, to come down to this situation, their case hanging by the threads of a statement made by a 38 year veteran of Uncle Sam's Navy, a highly decorated veteran, campaign ribbons weighing down the left breast surfaces of a uniform he most likely defended many times to within an inch of his life. How do you, or should you try to, discredit a man of this caliber?

"Well, guys, as much as I hate to do it, let's look into Percy's life, and let's do it in a hurry. We have 48 hours. Andrews, get with LCdr. Wilkens. Have her pull Kracklauer's ticket, let her help you review his sheets, then get back as soon as you can. Ed, anything more on the information the Marge Dillon lady passed on to you while in Chicago? We have to run down all leads, especially now. We may lose our prime suspects."

"No, sir, nothing new. I'm going to talk to Rusty Pattern, Peter Omar and Roger Bertron, men we already investigated, all having similar comments regarding one of the two unidentified men attending the late night card game aboard Yorktown. His M.O. seems much like the Jack person Marge talked about."

"Need any help on this project, Ed?" asked the lieutenant in charge.

"No, sir. That photo session stuff is over now. I have all kinds of free time."

§§

Great, thought a somewhat distressed Humphrey Craiger. Top Marine brass had been squeezing Cdr. Wilkens to free up as many Marine officers as possible, something brewing in the Solomon Islands, something big, could Humphrey help?

Sure, the service had been good to the Daukins' investigation. Help came from all quarters. If Ed Hill could handle the Jack situation by himself, most of the other leads had been run down, checked out, Craiger thought. Why not release the one Marine officer Humphrey had on his team, 2ndLt. Herb Shacter? Why not let an officer trained to lead men in battle do the job he was trained for? And so it was decided.

"Well, we'll miss you, Herb."

§§

Marine Sgt. Ron Milkusky had checked all Hawaiian telephone numbers and addresses from Daukins' little black book. Nothing. No girlfriends, brother, father, associated in any way or form with the Yorktown tour to Midway.

The sergeant had also looked into the court martial proceedings of Daukins' suspected statutory rape case of Nancy Phillips. Nothing, absolutely nothing to tie any of the players to Yorktown's last trip. Although not directly associated with Daukins' demise, Ron did check and found that Nancy's newlywed husband, 2ndLt. Charley Phillips, navigator on a Midway Island based bomber, was shot down over Nagumo's fleet, the lieutenant listed as missing in action.

"One slim lead though," commented the former New Jersey desk sergeant. "We keep talking about a couple of southerners who may have been friends of Fred Daukins, may be the two unidentified players in the late night card game. Well, in checking phone numbers, I talked and then visited with a cute Chinese girl who had dated Daukins one time, remembered him well."

"Daukins and this lady come out of Shanghai-Lil's bar having had a few, started walking along Front Street and ran into a couple of guys that Fred knew. One short, one tall good-looking fellow, she thought Fred might have called him Ron or Roy. Didn't have a name for his partner."

"The three fellas joked around for a few minutes. Then Ron or Roy said they'd rented a hotel room in town, would the two of them, Fred and Astelle, like to come up maybe have a party. They had plenty of booze back in the room."

"Well, this young lady was sharp. She was no fool. Not about to party in a room with three drunken sailors, so she and Fred took off for a few dances at the 'Bucket of Blood.' Never did see the two strangers again."

§§

The thoughtful lieutenant forced a weak smile, paused, then surprised the gathered group by asking Herb Andrews to include in his conference with Cdr. Wilkens a request that she have her people go through the files or records of men who had been aboard Yorktown at Midway. Pick out any files of men with first names like Jack, John, Ron, Roy or Ray.

"I know it's really groping, but, I'll tell you," he continued, "I'm shot down with this warrant officer business. If he's clean, our case goes down the drain. I know this Jack, Roy thing is thin, but what else do we have and why do a couple of rebels, one short, one tall, one ugly, one good-looking, keep coming up everywhere we turn? Could have merit. On the other hand, I really don't know what we would expect to accomplish should we locate the two other players. So far, that late night escapade has turned into nothing more than innocent gambling, no motive for murder."

§§

Rear Admiral Bill Fielder was not pleased when he received Humphrey Craiger's report on the Daukins' case. The lieutenant had made a point of keeping the former Yorktown skipper filled in as to the progress, or in this instance, lack of progress in the case.

Bill had been called to Washington soon after talking with Humphrey, called in to talk with Admiral King and Vice Admiral Jack Fletcher. This must be about my jeep carrier task group, figured the newly-appointed flag officer. Thought it might be a bit longer though before they would need his input.

To his surprise, the recall was about an entirely different matter, a subject that required the strictest secrecy. The outcome of the war in the Pacific could very well ride on the success or failure of the results of the proposed operation.

Early in 1942, it became apparent that Japan had plans for further expansion to the southeast Pacific beyond the area already conquered.

Tulagi, 300 miles south of Bougainvelle, had been seized and when a base was established there, it seemed to indicate that the aggressors would continue their advance down the Solomon's archipelago.

In June a surveying party crossed Sealark Channel from Tulagi to Lunga Point on Guadalcanal, and in July, the enemy began building radio stations, power plants, shops, barracks, wharves, and by early August had just about completed a long aircraft runway and hangars.

Australia, an ally, was nearby. Japanese takeover of an island chain off its northeastern coast presented a grave danger. In fact, as early as February, Admiral Ernest J. King, Commander, U.S. Fleet, had corresponded with General George C. Marshall, Chief of Staff, U.S. Army.

The Admiral thought that many of the islands in the South and Southwest Pacific should be taken over and occupied by the allies. These islands would be great stepping stones once the U.S. industrial might had time to shift into high gear, to supply the men, and to produce the machines, the carriers, tanks, and aircraft necessary to take back the Philippines as well as wage war on the home islands of the sons of heaven.

The Pacific had been divided into two specific areas, two major theaters. One was the Southwest Pacific area under General Douglas MacArthur, whose never-to-be forgotten statement, the statement uttered as he left his beloved Philippines, "I will return," had reverberated around the world. His command took in Australia, the Netherlands, East Indies, the Philippines, as well as the Solomons. The rest of the Pacific had been divided into three zones under Admiral Chester W. Nimitz, U.S.N. Commander of the Pacific Fleet.

Although there was continued controversy between Marshall and King, it had been agreed in early July that an offensive was to be mounted immediately, the goals the retaking of the northern Solomons, New Guinea and the Bismarcks.

The operation would be divided into three phases, with Phase 1 under Admiral Nimitz, who would appoint Vice Admiral R. L. Ghormley to head up the operation. His task would be to seize Tulagi, the Santa Cruz Islands and areas adjacent.

Nimitz had been given this assignment over the objections of MacArthur, the reason being he had the only force capable of establishing a beachhead, the 1st Marine division being assembled at Wellington, New Zealand.

MacArthur had three trained infantry divisions in the southwest Pacific area, the U.S. 32nd and 41st Infantry divisions as well as the Australian 7th division. These troops could support a landing once a beachhead had been established but were neither trained nor equipped to make such a landing themselves.

MacArthur was to command Phases 2 and 3, his troops to occupy the rest of the Solomon chain, the north coast of New Guinea and Rabaul as well as the New Britain-New Ireland area.

In addition to the Marine troops, whoever was to be responsible for the Phase 1 operation would need fighter support and available Allied airfields were too far off for land-based fighters to operate. Carriers, transports and other naval surface ships would be required.

There was another reason Nimitz was assigned Phase 1 of the overall operation. The Navy was reluctant to put its precious carriers as well as its equally precious 1st Marine division under the control of the Army.

§§

"And, Bill, this is where you come in. Nimitz and Vice Admiral Ghormley have assigned me TF61, the portion of the operation known as the expeditionary force," voiced a stern, concerned Jack Fletcher, "and I need someone I can trust to handle the carriers of TG61.1. When I heard you'd been given two stars, that you were up and around waiting for your next assignment, I asked Admiral King to let me talk with a man I really respect, a man I would like to have head up the carrier section of the air support force for this upcoming engagement. How do you feel, Bill? Are you up to the task so soon after coming out of the hospital?"

"Well, Jack, this is both an honor and a surprise. Sure, I feel great. My pins are still a little wobbly but as long as I don't have to chase tail hooks, my brain is functioning. I accept. When do we start?"

"The tentative date for Task Force 1 is August 1st. That doesn't give us much time. We've asked our joint chiefs for more time, especially to build up more air power, but they said no. They did say they'd try to supply further air support because we all feel it necessary to protect our surface ships against landbased aircraft during the approach, landings and unloading."

"By the way, Bill, you will have CV-3 Saratoga, CV-7 Wasp, and CV-6 Enterprise under your command. There will be one wagon, six cruisers and sixteen cans under Admiral Noyes supporting, quite a formidable armada."

Admiral Bill Fielder was pleased with the assignment, pleased with himself. Finally, after being passed over time and time again during peacetime, he would command his own flotilla of carriers. Could he handle the job, he asked himself? Sure, why not. He had worked under the best, Halsey, Nimitz, Fletcher, King, and this new guy, Spruance. He really liked his tactics, thought the spunky, wobbly two-star as he headed toward his new job.

§§

The trip from Honolulu to Wellington was a harrowing one for Marine 2ndLt. Herb Shacter. Jap submarines had shadowed his small convoy from the time it left Pearl Harbor until arriving in New Zealand. Seldom did the almost defenseless array of troop transports, tankers, and screening destroyers stand down from General Quarters.

Herb wasn't sure that he would cherish his new assignment, but it was good to plant his feet on good old terra firma again. Being part of Humphrey's investigative team had not only been a safe, cushy job, it was interesting. Herb liked people, all kinds of people, and the kind of work he'd been doing sure involved all sorts.

Time aboard Yorktown had been exciting also. Overseeing a number of 40 millimeter gun tubs during G.Q. carried a great deal of responsibility for the safety of his men as well as the safety of the ship.

What would this new task involve, wondered the husky, not-too-young, well-educated former college professor and crime fighter. From what he had been told, the new assignment would put him in the mud-marine class, the real Marines. Could a 90 day wonder, slightly out of shape body keep up with those 17 and 18 year olds as they hit the beach? Well, time would tell. Herb Shacter always welcomed a challenge. He was about to meet his match. He was now a part of the 1st Marine division, under the command of Major General Alexander Archer Vandegrift, U.S.M.C., TF62.8 Landing Forces.

The General had hoped for three months of training. Instead, his force was to be limited to less than a month after all echelons of his division had arrived.

Herb Shacter's first duty was an assignment to one of the organizationally loaded vessels that were to accompany the Marine division to its goal. It was his job to see that the ship's loading pattern be changed from economical use of vessel hold space to combat, in other words, that once arriving at its destination, the items aboard, trucks, tanks, supplies, etc., be unloaded in the order of need in an assault landing.

The New Zealand stevedores union was having labor difficulties. Time was of the essence, so Herb and his fellow officers would have the body of Marines assigned to them working eight hour shifts around the clock in cold, pouring rain, unloading and restowing cargo. You can believe members of the union were not popular with the men of the 1st division.

Wind, weather and labor unions had not slowed down the reloading, and the force sailed on schedule--at 0900 hours, July 22.

Little did the newly-reassigned Herb Shacter realize that he would indirectly fall under the command of two men to whom he had entrusted his life aboard Yorktown less than two months before, Vice Admiral Ghormley's, Officer in charge of Tactical Command, Vice Admiral Fletcher, and his air support force leader, Rear Admiral Bill Fielder, all heading into the jaws of the tiger, heading for that wet, hot, disease-ridden hell-hole known as Guadalcanal.

§§

"We know it seems sleezy, Commander, looking into the jacket of a 38 year veteran, but we have to be sure this man is honest, that his statement regarding Klein and Tarry is true."

LCdr. Wilkens was not a happy camper. To think that the JAG organization would not take the word of this old salt on its face value was distasteful to a lady known for her views regarding the highest moral standards.

"Mr. Andrews, I'll pull Skinney Kracklauer's records, but this will be a first, at least since I've headed up the office."

"You called Percy, Skinney, Commander. Why? Do you know him personally or what?"

"Yes, the Chief Warrant is well-known around the officers' club, like an old shoe. You can sit and listen to him spin stories for hours, especially if you get him oiled, buy him a few drinks and he'll not only tell you sea stories, but will go back to his childhood days in the mountains of West Virginia. Tell you about his family, dad a coal miner, mother caring for his brothers and sisters, how poor the family was, why he left to join the Navy at a young age. Great storyteller. We always kid him, ask why he doesn't write a book, that's if he knows how to write. Just kidding."

"Well, let's dust off the file, not as thick as I'd have thought it would be, depicting 38 years of a man's life."

The lieutenant commander and 2nd class yeoman would spend the next uninterrupted three hours reviewing Percy (Skinney) Kracklauer's life in the service, how he moved from an apprentice seaman boot to the coveted honor and rank of chief warrant officer in this man's navy, the ships and stations he had been aboard, the medals he had earned, his sinkings, his duties, but there seemed to be some voids, some lapses in the records. They didn't read like a book. Why, almost like someone had gone through the records and pulled sheets here and there.

"Who, other than you, would have access to Percy's file?" asked the confused yeoman.

"Heaven knows," commented the equally confused commander. "Over a period of 38 years that file has been in many places, many different people responsible for its safekeeping and updating. I just don't know."

§§

"Well, what you see is what you get," explained the disappointed Herb Andrews as he presented his findings to an equally disappointed Humphrey Craiger. "His record depicts the picture of a man who has done no wrong for the 38 years he's been in the Navy, nothing but honor and service to his country. LCdr. Wilkens says he is well-liked by all at the officers' club. I don't think we're going to discredit his statement regarding Tarry and Klein in any way or form."

"But you did find some discrepencies in his jacket, is that right, Herb?"

"Yes, sir, we did. Seemed as though for some reason or other, parts and pieces of his long, outstanding history were missing. Even Mary questioned this aspect of the file."

"You know, Lieutenant, this LCdr. Wilkens is a gem of a person. When I asked her would she have any idea of who we might approach regarding Skinney's background, someone who might have been around almost as long as he has, who just could have served with him, she thought for a minute, went to her card index and came back with the name and file of a veteran 30 year chief storekeeper presently stationed in Pearl at the commissary."

"Remembered Percy telling stories about this Willie Markham. They had pulled duty in the Philippines together. Seems General MacArthur was so impressed with Willie's ability to requisition things out of the ordinary, find things that Army Generals couldn't normally lay hands on, that the General borrowed slick Willie for a period of time, that was until Chief Markham was caught with his hand in the cookie jar, after which he was returned to the confines of the brig and eventually the Navy."

Did Craiger think the yeoman should talk with the wayward chief? "Hell, yes, Herb, and on the double. Time is fleeting."

"By the way, Lieutenant, I asked Cdr. Wilkens if she would have her people review the files of men who had served aboard Yorktown on the last cruise, men with first names like Jack, John, Ron, Ray or Roy. Should have something for us in a day or two."

§§

Ed Hill was just walking into JAG headquarters as Herb Andrews scurried off in the direction of the commissary on Ford Island.

"Good news, I hope, Bosun. Boy, I could use some."

"Well, sir, I talked with all three of the late night card players again, Rusty, Peter and Roger, nothing new. Roger did say he was sure he'd seen the ugly little southerner somewhere on the base just recently, but couldn't remember where."

"Well, that doesn't help, Ed, does it."

"No, Lieutenant, it doesn't. I also talked with Marge Dillon back in the States early this morning. Telephoned her after receiving this letter saying she remembered a photo, a snapshot, taken at Riverview Park by a roving photographer the day she had made the mistake of providing a blind date for this Jack person, this friend of Fred Daukins. Fred had paid the photographer a dollar for the picture and had given it to Marge. She didn't know why, but anyway she sent the photo along with others to her mother to be placed in one of the family albums."

Marge was sure all four, Fred, Jack, Virginia and her, were

on the picture. She asked should she have her mother send the photo to her and she, in turn, send it to Hill? She didn't remember how clear the picture was.

"Well, Humphrey, you can be sure I impressed on Marge that this picture could be of great importance, and once received, would she send it to me airmail, special delivery."

"Ed, this Chicago contact could be critical. As soon as the picture arrives, take it over to the base photo lab and have it enlarged, have copies made. If this Jack fellow is in Pearl or had been aboard Yorktown, we'll find him and hopefully, his buddy, also. Looks like things are starting to look up again," smiled the rejuvenated Marine.

§§

"Where might I find your chief storekeeper, Willie Markham?" asked an inquiring Herb Andrews as he approached a heavy-set seaman bent over a ledger, pencil in hand, intently checking the accuracy of figures scribbled on the pages before her.

"Might be back at Chief quarters or more likely the chief's non-commissioned officers club. He finished up here just half hour or so ago. He never tells me where he'll be, but that's usually where you can find him. Having a cold one."

§§

"Will you point out Chief Markham?" asked the sweaty yeoman as he approached the white jacketed, colored steward standing on the other side of the bar located against a far wall of this palatial hangout, this bastion of privacy, only to be occupied by those of the enlisted rank having reached the pinnacle of rate, chief petty officer, the foundation, the rock the Navy had been built on, "and while you're at it, how about drawing me a brew? I can use it. Hot as hell outside."

The Negro man gave Herb Andrews a more or less surprised, inquisitive look, as if to say, what are you, a lowly 2nd class yeoman, doing within these hallowed halls. You'd better get your ass out of here in a hurry, before it's kicked out.

Herb sensed the potential confrontation and quickly assured the purveyor of suds that he was here on official business. Now, would he, the barman, either point out the Chief, or better yet go over to Willie Markham and ask him to present himself, an official of the Judge Advocate's office was interested in asking him some questions.

"What can I do for you, Yeoman?" asked the big, red-faced Swede, as he strode across the room, glass in hand, sweaty wrinkled white uniform clinging closely to his belly, not in the best tradition of Uncle Sam's finest. "But first have a seat. Want a drink? Get the Yeoman a beer, Jim. Now, you're from JAG?" asked the Chief.

"Yes, Chief, I am. Thanks for seeing me," smiled the relieved feather merchant. "What can you tell me about a chief warrant officer named Percy Kracklauer?"

"You mean old Skinney? What'd you like to know?" asked the balding giant. "Skinney and I shipped out together many a time over the years. Great guy. Finished many a bottle with that rebel," laughed the outgoing old-timer.

Then in a more serious manner, the Chief asked, "Don't tell me Davey Jones locker finally caught up with the old devil, he went down with the Yorktown?"

"No, Chief, Percy is still alive and kicking. He's a witness in a murder trial and all I'm interested in is his character. Tell me about the man. Is he as honest and straightforward as people say? No vices? Goes to church on Sunday and so forth?"

"Church on Sunday, that's a laugh," echoed the storekeeper. "I don't think old Skinney's ever been in a church. In fact, the dam building'd collapse if he set foot in the sacred place. No, Skinney wasn't the churchgoing kind."

"What kind of man is he?"

"A good man, a brave man, likes his booze, but so do I. He's the kind of man I'd like protecting my back when things get tough. When Percy tells you a thing or two, believe him. He doesn't lie."

"Well, tell me, Chief, have you or Percy ever been up before the man, you know, Captain's Mast, or things of that nature?"

"Sure, what swabby with 30 odd years in hasn't? But so what, what's that got to do with me or Skinney?"

"Just wondered," commented Andrews. "The reason I ask, the warrant officer's package doesn't show any offenses, none at all, and from what you're telling me, Percy had to have had periodic run-ins with the Shore Patrol and such."

"Listen, Andrews, I don't want my friend to get his tit-in-a-ringer. I'm saying he's a square guy, a good honest man who likes a drink on occasion. I don't know anything about his records, but if you're asking me to be a character witness, right on. Percy is the greatest and if you won't take my word for it, ask the Bull. I'm sure he'd corroborate my statements."

"The Bull?" asked Herb.

"Sure, you know, Admiral Halsey. He and Skinney have been shipmates in the past. Great friends."

§§

"Back so soon, Mr. Andrews?" asked the assistant to Commander Wilkens.

"Yes, I am. Would you please ask Mary, I mean LCdr. Wilkens, if she could spare me a few minutes. There's something important we should discuss, and time is of the essence."

§§

"I can see why you'd want to review Chief Markham's package after what he's told you. It's hard to believe that Skinney could have participated in the escapades the Chief described and not been busted at least a few times, but where's the proof? No record of any such incidents in the warrant officer's past."

"Misty, will you bring in the file on Chief Storekeeper William Markham, please?"

"Yes ma'am, Commander," answered the dark-eyed, dark-skinned Hispanic Wave yeoman named Misty Clay, new assistant to the head of the Ford Island Personnel Pool.

"Pretty thick file, Commander, sorta heavy," laughed the yeoman as she placed the bundle of documents on her boss's desk. Herb Andrews couldn't help notice the glance he received, those flashing, dancing eyes, that flirtatious movement of her head as her short, black hair seemed to bounce with every movement of her swaying body as she left the compartment.

"What's the matter, Herb? Things changed in this man's navy?" asked a taunting Mary Wilkens as she noticed the undivided attention the investigator was giving another sailor.

"Sure have, Mary, and as far as I'm concerned, for the better."

"Well, maybe for you, Herb, but not for a certain chief warrant officer," commented the commander as she hurriedly thumbed through the papers that portrayed the history of a man who had experienced a long, turbulent sometimes exciting life, a man who had not always been on the right side of the law. Yes, Chief Markham's files made for interesting reading. Seems that the big Swede along with a buddy named Percy Kracklauer had been nailed, not once but twice, in the process of producing their own corn liquor, both times using a homemade still, both times while aboard ship, out to sea.

The chief's files would go on to indicate both men had not once but twice been reduced in rate, as well as spending time, hard time, in the brig. These same charges should have shown up in Skinney's files. But they hadn't. No wonder his life story read with gaps or lapses. Somehow, some time, somebody had gotten to the keeper of records and removed the unwanted, bad publicity so detrimental to a person's career.

"This is disgusting, Mr. Andrews. I apologize for a system that allows for such goings-on, but at this point my hands are tied." The lieutenant commander was visibly distressed. "You can count on my testimony, my support, should this deception be a factor in the investigation of Fred Daukins' murder."

§§

"You know, Herb, I'm amazed. It seems as though there's no end to strange happenings in this case." Craiger paused, then went on to say, "We still have a few hours before we have to appear before Admiral Ernest in defense of keeping Klein and Tarry locked up. You go back to the pool to see what if anything the men aboard Yorktown with names such as Jack, John, Roy and Ray might lead to, or help in identifying the two unidentified card players."

"Also, let Chief Markham know he is under a gag order, not to talk to any one about the case. I've asked that Chief Warrant Kracklauer meet me for lunch at the base officers club. Let's see what kind of answers he gives. Let's just see how honest he really is before we plead our case one way or the other."

"Sounds great to me, Humphrey. I'm going to catch some lunch over at the base chow hall, then go to pester the people at the pool again."

"Yeah, Commander Wilkens told me, Andrews, you're getting to be a pain in the butt, but all the time she had a big smile on her face. Nice lady, I could work under her."

§§

Humphrey Craiger was no fool. He had arranged to meet Kracklauer as stated, but only after discussing the possible meeting with Klein and Tarry's lawyers, Burns and Pastnu. They would attend the luncheon along with the star witness.

"Well, Percy, it's nice to meet you, especially after hearing such glowing reports on your 38 years of service, but you know, Percy, I was on Yorktown during her last run as you were. Funny we didn't cross paths in the wardroom or dining room if not in our everyday duties."

Lt. Craiger wanted to break the ice. He didn't have time to play cat and mouse with the wiley old veteran.

And speaking of old, this man sure looked the part. Every bit of six feet four or five in height, slender, I mean slender, like a rail. He couldn't have weighed over a hundred sixty pounds soaking wet. Thin, I mean really thin, drawn cheeks, wrinkles too many to count, his uniform just hung from his body like a uniform tunic hanging in a closet on a hanger. Have Percy wear a black top hat and tails and you'd swear Abe Lincoln had been reincarnated and joined the Navy. This man was just a bag of bones with some skin wrapped around.

"Thanks, Lt. Craiger. Thanks for your comments. It's nice to meet you also. No, I didn't get into Yorktown's officer's quarters too often, had a rack up in the aviation metalshop, liked to catch a few winks from time to time, but on the hangar deck or above. You've heard the story about a cat having nine lives. Well, I'm that kind of cat and I figure I've used up a number of those lives already. No use pushing my luck."

This man's from West Virginia? You wouldn't know it to talk to him. Slight drawl, but very slight. Seemed poised, intelligent, pleasant. Humphrey's quick assessment was that this fellow showed all the signs of being a gentleman.

The warrant officer had arrived at the table early, a good half hour before the planned meeting was to begin, and he was close to finishing his second manhattan. Craiger's next assessment, this man was a drinker.

Soon after all parties had been seated, a white-coated waiter made an appearance, passed out finely printed menus and asked if anyone in the party would like a cocktail or something from the bar before lunch. This is when the Marine investigator made his third assessment of the gentleman from West Virginia. This man was not a heavy drinker, he was a very heavy drinker. Percy Kracklauer had informed the waiter that he would have a third manhattan, hold the ice, just a dash of vermouth, heavy on the bourbon.

"You know a chief storekeeper by the name of Willie Markham, Percy?" Humphrey asked a slightly happy warrant.

"Sure do. The big Swede and I go way back. Think the first duty we saw together was on the Langley. Sure, it was the Langley. I can remember that tour like it was yesterday."

"Willie likes his booze. We'd been out to sea for a month or so and this dumb monster decided to make his own hootch. He was straining torpedo juice through loaves of freshly baked white bread. I told him that stuff would end his drinking habit in a hurry, that it was a form of wood alcohol, it'd kill him and whoever else might drink it. Willie was hard to convince. Some former submariner he'd met in a bar down in Norfolk one evening had cast the die, given him the recipe, told him to cut the product with pineapple juice, good as what you could buy during prohibition."

"It took some doing," laughed the skinny old-timer, "but I finally convinced the big lug that if the stuff he was making didn't kill him, it'd surely turn him blind. It wasn't 'til I agreed to set up a still in an out-of-the-way spot on the ship, that he agreed to abandon his project for our making some good old corn liquor. Heck, we were storekeepers. Had access to the tubing, cooker, all necessary ingredients. Before long we were in business. Not only had I satisfied Willie's and my needs, whatever was left over was easy to sell. There were plenty of takers."

"Are you ready to order?" broke in the patient waiter. Prime rib, turtle soup, and caeser salad sounded good to all members of the party except the warrant officer. He'd had a good-sized breakfast, an egg and toast, around 0600 hours this morning, he said. He really didn't care for lunch, but he would have another of those manhattans. Have the bartender make it just like the last one.

Skinney would continue his story. The listeners were all ears. The booze business was great until some shavetail ensign got wind of the operation, reported it to the exec and the next thing Willie and Percy knew, they were up before the Captain who happened to be Bill Halsey. The Bull was a great skipper, his men loved him, they still do, but turning the Langley into a rum-runner, well, that was too much. Halsey had the still destroyed, each man dropped a rate, and a week in the ship's brig, which never took place. Bull saw to that.

"I could tell you other stories about Willie, always enjoyed funnin with him. We'd have a couple too many and he'd wanta wrestle. Now, as you know they call me Skinney, and I am, but by the same token, strong. Guess that came from wrestlin bear up in those West Virginia mountains when I was a boy," laughed the slightly inebriated swabby. "Anyway, all I'd have to say to my good buddy was 'a thousand Swedes ran through the weeds, chased by one Norwegian' and all hell would break loose, clear the decks, the tustle was on."

What had been an afternoon lunch with a purpose, the purpose being to evaluate just how honest Skinney Kracklauer and his testimony were, or would be, turned out instead to be an afternoon of pleasure for the three members of the court. This man would spin one tale after the other, keeping Craiger, Burns and Pastnu in a constant state of stitches.

Finally, after two more manhattans and numerous tales, the long-time seaman would ask the Marine investigator why he had inquired about Chief Markham, was he a friend?

"No, Percy. You've been straight with me so I'll be straight with you. I'm the fellow investigating that Fred Daukins' murder case aboard Yorktown. As you know, you've given a statement to Captain Pastnu and Lt. Burns, saying both Jeffery Klein and Milton Tarry were in their racks, located in the aviation metalsmith shop, on the night and during the hours Daukins was murdered. That statement, if true, would clear both men of any impending murder charge. The investigating team felt that we had massive circumstantial evidence, good reasons for one or both of the men mentioned, to have put that knife into the victim's back. Your story shoots down that theory."

"We've talked with Chief Markham because he is your friend, you have served together over the years, he has been a sorta benchmark in our efforts to establish your credibility. I also wanted to talk with you personally having Tarry and Klein's counsel present. You've convinced me, Skinney, if I can call you Skinney, that you are an honest man. Therefore, I feel that your statement is true, and after giving you a lift back to officers quarters, I'll head for Admiral Ernest's office to ask him to release the suspected men."

§§

As Humphrey's jeep pulled up to a coveted private parking spot in front of the prestigious JAG headquarters, he could see both Burns and Pastnu mounting the stone steps leading to the massive oak doors at the entrance into this hall of justice.

"Hold up, guys," called the investigator as he raced after the pair. "I'd like to talk with you for a minute before we see the Admiral. Please accept my congratulations. You've both done a fine job and most likely saved a couple of innocent servicemen from a long prison term. But as I mentioned earlier, the Admiral will be asked to provide some form of relief for those two ladies who gave testimony regarding their husbands. I don't know how much Klein actually knows about his wife sleeping around, but whatever, he and Milton must be put on notice that if any bodily harm comes either to Marilyn or Rhonda, the Navy will come down hard on the former suspects, long prison terms for wife beating, and you can bet your ass that I personally will see that they're prosecuted."

§§

Admiral Ernest seemed relieved, pleased that Lt. Humphrey Craiger was satisfied that the defense witness, Percy Kracklauer, was telling the truth when he went to bat for the two men in question. He was relieved because he had telephoned Admiral Halsey while the three counselors and Skinney were drinking their lunch, the Bull giving a glowing report as to the Warrant Officer's integrity.

"If Skinney tells you black is black, it's black. Likes his booze, but he can hold it. No, Stephen, take him for his word. I'll vouch for him anytime. He's good people, and he's one of us."

You didn't want to go against the wishes of a man who possessed the power, the public respect, the political pull that a Halsey did. Maybe one other man, General Douglas MacArthur, was his equal when it came to the public's clamoring for a downright hero. No. Ernest didn't want to cross this fellow.

The Admiral was not happy about Humphrey's case suddenly being in a state of flux. "What now?" asked the distinguished mentor. "We have to produce some results. We're tying up a lot of good people. What am I going to tell Nimitz, and by the way, Lieutenant, forget about Skinney's jacket. Let's not open up a can of worms. If his record is clean, there's some good reason for it. OK? Let's leave well enough alone."

§§

Yeoman Andrews was licking his chops as he entered the base mess hall. Something smelled good. He hoped they were serving pork chops for lunch. Hadn't been happy with breakfast this morning, shit-on-a-shingle just once too often. Give me good old bacon and eggs anytime, easy over on the eggs, toast, fried potatoes, jelly, butter, two or three cups of that early morning java, he thought. That's living, maybe top it off with cook's freshly-baked sweet rolls, the ones with frosting swirled around.

Herb thought that the Navy in general served first class chow, even out to sea, unless at General Quarters. Oh, sure. Guys complained, always some bitching about the food. Should send these same fellows into combat with the mud-marines or maybe the army infantry. Let 'em live on "K" rations for awhile, he thought.

As Herb picked up his sectioned metal tray and started down the long line of spotless steamtables, he was grateful for the Navy's decision to serve vegetable soup today. And, no, it wasn't pork chops. That was breaded veal he'd been smelling. What gravy that would make, gravy for the creamy white, buttery mashed potatoes served by a swabby with an ice cream scoop. Herb always asked for a second scoop. He was never refused. Always plenty to eat. No, he didn't want two helpings of corn. Corn wasn't his favorite vegetable, peas, yes, not corn. And cherry pie for dessert. Next to apple that was his favorite.

As the hungry feather merchant approached the huge blue and white porcelain coffeepot at the end of the table, the pot that always intrigued Herb because it was suspended about 4 ft. above the floor, mounted on a pivot, allowing the fellow serving to apply minimum force to the pot's integral "U" shaped handle, and the good old Navy Joe would be metered out with ease in the quantity desired.

As Herb stuck out his large cream-colored porcelain cup, something struck him as being different. The dark-colored liquid flowed from the pot as usual. It was the ring on the finger of the fellow who was pouring the lifeblood of many a Navy man that intrigued the startled yeoman--large dark stone with some kind of letter or design on its face.

"Yeah, got enough, fella? Other people waitin' there, move on," grumbled the funny little guy responsible for Andrews' momentary pause.

"Yeah, yelled the bosun mate stationed at the end of the chow line, responsible for the smooth flow of the many hungry guys entering the hall and forming the never-ending chain, the human chain that would be fed like many products in industry in a manufacturing plant moving from station to station on a conveyer belt. Nothing should interrupt this belt or chain or the person responsible, in the case of the Navy, would answer to that guy with the star, that bosun mate at the end of the line.

Where had he seen that little fellow who was doing K.P. before, wondered Herb as he sat eating at one of the many wooden-topped metal-legged tables, so typical of both shipboard and barracks, mess hall furniture. And that ring. It looked familiar. Guess I'm seeing too many scary movies lately, he thought.

Herb couldn't get the image of the fellow pouring coffee out of his mind. He didn't know why but for some reason or other his face seemed familiar. As the deep in thought member of Humphrey's team finished the last of his cherry pie, polished off the last of the coffee, rose to his feet, headed for the depository for dirty tray and silverware, he would detour around the hall, forward past the steamtables and the coffeepot. Just one more look at the man who had aroused his curiosity. Was he from home? Had I done boots with this guy, maybe feather merchant school? No, that couldn't be. Why would he be doing K.P. if he was a rate? He'd get a better look, he thought. Maybe that would set his brain straight.

As Andrews passed the busy coffeepot for another look at the little man who had created so much turmoil in his aching brain, what little funny guy? What big, bold ring? The swabby pouring Joe was a good six feet tall, must have weighed over 200 pounds, sporting a wristwatch, but no ring. Was he going batty, wondered the concerned observer, as he took a second hard look. He thought maybe he should take the afternoon off, that perhaps he wasn't cut out for this detective work after all. He decided to have a talk with the Lieutenant when he got back, but to himself he said hell, the Commander is expecting me. Can't let the team down. My personal problems can wait.

§§

"Not as long a list as I would have expected, Commander, but that must have been quite a time-consuming job for your overworked staff."

"Let me worry about that, Herb. It's wartime, no nine to five, five day weeks out on the battlelines, none in my office either. Now, you know the list only covers personnel aboard Yorktown on its final voyage, and it covers men with first names of Jack, John, Ray, Roy and Ron. We found 22 Johns, 8 Jacks, 16 Rays or Raymonds, 6 Roys, and 3 Rons or Ronalds."

"You also asked that we break down our final list to names of the Johns and Jacks five foot, seven inches tall or less, and we have: 6 Johns and 2 Jacks. We then took the Rays, Roys and Rons, listed only men five foot, nine inches tall and over on a separate page. Again, our records showed 10 Rays, 2 Roys and 2 Rons."

"As a final step, alongside each name of a man killed or missing in the battle of Midway, we placed a star. In addition, I have placed a hold on transfer of men on the long and short list. If you find that your boss would be interested in a lineup, say the word. Give us a day or so notice and we'll gather the flock together."

§§

"Some good news, Herb. Only one of the men on the short list has been transferred out, a Jack Robinson, a colored stewards mate. Been sent back to the States. A Captain Fielder recommended him for the V12 program at Northwestern University."

They thought Craiger would go bonkers when he saw this data. Eight Jacks or Johns, 14 Rays, Roys or Rons, that's a total of 20 fellows. The list showed two of the Jacks or Johns missing or killed, and 3 of the Ray, Roy or Rons K.I.A. or M.I.A. That left fifteen suspects, and discounting the stewards mate back in the States, the final count is fourteen.

"What are we waiting for, Herb?" asked a jubilant lieutenant. "Let me call the lieutenant commander and thank her for a great job. I'll ask that she have the fourteen people in question on hand as well as Rusty Pattern, Peter Omar and Roger Bertron. Let's see if they can make an I.D."

Craiger also asked that the M.I.A. and K.I.A. list show where the fellows were from, and if they had been in trouble before, at the same time asking the fourteen to give home town and state. If anyone arouses suspicion, sheets would be pulled, remembering they were looking for southern or hillbilly accents and someone who might like to gamble.

All right, thought Yeoman Andrews! Things were on track again. He'd forget all about talking to Humphrey about his supposed problems.

§§

Jack Fletcher had come aboard Enterprise during an unsatisfactory Guadalcanal amphibious landing rehearsal at Kore Island in the Fijis on July 28th. He wanted to talk to Admiral Fielder. He was concerned. Things were not going well. Rear Admiral Turner and Major General Vandegrift were very unhappy. They were responsible for the amphibious landing forces of TF62, and while at a high level conference, Fletcher exploded a bombshell. He said he would not risk his carriers within reach of Japanese land-based air power for more than 48 hours after the landing.

The sinking of the Lexington at Coral Sea and Yorktown at Midway had made Jack Fletcher extremely reluctant to risk the valuable carriers. How would history look at a commander who had lost two of his nation's seven precious vessels in such a short span of time? Not well, he guessed, and to lose one or more of the three presently under Fielder's watchful eye would be a disaster.

At this same conference, Turner and Vandegrift had protested. They felt they would need at least four days to land the necessary tons of equipment and supplies, but without Admiral Fielder's air cover, this was more than a risky operation.

"I'm going to be busy as hell, Bill, as you well know. I don't want you to cater to our two friends, should the going get tough. I don't want you to put our carriers in Harm's Way."

§§

That sure as the devil puts me between a rock and a hard place, thought the always aggressive, fair-minded admiral. Was he supposed to hold back his fighter support when those poor bastards aboard the transports or on the beach were being bombed or strafed by the enemy? While thankful to Jack for his job, by the same token he wasn't made that way. If he could help, he would.

§§

Bill Fielder would have a few days to ponder his decision. On the 31st of July the fleet sailed. The Carrier Task Force would take up a covering position in the Coral Sea, to the south of Guadalcanal, while the Amphibious Force and its screen would steam straight for the target area, Lt. Herb Schacter one of the 19,000 Marines aboard the twenty-three transports.

The first U.S. amphibious invasion since the Spanish American War was about to begin. Marine troops would start landing on Tulagi and Guadalcanal at around 0800 hours on the 7th of August only after the first salvos from supporting warships had arched into the beach at Guadalcanal, beginning around 0600 hours.

Meanwhile, Bill Fielder's carriers had been maneuvering some 75 miles south of the islands. Almost simultaneously with the heavy surface vessel bombardment, his fighters began strafing specific target areas and providing CAP cover for the invading Marines, the transports and cargo vessels. It looked like the admiral and his carriers were here to stay.

§§

Fourteen sailors dressed in spic and span summer white uniforms, hats squared, shoes shined, stood at attention, in a straight line facing forward, the group on the right considerably shorter than their peers on the left.

Ed Hill and Herb Andrews had helped the personnel pool staff assemble the men to be scrutinized by Rusty Pattern, Peter Omar, and Roger Bertron.

Hill had just talked with Roger, Peter and Rusty the day before. Had they come up with any answers? Had they seen the two missing card players around the base? Anything that might help? The answer was a resounding no!

This could be an important occasion. Lt. Craiger, Lt. Greenberg, Corp. Spies, Sgt. Milkusky, Yeoman Andrews and BM1. Ed Hill were all in attendance, all seated comfortably, all waiting for the reactions of the men who would view the potential suspects. There was total silence in the large high-ceilinged room. You could hear a pin drop.

"How about you, Rusty? Recognize any of the men in the line up?" asked the calm, collected Wave lieutenant commander. Rusty paused for a second, got up from his chair to get a closer look, walked along in front of the men in the line up and reported that none of the faces were familiar to him.

Similar responses from Peter and Roger cast a cloud over the assembled investigative group. You could see the disappointment in their faces.

"Alright, men. I want each one of you, starting with the first man on the left, to call out loud and clear, where you're from, what city and state." Again to the group's disappointment, no rebels, no southerners, no drawls. This was a lost cause.

"Commander, I want to thank you for your trouble, and please thank the seventeen men who participated in the exercise just completed. They did a fine job, even if we had no results."

"You're welcome, Lt. Craiger, just part of my job. Now regarding the M.I.A.s and K.I.A.s on the list, in checking we found that none of the Jacks, there were two of them, came from suspected states. One came from Utah, the other from Michigan. Neither had been in trouble since enlisting."

She continued. "Checking the Ray, Ron or Roys was another story. One of the three, a Roy Bolton, was from the town of Mercy, in the state of West Virginia. His rap sheet showed he was up three times for gambling. S1. Bolton was six feet one inch tall, weighed 182 pounds, 22 years old. His duty aboard Yorktown had been plane pusher, was found dead on the hangar deck just after the first raid, both arms blown off."

"Was there a picture of Bolton in his file by chance?" asked Humphrey Craiger.

"No, sir, there wasn't, responded the conscientious, hard-working director.

§§

As the group began to disburse, Roger Bertron walked up to Ed Hill. "Excuse me, Bosun, but after we talked yesterday, I headed for the base mess hall, you know, noon chow. Well, I'm not sure but I'd almost swear that the little guy pouring Joe was one of the rebels in that late night game you're investigating. Again, I'm not sure. You know I see lots of people in my job."

"Wait here a minute, Roger. I want to talk to the lieutenant. Don't go away."

The rest of the group had started out of the room when the bosun hailed them, told them what the pharmacist mate had just reported. Further surprising the group, Herb Andrews, relief flashing over his face, announced that he had seen a little man sporting a large, dark ring pouring coffee at the same place around the same time.

"Ed, I want you, Herb and Roger to get right over to the mess hall, ask the chief cook to show you his roster. I want the name of each and every man working in the facility. Don't tip him off, or any of his people, as to why you're there. Let him know you're from JAG, so there's some authority. Keep an eye out for the fellow Herb and Roger might identify and if they spot him, bring him in for interrogation. We're still scratching, guys, but heavens knows, we need a break."

Asked why he hadn't mentioned the incident yesterday, Herb told his boss he didn't know, thought he was having hallucinations, didn't associate the fellow with the case, thought he might have known him from another world, but now in thinking it through, it must have been the ring not the person that threw him. That ring, big, black with a design in gold.

§§

"You wanna list of my help, Bosun? What are ya, nuts? I play hell trying to feed this bunch. You strikin' for chief or somethin', think you can come into my kitchen and pirate my cooks. S'pose you're looken to stock one of them repaired cans that just come in. Yeah, my cooks a real feather in your cap, well, lemme tell ya..."

"Hold it, Chief," smiled the understanding bosun 1st. "I'm not here to steal your cooks. I'm interested in one of your servers. And, by the way, I'm not striking for chief. Just made first class a few months ago." Ed Hill couldn't help laughing. This big, old fat guy was about ready to pick up a butcher knife and carve his initials on the torso of this rascal, a thieving rascal at that.

"No, Chief," he continued, "I'm from JAG and my friend, Yeoman Andrews here, is also from the Judge Advocate's office. We're part of a team making an investigation. Our friend Roger and Yeoman Andrews thought they spotted a person we've been looking for, a person we want to question. Thought this man might have been pouring coffee during your lunch hour mess, just yesterday."

The chief had begun to calm down, his blood pressure starting to return to normal, Ed hoped. This man didn't look as though added excitement was something his large, overweight body could tolerate. Good thing Roger was close by in case of a stroke.

"Come on back to my office. Sorry I got so dam exicted," apologized the purveyor of those good meals, as he quietly waddled ahead of the three-man contingent, leading them into a small compartment. Nothing fancy, metal grey-colored desk, a few metal chairs with leather seats, the bulkheads plastered with sheet after sheet, lists of menus, breakfasts, lunch, dinners, who was on watch, and when, duty rosters, finally, a list containing all men assigned to Chief Curro's kitchen and their duties.

"Let's see," mused the now calm chef. "S2. Jerry Kostof had coffee duty yesterday lunch."

"Chief, is he a short, slender sailor?" asked the inquiring bosun.

"Hell, no. Jerry's a good-size guy. Been boxin' heavyweight on our base squad last three months or so. Had been light-heavy, but still growing. No, Kostof's no little guy."

Roger, Ed and Herb were disappointed. How could this be? Not one, but two men thought they had seen a slight, short sailor doing coffee duty.

"Chief, could this be a mistake?" asked an anxious Herb Andrews. "Both Roger and I had lunch in your mess hall yesterday noon, and we both noticed a smaller man pouring coffee. This fellow was wearing a large, dark-colored ring on his right hand."

You could see the color starting to rise on the cheeks of the kitchen wizard, as he looked the yeoman straight in the eye and declared his lists didn't lie. Unless Jerry Kostof had come to him personally, had asked to be excused from duty, well, he was the one pouring coffee at the time. But wait, he said, Jerry could have had a piss call, maybe been away for five or ten minutes. Well, then someone would have stepped in, no holding up the chow line because nature called.

"Could we talk to Jerry?" asked the vindicated bosun.

"Why not? You should find him over at the base gym, always workin' out when he's not doin' his job here in the kitchen, just ask for Jerry Kostof," Curro said, "everybody knows him, next heavyweight champ of the fleet. Really gotta punch, a real left hook."

§§

The trio started to leave Chief Curro's kitchen when Roger shouted, "There he is, peeling potatoes!" All hands stopped what they were doing, looked up.

"Where?" asked an excited Herb Andrews.

"Over in the corner," exclaimed the equally excited Roger Bertron, as he pointed toward a man seated before a huge metal tub filled with what turned out to be peeled potatoes. Roger was right. There was a swabby dressed in a white Navy t-shirt, white pants, white sailor hat, and a long white apron in the process of turning out the prime ingredient necessary for that great end product, be it mashed, fried, boiled or whatever.

A rather short, slightly built young man rose from his stool as the trio approached.

"You're right, Roger," exclaimed Andrews. "He's the fellow I saw pouring coffee yesterday. He's the one with the ring."

"Whad Ah do, ya guys? Why ya'll afta me?" asked the scared man.

"Just want to talk with you, fella," answered Hill. "Nothing to get excited about. My two friends noticed you serving yesterday and you answer the description of a man we want to talk to."

"Bou' whaat? Ah haint duyun nuthn."

"We didn't say you'd done something. We're looking for information and feel you might help. Let's get that apron off, put on your jumper. I'll clear your leaving with cook. Got a jeep waiting."

"All set, fellows?" asked the authoritative bosun, as four members of the cast of a new adventure about to be played out left the mess hall and headed for JAG headquarters.

§§

Lt. Craiger's crew had hardly gotten settled when Hill, Andrews, Bertron and the fourth member, the guest of honor, the spud peeler swabby from the mess hall, made their appearance at the island's Hall of Justice, and tromped into Humphrey's office.

"Lieutenant, I'd like you to meet Ben Kiter. He's the man who pours coffee for Chief Curro's crew."

"Tain't so, Bosun. Ah peeels taders."

"But Mr. Andrews and Mr. Bertron saw you pouring yesterday during lunch."

"Ah onne duzzat ifn Jerrah tooknah leak er grabbenah smokes."

"Well, that's not important, sailor. Were you aboard Yorktown when she went down?" asked the lieutenant.

"Yeaah, 'mos drownded, din't havenah lihhf beyalt, sliyupd offen ah liyun wheyun ah weyun offada siyud. Gooyudting ah kin swiyum, goyuutaah tiyun cayun ahnde fiyush meh ouyut."

"I notice you speak with a little drawl, sailor. Where you from?" asked Humphrey Craiger.

"Ahsfrum Wes Vaginni, Luutenaan."

"Where?" asked Humphrey again.

"Wes Vaaginni," Kiter answered, this time louder and plainer.

Herb Andrews had started to question the scullery mate on the trip from the mess hall to JAG headquarters. Found out his name, that he was berthed at barracks #31 on Maui Drive, only a stone's throw from the mess hall. Ben Kiter was an apprentice seaman, the lowest rate in the Navy. Seemed a little old for having just entered the service, or had he?

"How long you been in the Navy, fella?"

"Sehvun yarrs," answered the potato peeler.

"Seven years, wow!" cried the Yeoman, "that's what I really call being passed over."

"Yeaah, tiyungs 's ruyuff," scowled the little man.

Yeoman Kathy Kite had called over to administration, asked that Seaman Kiter's records be pulled, she would be on her way over to retrieve them.

"You play cards, Seaman?" asked the interregator.

"Yeaah, Ah duz, Luutenaan. Y'all pullenmeh offn da joyub so's ah mayukeah fiyuth fer sehvun caard stuyud?"

"No," smiled Humphrey as he thought, the kid's got a sense of humor. That's one for his side; that's not all bad.

"Just wondered if you might have been a player in a game aboard Yorktown, the night she sailed for Midway, you know, you were aboard."

"Naw, nommeh, Luutenaan. Ah jiscumoffn leebatee bufo' we'all sayuld. Ahs deyud broke."

"You're sure of that, Ben? You don't want to think back? Maybe search your memory? You know that was sometime ago, sometime in the past. Tell you what, Seaman. I'm going to have Bosun Hill take you over to another office, get you a coke and cigarette. Do you smoke, Ben?"

"Yeaah, Ah duz."

"OK, Ben, Ed'll fix you up with that cigarette, you relax in that comfortable office, search your memory about what we talked about. I'll be in to talk some more in just a short time."

§§

As Hill and Kiter left Humphrey's office and headed for the compartment known as the box, that dreaded spot where friend and foe battled it out for the truth, Roger Bertron would assure both Andrews and Craiger that this Ben Kiter was one of the two rebels who sat in on the fateful card game.

"But his name's Ben, not Jack," agonized the involved pen pusher.

"I'm not sure, Herb, if we caught the right name the night of the game, but I am sure of the guy, especially the face."

"You say you see a lot of guys at sick bay. Could you be confusing the incidents, Roger?" asked the fair-minded lieutenant.

"That's always possible, sir. Maybe you should ask Rusty and Peter to pick him out of a line up. I'd feel better if you did."

§§

Peter Omar and Jim Pattern had no more than had lunch, then stretched out on their sacks when the call came in from JAG headquarters.

"Get your butts over here on the double. Another line up."

Ron Milkusky had gathered together a half dozen white-uniformed seamem picked from the various departments supporting the many JAG factions, explained the task and then had them seated around the table with Ben Kiter, explaining to the seaman that they were on break and the box was the only place you were allowed to smoke.

A large one-way picture window looked directly into the compartment from an adjoining passageway window. It allowed participants standing in the passage to observe the occupants in the compartment, but did not allow the occupants to see the observers standing in the passageway.

Peter and Jim were ushered into the compartment one at a time, Peter first.

"That's one of the rebels sitting next to Ed Hill, the short ugly one, the guy that was always broke!" cried the machinist mate.

"Wait til he talks, Peter," ordered the smiling lieutenant.

With a push of a button, compartment speakers allowed the conversation being held within the interrogation room to be heard out in the passageway.

"Yeah, that's Jack alright. Sure as hell is. I'll verify that."

Jim Pattern took a few seconds before he would confirm both Roger's and Peter's findings. "That's him," commented Rusty, "only thing being, I thought his name was Jack, not Ben, but hell, both those guys talked like they had a mouth fulla shit! Sorry, Lieutenant. I mean mouth full of marbles."

§§

"Admiral Ernest has appointed a Marine Major General named Herman Trusock as the judge to oversea the Daukins case, should we come up with more evidence or a suspect," commented Craiger.

"This Ben Kiter is about all we have, and we don't want to screw up. I'll ask the judge to appoint counsel for the seaman before we interrogate him any further. That way, should we eventually find him a bonafide suspect and go to trial, we've dotted all the i's and crossed all the t's. In the meantime, Herb, get in there and help Ed keep the little guy busy."

§§

Once Klein and Tarry had been released as well as cleared as suspects, their lawyers, Marine Captain Roger Pastnu and Wave Lt. Hilda Burns, were free to counsel other members of the service.

When Craiger went to Judge Trusock with the Kiter situation, Judge Trusock immediately appointed Pastnu to represent the seaman, to sit in on the upcoming interrogation to begin within the next day or so.

Isaac Greenberg and Humphrey Craiger were well aware of the fact that from a legal standpoint they had pushed the envelope when interrogating Klein, Tarry and their wives. They had ferreted out much information before the suspects and/or witnesses had been read their rights or been provided counsel. Both had worried should the two metalsmiths have gone to trial, much of the evidence would have been thrown out.

§§

Humphrey Craiger continued to find Isaac a real asset to the overall case. His legal knowledge reached depths far greater than would be expected of a man so young and with such limited experience. Isaac's youthful, casual appearance had caused more than one opponent to underestimate his capable legal talents as they did battle in the arena of right or wrong.

As Isaac would think back over his career and life, he would attribute much of his moxie, his know-how, to growing up an only child, with a mother who was a doctor considered by many one of the best in her field, and a father, the lawyer whose foes would cringe in their boots when this talented, magnificent orator would challenge them before the bench.

A constant battle seemed to be going on between mother and

father. Not an open battle, but an effort by each to sway the direction the young Jewish boy might take as he grew into a young man, as he searched for a profession. This was a behind-the-scene situation, but it always was there. Isaac could feel the tension, the desire by each parent to have their only offspring follow in their footsteps.

From a very young age, this nerd, this bookworm would be absorbing his parents' know-how by a form of osmosis. For his brilliance this young man would suffer though, at the hands of his peers. Other students were jealous. They didn't like the kid who had all the answers, who raised the curve when it came to grading and evaluating progress. No, Isaac would have few friends as he climbed the ladder through grade school, high school, and college.

Law school was another story. Here, fellow students recognized and appreciated his talents, knowing association with the Jewish kid would result in benefits as they progressed in their chosen field.

§§

Isaac had recommended that Humphrey contact the Bureau of Naval Architecture in Washington, D.C. asking for blueprints showing the hangar deck layout aboard Yorktown, as well as details of the aviation metalsmith's shop and nearby head. This request was made soon after Warrant Officer Percy Kracklauer swore in his deposition that Klein and Tarry were sound asleep during the period Daukins was murdered, this while he was lying awake reading in the rack below.

The head was located opposite the metalshop. The warm Pacific night most likely warranted that the hatch cover both to the head and shop be left open. If the alignment was such that an avenue of sight had been provided to Percy, he might have noticed who had been coming in or out of this much-needed relief station aboard ship.

The metal hangar deck curtains were always drawn or closed at night when a ship was out to sea, in the battle zone. There was always a low intensity form of night light provided so that anyone stirring could find his way about, yet because of the curtains, not providing signals to any lurking enemy.

§§

It was Greenberg who had suggested that LCdr. Mary Wilkens write to the parents of the young man killed aboard Yorktown during one of the raids, the man identified as Roy Bolton, possibly one of the two unidentified card players. Mary would ask if they might have a photo of their son, as the Navy was planning a memorial and would like his picture as part of the service.

"You know, Mary, you can't very well write and ask grieving parents for their son's picture, because you want to use it as a means of identifying some guy as a participant in a murder investigation."

"I know, Isaac," commented the base personnel director, "but it seems so devious, not a nice thing to deceive people who have given a son to the war effort, but you're right, and the request will be made."

Privately Mary thought that maybe the shyster lawyer has more than Yeoman Kathy Kite's legs on his mind after all. That was a good idea.

"Misty, will you come in, please. I'd like to dictate a letter."

"Yes, Commander, on my way."

§§

"Ben, before we talk more, I thought you should have counsel handy."

"Whaddy'all meyun, cowensul, Luutenaan? Wazzayut?"

"Well, Ben, Marine Captain Roger Pastnu is a lawyer. We use the term counsel in a sort of interchangeable way, but anyhow the Captain is here to help you with answers to the questions I plan on asking you."

"Whakinah quishuns ya'll gonna ayusk? Ah ain't dyun nuthin!"

"Ben, I didn't say you did."

"Ya know, Luutenaan, yer guyh cuminta da keetchin yisterdayn upseyutsda whoyuul applecarrt. Mah boss, Chief Curro, he thiyunks ahminsumkinna trublean ah ain't hayuda driyunk in morana weyunk, no leebetee, no nuthin!"

"All I'm asking, Ben, is were you in a card game aboard Yorktown the night or morning she sailed for Midway?

"Anahstellinya guyusagin, no, no waay, ahs flayut broyuk."

"Ben, because you are under oath, any question I ask you, that we find you have not answered truthfully, can be held against you. We call that perjury."

"That's right, Ben. What Lt. Craiger is telling you is straight dope. You must give truthful answers to his questions," replied Captain Pastnu.

"Ahthoyut yer s'posetubee onnmah siyud, Capn?"

"I am on your side, Ben, but that doesn't mean we don't answer questions in an honest manner."

"Once more, Ben. You've had a day to think about my question. Remember yesterday when you were in that little office with all the guys having a break, I asked if you had played cards the night the ship left Pearl."

"Yeaah, ahmembeer anah tol' y'all no, an it's no agin today!"

"Well, Ben, you had your chance. I believe Captain Pastnu will agree with me. You're in trouble, deep trouble, because you just lied, gave me some bum dope."

"Now whatcha mean, lied, bum dope? Ahsays ah warn'tinna game an that's true. Was y'all there, Luutenaan? Didy'all see me?" scowled the little man, glancing from interrogator to counselor and back.

"No, Ben, I wasn't there, but I have three witnesses, three men who took part in the game. All three said you played, you took part in the gambling also."

"That'sa buncha crap, Luutenaan. Y'all ain't got no guyus that seen me there, an iffn y'all did, those guyus'd be lyin. It'd be their word agin mine."

Hands trembling, lips quivering, the pathetic apprentice seaman looked to the man who had been declared his counsel, his friend, for help.

"Lt. Craiger, I'd like to talk to Ben alone, just for a few minutes. What do you say you step out of the compartment."

"Sure, Roger, take your time. Ben needs your help."

§§

Once alone, Roger Pastnu made no bones about setting the record straight with his confused client.

"Listen, Ben, first off, know that my job is to give you all the help necessary, if it's necessary. All the lieutenant has asked you, were you or were you not in a card game aboard Yorktown the night she sailed. If so, no big deal. He has three other men who were in the game, no problem. He's not out to give them or you a summary court martial for gambling. He's investigating a murder. He's interested in talking with fellows who might have been some of the last to see the murdered man alive."

"Now, believe me, there are three sailors who were in the game. I've talked to them, they're real, and all three picked you out of a line up. Those fellows who came in the office yesterday were not on a break. They were sent into the compartment so there would be seven people for the three men to view, all legitimate, and again the Lieutenant's witnesses said you were in the game. They picked you out, no strain, no pain."

"Ben, I'm going to ask the lieutenant to give you another chance to answer the question. If you weren't in the game, say so, but don't lie, because if you do, the truth will catch up to you, and instead of a little gambling, big trouble."

"Come on back in, Lieutenant," called the counselor. "Please ask Ben the question again."

"OK. Ben, did you play cards with six other fellows the night before or next morning Yorktown left Pearl?"

"Same answer, Luutenaan. Those guyuser mixin' me up with nother guy. Naw, ahwas inmah sack."

"All right, Ben, then another question, and remember, you're under oath. Did you know a Fred Daukins?"

"Naw, notme. Ah nevva knowsat guy."

"One last question, Ben. Did you know a plane pusher by the name of Roy Bolton?"

"Naw, not him neither, nivver heerd offim. Ah din't knows no airedales."

"Ben, you relax, have a cigarette while Captain Pastnu and I go into another office and have a talk. I'll send one of our people in with a coke."

§§

Isaac Greenberg joined the two who had just spent the last half hour with the person suspected of being one of the members of the infamous card game. As the three settled into chairs in Craiger's office, Humphrey wasted no time in informing Captain Pastnu that his client was lying through his teeth, and why, he asked? He was beginning to think there was much more to this than meets the eye.

"This fellow is not only positively identified by three men who were there, who played cards with him, but he claims he doesn't know Daukins, never met him, yet he matches the description of a person seen with Fred by two different people. First off, this friend of Ed Hill, this Marge lady, described him to a T; then the Chinese lady Ron Milkusky talked with places a man with Kiter's description and a man we think was Roy Bolton together on Pearl."

"In addition, Captain, you've seen Kiter's jacket, you reviewed his record. In the service seven years and only an apprentice seaman? That's ridiculous. This fellow's been in trouble since day one, gambling, drunkenness, fighting, you name it, he's been a part of it."

"Herb, you make some good points, but have proved nothing," challenged the defense attorney. "Let's go over the case you're making, point by point."

"First, after reviewing the records of the three sailors who claim that Kiter was a participant in the card game aboard Yorktown several months ago, I don't know. I would challenge the honesty and integrity of at least one, maybe two, of the fellows, and then their effect on the third member of the trio. Could be their choice was an influencing factor in his picking Ben."

"You claim you have two different ladies who describe a man answering Kiter's description as being seen with Daukins, yet my client claims not to know the deceased. You know as well as I do, gentlemen, that there are thousands upon thousands of men who could answer to Kiter's description. No case there either."

"As to Kiter's seven year Navy record, it proves nothing. Sure, only a lowly apprentice seaman, so what. So he likes to gamble, so do the other six fellows who were part of the game in question. Likes to drink, so does our friend, Warrant Officer Kracklauer; we think he's a hero. He's a scrapper. We want our fellows to be aggressive. We teach them to fight, that's their job."

"And the last point, this Roy Bolton person, the man killed in the attack on Yorktown. That's really thin. How you come up with him being a suspect and friend of Ben is actually comical, funny. No, gentlemen, you have no case against my client. I want him freed and returned to duty."

§§

"I agree with the defense in this case," judged the placid Major General, as the two opposing attorneys stood toe-to-toe, each voicing his reasons as to why Seaman Ben Kiter should or should not be held over until a board of inquiry could be impaneled.

"No, Lt. Greenberg, I feel Captain Pastnu has made some good points. The seaman goes back to the galley for the time being. Good day, gentlemen. Unless you have something further, I have work to do."

§§

The General had been called into JAG headquarters from a high level meeting he had been attending, called in to referee the Kiter situation, minor he thought compared to the information being reported by members of the team of officers who had just returned from the Guadalcanal front.

Things were not going well. Oh, the first few days saw minimal opposition. The Japanese forces on the Tulagi-Guadalcanal area had been greatly overestimated by Naval intelligence.

The 500 defenders of Tulagi gave the invading Marines a taste of their fanatical bravery and tenacity, but the American troop strength was overwhelming.

Forces landing on Guadalcanal saw little, if any, initial opposition. The big problem was bringing supplies ashore from the waiting transports and the area itself. The heat, the mosquitoes, the thick, steamy jungle slowed the progress of troops heavily laden with equipment, not enough salt tablets and drinking water.

Supplies began to pile up on the beach. Few of the landing boats had ramp bows and materials had to be lifted out over the gun wales, had to be handled by sailors and Marines; machines capable of the task were not ashore.

Also as expected, news flashed from Tulagi brought immediate reaction from high level Japanese on Rabaul. Twin engine Bettys and their Zero escorts responded and would be met by Bill Fielder's fighters flying CAP over the islands. Fierce dogfights and numerous losses would be registered by both sides. The battle had really begun.

But as the days went by things would change. Fletcher had kept his word. Forty-eight hours after the fracas had begun, he insisted on retiring his valuable carriers and air support. The devastating battle of Savo Island would follow and finally, while the Marines on shore watched in disbelief, the invasion armada sailed away, taking with it food, ammunition, tools, hundreds of items, all necessary to fight this war.

Rear Admiral Turner claimed he had been left with a bare behind while Major General Vandegrift insisted he was practically naked. No air or sea cover, food for about a month for the roughly 16,000 Marines on the islands of Tulagi and Guadalcanal. This was a disaster.

Then came the nightly Bonzi attacks, unopposed Japanese capital ship shellings, and finally, the antics of "Washmachine Charley" and his fellow airmen. This was too much. The physical and psychological damage to the brave Marines on this godforsaken island was almost unbearable.

§§

The officers reporting had stopped at Pearl on the way back to Washington. Casualties were high. There was a dire need for non-coms, commissioned personnel also, but especially non-commissioned officers, corporals and sergeants. Could the staffing facilities on this island help, they asked?

The Guadalcanal people were bearers of more bad news. A partial casualty list reported that Marine 2ndLt. Herb Schacter had been killed, gunned down on the beach at Guadalcanal. On the third day of the landing, Herb had been transferred off his cargo ship to the beach, assigned the job of assistant beach-master. His job was to get supplies and men moving inland. Out of nowhere, a Val dive bomber, its 7.7 MM guns blazing, roared in strafing the long line of material and unsuspecting men, several shells ripping at the brave lieutenant's mid-section, almost tearing him in two.

Humphrey Craiger would experience many sleepless nights agonizing over his transferring the helpful Marine officer from a safe desk job to combat. He could have balked at the request, said Herb was necessary to the investigation, but then again, he thought, that was no way to win a war.

Now he was being asked to give up two more of his team, send Corp. Gene Spies and Sgt. Ron Milkusky into Harm's Way. Admiral Ernest had called the lead investigator into his office, sat him down and given him the poop.

"Humphrey, you have 30 days to clean up the Fred Daukins case. If after the 30 days all leads have dried up, we will consider the murder unsolved. Happens every day out in the real world."

The admiral went on to say the team would then be dissolved and men assigned other duties, but for now, there is a convoy of transports leaving for the Solomons in a few days, he said, and he'd like Gene and Ron to be a part of that convoy.

§§

"Well, fellows, there are only four of us now and time is of the essence." Humphrey Craiger was going about his usual Monday morning meeting, summing up the case, reporting on the admiral's now or never statement, the results of Greenberg's request before Major General Herman Trusock, that the naval architects in Washington, D.C. had forwarded a blueprint of Yorktown's hangar deck and adjoining head. The print showed that a person lying in the lower sack in the metalshop could not view the entrance or hatch of the head. The person might view a portion of the passageway between the two compartments, but that was all.

§§

Herb Andrews reported he had checked with the personnel pool. No word, picture, or letter yet from Roy Bolton's folks. He would keep on this aspect of the search.

§§

Ed Hill reported that the picture being sent him by Marge Dillon could arrive later today. Once received, he would have the base photo lab blow up the picture. He continued to feel that this Ben Kiter's face and voice were giving him nightmares. He had seen this fellow before somewhere, but couldn't remember where. Humphrey suggested Ed spend some time reviewing Kiter's file. The records just might jog his memory.

§§

"Marine Corp. Spies and Sgt. Milkusky here to say goodbye, if you have a minute, Lieutenant."

"Have a minute! Gosh, Kathy, no formality here. Show those two Gyrines in on the double!"

All four members attending the morning meeting had sprung to their feet, eager to shake the hands of the departing Marines. This had been a close couple of months, friendships had sprung up, lots of camaraderie. Ron and Gene would be missed. Godspeed, Marines, they all echoed.

§§

"You won't believe the likeness, Lieutenant, even the scar on his chin."

Ed had received the picture Marge had sent in the afternoon mail. It was a 5 x 7 print, larger than he had guessed it would be, and the lab had done a fantastic job of blowing up the suspect's face. This fellow Jack was Ben Kiter, or a twin.

"Wait til Marine Captain Roger Pastnu gets a shot at this picture. And this guy, this seaman, claims he didn't know Daukins. This is proof, real proof, that the kid is lying through his teeth."

"And you know, Humphrey, after leaving the meeting this morning, I spent time going over Kiter's records. Now I know where I knew him from -- the base hospital."

Kiter's records showed he was assigned to the Ford Island Base Hospital from the first part of December, 1941, through February of 1942. Ed Hill was a patient in that same hospital about that time and remembered like it was yesterday a crummy little seaman assigned to his ward, supposed to empty bedpans and ducks, help feed patients who couldn't help themselves, in general, a goffer.

"Well," Hill said, "this bastard not only took to demanding money from the injured he was supposed to be serving, you know, two bits to bring you a pack of nickel sea-stores or half a buck for a coke, he was also peddling rat-gut whiskey on the side."

"LCdr. Hilton Chamer found out about this crummy kid's antics and the next day this preditor was gone. We never knew where. We heard no more about him and he sure as hell wasn't missed."

"Ben's records don't mention the incident, only that he did duty at the hospital at that time, but I tell you, Lieutenant, that kid was Ben Kiter."

"I'm going to stop over to the base pathology lab later this afternoon, see if the commander remembers the incident." Ed was adamant. "This kid has all the makings of a killer. He's lying about the card game for some damn good reason. Hell, his sheets show he's been involved in major crimes. A little gambling incident wouldn't be that big a deal. He's got to be afraid of something bigger, and that something could be murder."

§§

Herb Andrews had talked with Humphrey yesterday evening. He, too, had gone through Ben's records and had feelings similar to Ed's. What was this guy hiding?

The seaman's records showed that he could be violent. There was that incident in Honolulu about a year ago. Ben had tried to drag the line leading into a Front Street can house. He couldn't wait to pay his two bucks to spend three minutes with one of the house ladies of the night. That city block long line leading up the outside flight of steps was just too much, too long.

No, the drunken seaman would try pushing his way past several Marines half way up those same stairs, and that was a mistake. One Marine reached for Ben's feet, the other for his jumper collar. They had planned on lifting him up bodily and hanging him over the railing. Scare the hell out of this crusty swabby. But before that could happen, the sailor had pulled a sheath knife from under his jumper, made a number of passes toward cutting the men who had tried to grab and restrain him, only to be disarmed and turned over to nearby Shore Patrol.

§§

Bosun Hill had not mentioned that the envelope with the Daukins/Dillon/Koler/Kiter photo also contained a letter, as well as a newspaper clipping from The Chicago Tribune. The clipping was an article about Hill's rescue of the Dutch sailor, as well as a shot of the bosun with a senator on one side and a congressman on the other.

The letter was a little more personal. Marge thought the bosun took a good picture and that she was very proud to know him. Yes, she said, she would like to continue to correspond with the naval hero, and, yes, she would send Ed her photo, an $8\frac{1}{2}$ x 11 portrait mounted in a gilt-edged frame.

This could lead to something, thought the happy investigator as he set sail for the pathology lab and a talk with Dr. Chamer. You know, he thought, maybe he should strike for chief. Might just need that extra dough in the future. Yes, Ed Hill's head and thoughts were in the clouds. Maybe he had finally met that special girl.

§§

"It's good to see you, Bosun, good to know you were able to get off the ship safely."

"Well, thank you, Commander. Herb Andrews and I were assigned the job of seeing that the Daukins' murder evidence made it safely back to Pearl, and the two of us, along with that container, were treated like VIPs."

"Cdr. Chamer," he continued, "I know you're a busy man, many important things on your mind since that fateful day December 7th, but I wonder if you would by chance remember that little bastard who had been taking advantage of patients in the ward you oversaw at the Ford Island Base Hospital, the kid who was assigned bedpan duty and ended up operating a still somewhere on the island as well as selling bootleg hootch to hospital staff and patients."

Hilton laid back in his swivel chair, smiled, then more or less laughed as he assured Ed Hill that, indeed, he did remember the incident and especially the man involved. In fact, he was so impressed, he still remembered the fellow's name, a Ben Kiter.

Why did he remember Ben so well, Ed asked, why had the dirty, little shit made such an impression on the well-educated, worldly doctor? What Kiter had done was disgusting in the mind of the bosun.

"Ed, I'll tell you why. Here's a kid right out of the hills, only a 4th grade education, hardly able to read or write, dozen brother and sisters, had to scratch to eat, no shoes, froze his feet in the winter, yet smart enough to find a family to support him, the Navy."

"Sure, the way he was working patients at the hospital was wrong, but by whose rules? Not his. He figured each and every task he performed for someone or something merited a fee. That's how he lived, that's how it was done up in the hills when he was a boy, a young man."

"Stoking a still was his way of making a living. He saw an opportunity to go into business and I give him credit. He took that opportunity. He designed the product, made the product, and sold the product. In our world, we would call him an entrepreneur."

"But, Doc, he's living in our world now, he has to follow our rules," countered the surprised bosun, surprised that this good man could or would have condoned Ben Kiter's deeds, that he would in a sense stick up for this preditor.

"I suppose you're right, Ed," smiled the thoughtful pathologist, but having been born into a family that gave me everything, good home, food, clothes, cars, education, love, especially love, I didn't have to scratch for anything. It was easy to live by the rules. Ben didn't have the food, clothes, education, had to share what love there was with twelve brothers and sisters. Maybe your rules, and my rules, weren't or aren't that easy for him to accept."

"Because I think the good Lord sets different rules for different people and not necessarily the same rules for each and every person, I, in Ben's case, did not put him on report. Instead gave him a good lecture, a good going-over, and sent him on his way. That's why the hospital incident doesn't appear in his files or records."

"In your opinion, Doctor, could this man kill?" questioned the bosun.

"Ed, I'm not a psychologist or psychiatrist, as you well know. I'm a pathologist. But in my opinion, should Ben be trapped in a corner, or his lifestyle challenged as in the example you portrayed to me, the Honolulu whore house episode, yes, he could very well lash out with vengeance, as he did with those Marines."

§§

"More good news, Humphrey. I'm just leaving the personnel pool and have the photo Roy Bolton's folks airmailed to the Commander from Mercy, West Virginia."

Misty Clay had telephoned Herb Andrews earlier in the day, asking that he stop over to pick up the picture. She mentioned that the Commander was tied up with the ever-important Guadalcanal replacement program. They would talk later.

§§

"Talk about damning evidence! Well, this takes the cake." Herb Andrews and Humphrey Craiger had just finished viewing the snapshot sent by Roy Bolton's folks. The picture showed two sailors posing with an Hawaiian girl, the girl outfitted in the typical hula outfit, grass skirt and all.

Herb Andrews had seen many snapshots of this type over the years he had spent in Honolulu. Walk down Front Street on any afternoon and there were a dozen or more open store front buildings, each offering to take your picture with a grass-skirted young Hawaiian beauty seated on your knee. All it took was a quarter, only 25¢, and voila! something to remember for the rest of your life.

But as Humphrey had mentioned to Andrews, this particular photo was damning evidence that Ben Kiter was a pathological liar. Roy Bolton had written the following on the back of the photo: "Hi, ma and pa. This is Applejack and me with a hula babe. Love, Roy."

The Boltons had enclosed a short letter along with the photo, asking that the picture be returned. It was the only one they had of Roy. They went on to say the other fellow was their son's lifelong best friend, Ben (Applejack) Kiter who lived in the next town over, just a few miles down the road in Aliston, West Virginia.

"Herb, get this picture over to the lab for a blowup. Be sure to insist on the same quality work Hill got on the picture Marge Dillon sent. And, Herb, get in touch with that Astelle Lu lady Ron Milkusky talked with earlier. She lives in Honolulu. Have her come in to identify both the men on the picture, and, if possible, "Applejack" himself."

The lieutenant and Herb stood speechless for a few seconds, then smiled at each other, Humphrey finally saying no wonder they didn't tie that little shit into the personnel pool investigation. That Jack business was not a first name but part of a nickname. No wonder it threw them off.

§§

Ed Hill had borrowed the lieutenant's jeep for a quick trip into town to pick up the Lu lady. She had agreed to come in, take a half day off from her job as a clerk in one of the better ladies' clothing stores located in the heart of the city.

Sure, the tall, good-looking sailor was the Roy fellow, no question about it, and, yes, she recognized his slightly inebriated friend, the short man, the one with the hula girl sitting on his knee.

And, yes, that was Fred Daukins on one side of the four people shown lined up on Marge Dillon's picture, and the same little man shown on the other side.

"What now, Lieutenant," asked Herb Andrews, "should we bring in Kiter? Let him face Miss Lu?"

"No, not yet, Herb. I think Ed, you and I are sure that we have positive identification of the two previously unidentified card players. We know that Ben will continue to lie about being part of the game. He will continue to deny knowing Bolton and Daukins."

"But lying or not, knowing Bolton and Daukins, playing in the late night game, all of which does not make Applejack a killer, we need more evidence, if possible, physical evidence."

"Let's think back. Herb, you mentioned that Ben was wearing a large ring when you first noticed him in the mess hall serving line. In fact, if I remember right, it was the ring, not the fellow, that first and foremost came to your attention, caught your eye."

"That's right, Lieutenant, a large ring, dark background with a shiny design, maybe gold."

"And, Herb, none of us, including you, noticed Ben wearing a ring when we brought him in for questioning. Is that right?"

"Yes," nodded both Herb and Ed.

"Let's think back to an earlier time in the investigation. Didn't one of the fellows we interrogated say Daukins was wearing a large ring the night of the game?"

"That's right, Humphrey. That was mentioned. In fact, the comment was Daukins was being kidded by the guys for wearing a ring so large, they said it was his means of hiding his hand, you know, his cards, from the other players. Right, guys? Right, Lieutenant?"

"And didn't Cdr. Chamer's autopsy report indicate that Daukins was not wearing a ring at the time he was found murdered, but that the ring finger of his right hand showed physical markings indicating a large ring had been in place not too long before the body was found?"

"Right on, Lieutenant, and you've put two and two together. I see where you're going with this. Let's get Isaac to talk with the Judge right now," commented an excited Ed Hill. "Let's see if the General will issue a search warrant so we can inspect our friend's locker."

§§

It was very hard for Herman Trusock to disregard the new evidence Isaac Greenberg had set before him, the two photos, the letter, Astelle Lu's positive identification of Bolton and Kiter, Kiter's lies, his long record of deceit while in the service and, in conclusion, Dr. Chamer's assessment. "Here's the order, counselor. Use it in good faith."

§§

Being a bosun mate meant that it took Ed Hill a very short time, only minutes, to come up with a bolt cutter. Also armed with a search warrant and the use of Craiger's jeep meant it would be a very short time before Hill and Andrews appeared before Ben Kiter's locker. The bolt cutter made short work of the protective combination lock. The two investigators were soon methodically inventorying the contents of the locker.

"Yes, Humphrey was right, and so were you, Herb," commented the husky bosun. There was the ring, large dark onyx stone, with the initials J.B.S. in gold, embossing its surface. Further scrutiny of the ring showed the initials F.W.D. '39 engraved on its underside.

"Where does a fellow by the name of Ben Kiter, initials B.K., come up with a ring having initials of F.W.D? Something rotten in Denmark, and this badly wrinkled snapshot? That's a carbon copy of the one the Boltons sent, picture of Roy and Ben taken in Honolulu, and, my God! A roll of 3/8 copper tubing. Where in the hell did he get that? That stuff's expensive. What would he use that for?"

"I don't know for sure, Ed, but I think I have a pretty good idea," answered the yeoman. "Let's stop at the mess hall and pick up the potato peeler. From what we found in his locker, I'd say Applejack has some explaining to do. My guess, the charge will be murder, not participant in late night gambling."

§§

"What right did you have to pick up my client? Judge Trusock released him, you know. I have a signed order to that effect." An angry Captain Pastnu was upset, for more reasons than one. He had been enjoying cocktails and dinner with a pretty Army nurse at the officer's club when Humphrey's call came through for Roger to appear before this same judge, Major General Herman Trusock.

This was the captain's first opportunity to be exposed to the massive new evidence being presented, evidence which the prosecution felt would show Ben Kiter as not only a liar, participant in the Yorktown gambling fiasco, but as number one suspect in the murder of Fred Daukins.

Captain Pastnu was taken aback. He wasn't prepared for this backlash. He felt that his client being released several days ago in lieu of suspect findings or evidence would more or less discourage the prosecution from further investigation. That, coupled with the Klein/Tarry defeat, should have put Craiger's team on notice. There is no case here, no concrete evidence, get on with your life, fellows. Let the Daukins' murder case go into the record book as unsolved.

"Well, Judge, I need time to review the prosecution's findings and charges. Just a quick glance at what they're presenting surely does not warrant suspected murder. Lying maybe, gambling maybe, that's all." Roger was adamant. These bumblers had put one over on him, but these hayseeds weren't going to prevail, not against this city slicker.

"Judge, I would like my client released back to duty, while the prosecution's charges are being looked into."

"Not a chance, counselor. Mr. Kiter is to be held in custody until a week from today when I will hear motions and findings from both sides. Let's get with it. We're all aware of Admiral Ernest's deadline regarding this case."

§§

"Let's not count this Roger Pastnu out. He's a heavy-hitter, and no dummy. He knows we have damaging evidence and testimony against Kiter. He's asked for help and gotten it. Lt. Hilda Burns has joined his team as well as several former detectives now with the base Shore Patrol."

No, Lt. Craiger was no fool. Although he wasn't crazy about the Marine captain's tactics and reputation, he did respect him.

"Humphrey, I'd like to talk with this Applejack fellow before we appear before the Judge again. I'd like to hear his answers to several questions I have. Would feel better prepared to present our case."

"Sure, Isaac, let's bring Kiter, Pastnu and Burns in tomorrow morning."

"Let's get right on it," replied the lieutenant.

Then, as he left JAG headquarters, heading back to officer's country, Humphrey smiled to himself and thought that Isaac couldn't wait to get back in the ring with the former high-priced barrister. If he were a betting man, his money would be on his mild-mannered friend.

§§

"Good morning, Ben. Did you sleep well last night?"

"Whaat? Y'all some kinda wise guy, Luutenaan? Who sleeps good in jail, an why y'all on my back agin? Ah's tol y'all ah knows an it ain't nuthin."

"Well, Ben," continued the smiling interrogator, "we don't believe a word you have told us, but let's go on. We found this ring in your locker. Where did you get it, Ben?"

"Whatch doin in m' locker, Luutenaan? Ain't dat gainst da law, Mr. Pastnu?"

"Answer the question, Ben. Lt. Greenberg had permission to search your locker. You can be sure that Miss Burns and I are on top of your case. The Lieutenant would not have been able to go through your things without Judge Trusock's permission."

"Ah goddat ring when ah finish school."

"You finished high school, Ben?" asked the slender interrogator.

"Yeaah, Ah diyud, inda Navy."

"Tell us about that, Ben. When did you finish high school in the Navy?"

"Took me a test in boot camp, den ah finish high school an gotda ring."

"Gee, Ben, I have all your Navy records here. Funny they don't show you having taken an equivalency test where, if you had been successful, you would have been awarded a certificate. You have that certificate, Ben?"

"Naw, ah los dat paper. Yeaah, ah los it when da ship weyunt down."

"OK, Ben, let's go on. Just a point of information, your Navy records show that you were in the fourth grade when you left school."

179

Ben looked at Pastnu, then at Hilda Burns, squirmed in his chair as if to ask why don't you help, you're my counsel, you're here to help me.

"Ben, let me tell you," went on the Lieutenant, "the Navy does not give out rings when one of their people is successful in completing an equivalency course. They do give diplomas. Now, where did you get that ring?"

"Mebbe dey don't give rings all da time, but de give it ta me. See, y'all got it."

Greenberg moved his focus from the accused to the lawyers of the accused. "Anything to say, counsel? Anything to add to Ben's answer?" No comment was the reply.

"OK, Ben, then let me tell you where I think you got the ring. I think you murdered 3rd class aviation metalsmith Fred Daukins on the night or morning of that big card game. Then you removed his high school ring from his finger, put it in your pocket and walked away."

The slight, short, homely kid turned pale, got up from his chair, clenched both fists, jaw out, saliva running from the corners of his mouth, proclaiming to all involved that the lieutenant was one peckerhead liar, that he wouldn't kill no one, that he didn't know no Daukins, and maybe he bought the ring in a pawn shop, or won it in a crap game.

"Yeaah," he said, "now ah member. Won mah ring inna crap game."

"Sit back, Ben," demanded Captain Pastnu, "no more outbursts. And you, Lt. Greenberg, careful with your questions. You have no evidence that my client killed anyone."

Yeoman Kathy Kite looked up from her shorthand pad, glancing quickly from the defendant's counsel to the interrogator.

"Did you get all of that down, Kathy?"

"Yes, sir, I did, Lieutenant."

"Then let's proceed," went on the smiling attorney.

"Bosun Hill, will you please bring in the enlarged version of the photo Marge Dillon sent us from the States?" Ed had been quietly sitting at the back of the interrogation room, prepared to assist Isaac when and if he needed help.

"Recognize the people in the picture, Seaman Kiter?" asked the still smiling Greenberg. The accused stared at the large, clear forms represented in the photo, looked surprised, took fifteen to twenty seconds before answering with the now familiar resounding, "Naw, why should I?"

"You don't recognize the fellow over on this side?" asked Isaac, pointing to the sloppily-dressed sailor glaring at a pretty young lady at his side.

"Hell, naw. Ah knows none of 'em."

"You don't remember Riverview, Ben? Remember the blind date you went on? Remember Fred and Marge fixed you up with a nice young lady named Virginia Koler? She's the lady in the picture you're looking at, the lady standing right next to you."

"Ah says tain't me. Knows no Vaginni. Knows no Fred. Whatcha tryin ta pull, Luutenaan, tellin all dese people dat's me. Ah ain't ever bin ta any Riverview."

The accused paused again, looked over at his counsel, and asked, "ain't ya gonna help me?"

Hilda Burns spoke out for the first time. "You sure the fellow Lt. Greenberg is pointing to is not you, Ben? It sure looks like you."

"Tain't me, ah sed tain't me befo, an whose side ya on anyways, lady?" an agitated Seaman Kiter asked.

"I'm on your side, Ben, and so is Captain Pastnu."

"Will you please bring in the other enlargement, Bosun? I'm sure Ben will recognize the two fellows on this picture." Isaac was not upset with Kiter's answers. Although all negative, they showed a pattern of deceit, a pattern of lies, a testimony weaving untruth after untruth into a circumstantial case against which his counsel would find it hard to defend.

"Let's assume you were right in the past, Ben, that you didn't recognize the people on the large picture we showed you before, you know, the one sitting next to this new one I'm going to ask you about. Recognize these two sailors?"

All color drained from the face of the Applejack fellow, followed by a look of compassion. Kiter didn't answer the inquiring lieutenant.

"Let me ask you again, Seaman. Recognize the two men I'm pointing to?"

"Naw, jista coupla swabbies with some Hawaiian broad. Evry guy in da Navy has a pitcher wid 'em."

"What would you say if I told you Roy Bolton's folks sent us the original of this particular picture, Ben?" asked the beaming prosecutor. "Here's the original, read what it says on the back, read it out loud so we can all hear the message."

"Ya knows ah don do no readin, Luutenaan."

"You don't read, Ben? I thought you told us you graduated from high school. Hard to believe a high school graduate doesn't know how to read."

"Ah don't an dat's it."

"Let me read it for you, fella," said the prosecutor as he took the picture from the shaking hands of a very upset, scared member of this man's navy. He went on to say that the Boltons stated that the picture shows their son, Roy, with his best friend Applejack, then continues, the friend Applejack is Ben Kiter from the neighboring town of Aliston, West Virginia. They were in the Navy together.

"Now once again, Seaman, who are the two men in the photo?"

"Ah tol ya, ah don know. Quit harpin at me, Luutenaan. Ah'm gettin pissed off atya, ah don know no Boltons either. Ya mus be framin' me!"

"How about this companion picture we found in your locker, Ben? Same picture, carbon copy of the one the Boltons sent, only wrinkled like you may have carried it in your wallet at one time or other. Do you think I'm framing you with the picture we found in your locker?"

"Yeaah, Ah do, it'salla frame."

"Just for the record, Kathy, would you please indicate that both a Marge Dillon from Chicago, Illinois, and an Astelle Lu from Honolulu have identified Ben Kiter as being seen with aviation metalsmith Fred William Daukins? Thanks. I won't waste time asking Applejack if he knows the two ladies, and say, Ben, by the way, why do they call you Applejack?" asked the lieutenant.

"Summore bum dope, m' name's Ben."

"Are you through, Mr. Greenberg?" asked Roger Pastnu. "If so, I think Mr. Kiter has been asked enough questions for one day."

"Yes, Captain, enough for one day," replied the prosecutor.

"Oh, wait, one more question. Ben, where did you get that roll of 3/8 copper tubing we found in your locker? Did you steal it?"

"That does it, Isaac. No more! What right do you have to accuse this man of such a deed without any evidence, no evidence at all?" demanded the defense counsel.

"Ah'll answer dat," yelled out the defendant. "Ah nivver stole nothin. My uncle give it ta me. Yeaah, Ah don't steal. My uncle's a storekeeper. He give me da tubin."

"Your uncle owns a store, Ben? Is that what you're saying, a store here in Honolulu, and he sells copper tubing?"

"Naw, he don't own no store. He's a storekeeper rate. He give me da tubin outta his warehouse. He gottall kinds."

"Ben, you say your uncle is a storekeeper. Is he on the Island?"

"Yeaah, he is."

"Ben, I believe you," responded the cagey lieutenant. "Who is your uncle, what's his name?"

"He's Skinney Kracklauer, ya know, Chief Warrant Kracklauer from da Yorktown."

A long deadening silence came over the room. You could have heard a pin drop. Lawyers for both the prosecution and defense looked at each other with dismay. Finally, Greenberg was able to utter a weak, "Let's call it a day, ladies and gentlemen. Enough is enough."

§§

"You have some more questions about Klein or Tarry?" asked the Chief Warrant once the conference got down to the business of the day.

"No, sir, Percy," answered a somber Lieutenant Craiger. "We've been talking with a young man who claims to be your nephew."

Minutes after Greenberg contacted him, Humphrey Craiger had placed a call to officer's quarters asking that Chief Warrant Officer Percy Kracklauer please do the JAG members the honor of his presence. Bosun Hill would be right over to pick him up.

"You mean a fella on the island told you I'm his uncle? Well, that could only be Applejack, unless another of my younger sister's kids has joined the service."

"Yes, sir, the man is Ben Kiter, and I believe he has been referred to as Applejack. Claims to be from Aliston, West

183

Virginia."

"That's our home, Lt. Craiger, and Ben is the first family member to follow in my footsteps. What's he done now?"

"Well, Percy, we thought he stole a roll of 3/8 inch copper tubing, but he claims you gave it to him out of your warehouse."

"Applejack's telling the truth, Lieutenant. I did give him the material. One of my suppliers did me a favor, you know how that works, you scratch my back, I'll scratch yours. Told this Bill Meyers from Catch Bronze and Brass that I needed some tubing for a family member and next day it's waiting on the doorstep. I buy lots of product from him, small gesture, but it pays off."

"Just for my information, Percy, what is a fellow who works in the base galley going to do with copper tubing?"

"I didn't ask him, Humphrey, you know the old saying, what you don't know won't hurt you," laughed the wirey old-timer. "But I can guess. As you know, booze is hard to get here on the island, and I'd think the kid is going to build a still, you know, go in the business like that Capone guy in Chicago."

"Percy, to change the subject, did you know that your nephew was aboard Yorktown its last trip out?" asked the lieutenant.

"I didn't at first," answered the 38-year veteran, "wasn't until we were out to sea that first night or early the next morning when Ben and a couple of friends came by the metalshop, stood at the hatch and motioned me to come out in the passageway. Gave 'em the keep quiet sign, cause Klein and Tarry were sound asleep. Well, you remember. That's what all the hullabaloo was about, my swearing those two fellas were in their sacks between 0330 and 0400 hours."

"Anyway, Ben said he and the other two were just on their way into the head to take a leak before turning-in and he noticed his uncle reading, wanted to say hello."

"Percy, did Ben introduce you to the other two sailors?"

"No, he didn't, Lieutenant. Just said they'd come from a card game. Kid doesn't have too many manners. Anyway I didn't see my nephew for about a week after we were returned to Pearl. That's when he asked for the tubing."

"Well, thanks, Percy. You were a great help. I'm going to ask Lt. Greenberg to drive you back to the officer's club and buy you a couple of manhattans on me."

"Thanks, Lieutenant, sure glad we straightened that tubing deal out. I wouldn't want Applejack to get into any trouble over that. Seems like trouble finds the kid anyway."

Little did Percy realize at the time just how true his last statement was. This kid was in real trouble. Humphrey was convinced the murder aboard Yorktown was about to be solved.

§§

Major General Trusock wasted little time in putting the prosecution's case before Ben Kiter's two lawyers. The five, Trusock, Greenberg, Craiger, Burns and Pastnu, were gathered around a table in his chambers.

"I agree with Lt. Craiger's charges of murder against Seaman Kiter. I think the evidence is overwhelming and that your client is a pathological liar. Once again, let's lay out the evidence," instructed the stern Judge.

"Four sailors have positively identified Kiter and Bolton as players in the late night card game. Two ladies have positively identified Kiter and Daukins as knowing each other. One lady puts Kiter, Daukins and Bolton together. Bolton's folks identify Kiter as a lifelong friend of their son. Daukins' class ring is found in Kiter's locker along with a copy of the same picture Bolton's folks sent and in which Kiter claims the fellow in the picture is not him."

"But the kicker, the final nail in the coffin, is Chief Warrant Officer Kracklauer's honest testimony that his nephew, Ben Applejack Kiter, along with two friends, was seen going into the head, the same head in which Fred Daukins was found murdered, at about the time pathology reports the murder occurred."

"Now, ladies and gentlemen," the Judge continued, "I believe there are really only two unanswered questions here. The first, was Roy Bolton a party to the murder? And seond, why? Why was the aviation metalsmith murdered? I along with Humphrey Craiger and Isaac Greenberg feel that only one person can answer those two questions. The murderer, Ben Kiter."

Roger Pastnu began to speak, but the Judge silenced him before he could get started. The Judge hadn't finished.

"Sit back, Captain Pastnu. The prosecution has agreed to terms I feel are more than fair. If Ben Kiter admits to the murder, saves us an expensive time-consuming trial, they, the prosecution, agree not to ask for the death penalty, but will consider a sentence of life in prison."

"Now, I want both of you, Captain Pastnu and Lieutenant Burns, to take this offer back to Seaman Kiter, explain the terms and situation to your client in detail, be honest with him and yourselves. You know as well as I do he's guilty. Now do him a service, save him from a firing squad, get him to confess."

1stLt. Hilda Burns rose from the table, thanked the judge, and started to leave the room. Roger Pastnu rose, nodded to his Honor and followed his associate.

As they walked down the marble steps toward the lockup, Hilda broke the silence. "I'm convinced he's guilty, Roger, and I hope you feel the same."

"Yes," nodded her compatriot, "guilty as sin. I've felt that way for a long time. Just hated to give up, but this last evidence is damning. That honesty label we were guilty of applying to Percy has backfired. His testimony would be considered valid and believable."

"Let's get it over with. We could wait until morning but that would mean another sleepless night. No, Roger, let's face up to the fact that we have to convince Ben that only the truth, a confession, will save him from the death penalty."

§§

"Ya's got good news?" asked the sleepy-eyed mountain boy as he was ushered into the room, a room containing a table, three chairs, bare deck, overhead and bulkheads all painted a dull grey. Seated in two of the chairs was Applejack's hope for redemption, the two people who would get him out of this jam. He told them he done nothin and they believed him.

"Are they treating you alright, Ben?" asked a serious Captain Pastnu.

"How's the food, Ben, good or better than they serve in the base mess hall?" asked a smiling Lt. Burns.

"Yeaah, Ah'm OK," responded the unkempt seaman. "Whatcha got fer me?" he asked again.

"Well, Ben, we spent the last several hours going over the evidence the Navy has against you."

"Agin me, fer what? A lousy card game? Dey still handin out dat bum dope? Dat's crap. Ah wan outta here!"

"Ben, sit back, relax, keep your mouth shut, and listen to what

186

we have to say. It could save your life. Hilda and I are the only friends you have right now. Believe me, we want to help you, but we can only help to a point and only if you let us and agree to tell the truth."

"First off, Ben, everyone involved, including the lieutenant and myself, knows you have been lying and not doing a good job at that."

The defendant settled back in his chair and looked down at his folded hands. A look of relief seemed to come over his face. He said nothing.

Captain Pastnu continued. "As I said before, Ben, the evidence is overwhelming. Four sailors have positively identified you and your friend Bolton being together with Daukins. Two ladies have identified you and Daukins as friends. One lady puts you, Bolton and Daukins together, and Mr. and Mrs. Bolton know you as a boy who grew up with their son, played together, hunted together."

The defendant didn't speak; he did look up toward Hilda Burns.

"The Captain is right, Ben," she said, "all parties agree that you knew Daukins and Bolton and that you were a part of the card game in question. And, Ben, those photos. They had to be of you. Every detail the same, to the scar on your chin."

Applejack kept looking up at the lieutenant as she continued to talk, then inadvertently reached up and touched the scar she had mentioned.

"Now, Ben, look at this. It's Fred Daukins' yearbook, and on the first page is a picture of the ring each graduate can purchase once they graduate."

The lieutenant had pulled out the 12 x 14 leather-bound remembrance, turned to the picture, the enlargement being discussed, and compared the picture with the ring found in Kiter's locker, the ring the prosecution was kind enough to allow the defense to use, the ring with Daukins initials engraved on its underside.

"But you know, Ben, what really convinced all of us involved," went on the Wave lieutenant, "was when your Uncle Percy told Humphrey Craiger that you and two other fellows, whom we assume were Bolton and Daukins, went into the head together about the time Fred was killed."

"Ya talked ta my uncle about dis?"

"We didn't. No, the Captain and I didn't, but as we mentioned, Lt. Craiger did."

"An my uncle ratted on me an Roy?"

"He didn't rat on you, Ben. He just told the truth. Your uncle is a very respected man. The Navy takes his word as fact. That's why you have to be truthful and admit that you, Fred and Roy were together when the killing took place."

What little fight remained in the more or less pathetic young man seemed to drain from his slender body. He looked up at the lieutenant and asked, "If I tell ya the story will ya get me off?"

"Ben, we can't get you off. Tell us the story, the truth, and depending on the facts, both Captain Pastnu and I will do everything in our power to get you the best deal possible."

"OK an dis is da truth."

§§

"Wait, Ben, we want a stenographer to come in and take down your story."

"First off, dis Daukins was a bad person, smartass, always lorden it over me 'n Roy. Thought he was so good looken, could take our girls away from us. Nivver paid us fer his booze."

"Wait one second," asked the lieutenant. "What booze?"

"Roy 'n me always had us a business wherever we was. Made hootch, corn licker. What we din't drink, we sold," answered the seaman.

"Go on with your story, Ben. You're doing fine," smiled the unpretentious Navy lawyer. "Sorry I interrupted you."

"Well, anyways, dis night da metalsmith asks me ta bring Roy ta da game, ya know, Roy always had a few bucks on 'm. Met de otter guys, had a good spot, an' we dealt a few. Said we quit by 0330 hours and we did. Roy an' some otters had 0400 watches."

"We breaks up, me, Fred and Roy head aft on da hangar deck, Fred asken 'bout our booze business, said ain't it time we took 'm in as a partner. Roy looks at me, me at him, ya know dat look, dat'l be da day look, anyways when we passes the metalshop I notices Uncle Skinney readen in his rack. Ah motion him out in da passageway, we talks fer a few minutes, den Fred says he gotta take a leak, my uncle goes back in da shop, and da three of us odder guys goes in da head."

188

"Well, dat's when it happens. Daukins pulls down his drawers, was getten ready ta sit on da john, den says if he warn't in on our corn licker deal, he'd talk ta Uncle Skinney, cause he works where Uncle Skinney sleeps, maybe Skinney could get da stuff cause he's a storekeeper, ya know, da stuff ta build da still, Fred says he has da know-how ta do da builden cause he's a metalsmith."

"Dat's da last straw. Ah looks at Roy, him at me, den all hell breaks loose. Roy takes Fred inna headlock wit one arm, da otter over da bastard's mouth. Ah pulls out my pig-sticker, and really cuts him, Ah mean cuts him, buried dat sucker upta its hilt."

"Roy sets Fred down gentle like, looks like he's taken a crap. Ah warn't no dumbbell. Ah rubs da knife handle clean, dere was hardly no blood comin outta dis guy. Roy an me was clean, so we took off up da ladder on da portside of da metalshop, no one round, got ta da flight deck, it was pitch dark, Roy goes on his watch, Ah heads forward on da deck ta da island hatch, den down ta da galley an my rack. We got rid a dat peckerhead real easy, jist like me an Roy useta practice back home."

The two attorneys sat quietly stunned. The stenographer looked up from her shorthand pad for a second, then looked away and toward Ben's counsel, as Kiter finished.

"Well, dat's it, dat's da truth." Ben was perfectly calm, relieved, like a load had been lifted from his shoulders. Finally, Lt. Burns asked Ben what he meant when he said that he and Roy had practiced the killing at home.

"Oh, Ah don't mean killin Daukins at home," laughed the seaman. "I mean Roy n me, ya know when we was kids, when we playin' in da hills, we plays dat game like we practice what iffa bear comes on us, when we din't have our pieces, ya know, our guns, well, wid da bear sucker on his hindlegs, say comin at Roy, he's get da bear inna headlock an Ah comes in back an let dat varmit have it wit my sticker. Ah'd cut 'em thru n thru."

§§

It would be the next morning before Judge Trusock could assemble the four attorneys to discuss the Kiter confession. There seemed to be an air of relief in the room as Lt. Burns finished reading the signed document. Now to the charge and sentence.

"Because there was a form of blackmail, Daukins insisting on a third of the business or else, we, Lt. Burns and I, feel the charge should be second degree murder, with a sentence of not more than twenty years in the federal penitentiary," voiced the articulate Captain Pastnu.

Greenberg was adamant. "Roger, you must be out of your mind to suggest a sentence of twenty years. These two fellows, Kiter and Bolton, took a man's life, a shipmate's life, killed him in cold blood, actually without hesitation. We know Bolton has gotten his, but Kiter, he really should be put before a firing squad."

"Isaac, you know we had an agreement. Bring in a signed confession and the death penalty is out. Well, there's the confession. Now let's hold to our bargain!" demanded the Marine captain.

"Captain Pastnu is right," agreed Major General Trusock, "if Kiter confesses, no death penalty. That was the agreement between prosecution and defense counsel."

"Lt. Craiger and I don't feel as though there was blackmail involved," replied the prosecutor. "But you're right about the death penalty agreement. We will settle for life in prison."

Pastnu shook his head, no. Judge Trusock chimed in with what he thought a compromise sentence should be and after some discussion, all parties agreed.

The Judge felt that there was a degree of blackmail involved, that the two parties responsible for the heinous act had not conspired to murder Daukins but acted on impulse, a spur of the moment decision on their part. But by the same token, they had taken a man's life. The sentence should be a hefty one. He suggested forty years at hard labor in the federal penitentiary at Leavenworth, Kansas.

§§

As Pastnu and Burns left the Judge's chambers to pass on the news of the verdict to their client, Greenberg and Craiger headed for their offices at JAG headquarters. Herb and Ed would be waiting patiently.

"Well, fellows, our work is done. Our little task group is now disbanded. Would think we'll have our next assignment within a day or so."

"I've asked for the Solomons," announced a more or less anxious Craiger, "believe that request will be granted. And by the way," continued the former leader, "as a small token of my appreciation for all you have done over the past months, I'm inviting the three of you to have cocktails and dinner with me this evening, dinner at the main dining room of the Royal Hawaiian Hotel."

"I'd like to, but have a previous engagement," commented the young Jewish member of Craiger's group. "I'm sure, though, the four of us will be able to get together at another time before we leave Hawaii."

"OK, Isaac, you're off the hook, but our next meeting's on you," laughed the lieutenant.

§§

Later that evening, as a Marine 1st Lieutenant along with a 2nd class Yeoman and a 1st class Bosun sat sipping cocktails while listening to the strains of a five piece band, seated amongst the palms set ever so carefully in a dining room furnished for royalty, fit for a king, Ed Hill happened to look over at a nearby table located next to an open window, the view facing the white sands and blue waters of Waikiki beach.

Seated at the table, watching the setting sun touch the horizon, was a slight, younger man dressed in civilian clothes, holding hands while sitting across from a beautiful young lady in a black strapless dinner dress. A candle glowing ever so gently provided just enough light to allow the observers to make out profiles.

"Damn, fellows. If I didn't know better, I'd say that's Lt. Greenberg, out of uniform, with, who else, but Yeoman Kathy Kite!"

Humphrey smiled, rocked back in his chair, and said, "Wouldn't old Isaac wish he was smart enough to come up with such a scenario. Finally, a way for an officer to fraternize with an enlisted person."

§§§§

To order additional copies of **Murder Aboard Yorktown,** complete the information below.

Ship to: (please print)

Name_____

Address_____

City,State,Zip_____

Phone_____

_____copies of **Murder Aboard Yorktown** @ $23.95 each $_____

Postage and handling @ $2.75 per book $_____

Total amount enclosed $_____

Make checks payable to Roy Latall

Send to: L & L Publishing, 2314 Lakeshore Drive, Pier Cove, Michigan 49408

To order additional copies of **Murder Aboard Yorktown,** complete the information below.

Ship to: (please print)

Name_____

Address_____

City,State,Zip_____

Phone_____

_____copies of **Murder Aboard Yorktown** @ $23.95 each $_____

Postage and handling @ $2.75 per book $_____

Total amount enclosed $_____

Make checks payable to Roy Latall

Send to: L & L Publishing, 2314 Lakeshore Drive, Pier Cove, Michigan 49408
